Praise for *New York Times* bestselling author

CHRISTINE WARREN

HOWL AT THE MOON

"Warren delivers a rapidly paced tale that pits duty against honor and love. Populated with intriguing characters who continue to grow and develop, it is fun to see familiar faces in new scenarios." —*Romantic Times BOOKreviews*

"A fantastic addition to the world of The Others...grab a copy as soon as possible. Christine Warren does a wonderful job of writing a book that meshes perfectly with the storylines of the others in the series, yet stands alone perfectly." —Lori Ann, *Romance Reviews Today*

"Warren weaves a paranormal world of werewolves, shifters, witches, humans, demons, and a whole lot more with a unique hand for combining all the paranormal classes." —*Night Owl Romance*

"*Howl at the Moon* will tug at a wide range of emotions from beginning to end...Engaging

MORE...

banter, a strong emotional connection, and steamy love scenes. This talented author delivers real emotion which results in delightful interactions...and the realistic dialogue is stimulating. Christine Warren knows how to write a winner!"   —*Romance Junkies*

THE DEMON YOU KNOW

"Explodes with sexy, devilish fun, exploring the further adventures of The Others. With a number of the gang from previous books back, there's an immediate familiarity about this world that makes it easy to dive right into. Warren's storytelling style makes these books remarkably entertaining."   —*Romantic Times BOOKreviews* (4½ stars)

SHE'S NO FAERIE PRINCESS

"Warren has fast become one of the premier authors of rich paranormal thrillers elaborately laced with scorching passion. When you want your adventure hot, Warren is the one for you!"
—*Romantic Times BOOKreviews*

"The dialogue is outrageous, funny, and clever. The characters are so engaging and well scripted...and the plot...is as scary as it is delicious!"
—*Romance Reader at Heart*

"Christine Warren has penned a story rich in fantastic characters and spellbinding plots."
—*Fallen Angel Reviews*

WOLF AT THE DOOR

"A great start to a unique paranormal series."
—*Fresh Fiction*

"This book is a fire-starter...a fast-paced, adrenaline- and hormonally-charged tale. The writing is fluid and fun, and makes the characters all take on life-like characteristics."
—*Romance Reader at Heart*

"Intrigue, adventure, and red-hot sexual tension."
—*USA Today* bestselling author Julie Kenner

ONE BITE
WITH A
STRANGER

CHRISTINE WARREN

St. Martin's Paperbacks

This is a work of fiction. All of the characters, organizations, and events portrayed in this novel are either products of the author's imagination or are used fictitiously.

ONE BITE WITH A STRANGER

Copyright © 2008 by Christine Warren.
Excerpt from *You're So Vein* copyright © 2008 by Christine Warren.

All rights reserved.

For information address St. Martin's Press, 175 Fifth Avenue, New York, NY 10010.

ISBN: 0-312-94793-3
EAN: 978-0-312-94793-4

Printed in the United States of America

St. Martin's Paperbacks edition / October 2008

St. Martin's Paperbacks are published by St. Martin's Press, 175 Fifth Avenue, New York, NY 10010.

10 9 8 7 6 5 4 3 2 1

As always, to my best girlfriends— JoJo, Kim, and Sham. Because they always put up with me. Even when they shouldn't.

CHAPTER 1

"GOOD LORD, YOU SHOULD HAVE SEEN HER FACE! I thought her eyes were going to pop right out of her head."

Regina McNeill laughed along with the friends gathered in her apartment for their semimonthly girls' night ritual. As said ritual had already involved several bottles of truly exceptional wine, Reggie was currently stretched out on her living room carpet with her head resting on a sofa pillow and her gaze fixed on the ceiling, which spun in wide, gentle swirls overhead.

True to form, her friends noticed her distraction and reacted by setting her wine glass on the edge of the coffee table near her shoulder and continuing the conversation.

"Are you kidding? And miss one second of staring at that gorgeous hunk of a man? Our Corinne would never be that stupid." Danice topped off her wine glass from a nearly empty bottle of cabernet and grinned slyly. "Besides, if her eyes had popped out, they probably would have just landed on her chin. I think it was on the floor by that point."

Missy laughed. "That accounts for the puddles, then!"

"Hey," Corinne protested with mock dignity, finishing off the white wine in her own glass. "There were no puddles involved. At least, not that early on."

"And they didn't consist of drool anyway," Ava quipped as she selected a chunk of havarti from the plundered plate of cheese on the table in front of her. "I hope those sheets of yours didn't stain, Corinne, darling."

"If they did, I don't want to know about it." Reggie laughed and pushed herself into a sitting position. It took enough effort that she figured she should forget another glass of wine.

Reggie wasn't normally a heavy drinker, but if tonight's company hadn't provided enough of an excuse to relax that rule a little, the damp, dreary spring weather had. She'd had three and a half glasses of pinot grigio, which was two more than it took to bring her solidly past tipsy. "There's such a thing as too much information, you know."

"There is not," Danice protested, her pretty brown eyes sparkling with wine and mischief. "Friends share everything, Reggie!"

"Mm, especially the dirty parts," Ava purred.

Her sleek, dark eyebrows wriggled suggestively and drew another laugh from the group.

Even Reggie laughed while she snagged a cracker from the coffee table full of munchies. Predictably, it had only taken four hours and a bit of alcohol to send the conversation among the five close friends straight to the gutter. As the self-acknowledged prude of the group, Reggie had been figuratively dragged along behind the others.

"I don't get the dirty parts," she commented for probably the hundredth time to this particular audience. "I thought that's what blue movies and romance novels were for. I mean, who wants to hear about the sex lives of people they actually know? It's like watching your parents get freaky. Ick."

Danice gave a theatrically disappointed sigh. "Regina Elaina, where did we go wrong with you? All sex is interesting, sweetie, 'cause hearing about it is the next best thing to doing it."

Reggie rolled her eyes. "I've heard that argument before, Nicie, and I'm still not buying. If I'm not having the sex, I'm not interested in hearing about it."

"And that brings up something I've been wanting to talk to everyone about," Ava interrupted, her mouth curving in the kind of smile that always made the hair on the back of Reggie's neck stand up. "Thank you for the lovely segue, Reggie dear."

Unease pushed Reggie into an automatic protest,

but Ava characteristically plowed right over her like a Prada-wearing steamroller.

"It has come to my attention," Ava continued, "that you, Regina, are the only one of our little group who has yet to take part in her very own Fantasy Fix."

The suggestion was met with a half second of silence followed by a rousing cheer from everyone but Reggie; because *she* was too busy snapping into instant sobriety and experiencing a sudden and debilitating empathy for trapped lab rats around the world.

And were those cat's whiskers she could see sprouting from Ava's nose?

"Oh, no," Reggie protested, holding her hands out in front of her as if she could beat back her best friends' intentions. "I'm not going to be your next victim. I was never wild about the Fix idea in the first place, but you guys ignored me back then. You said I was being a silly Puritan and that I'd get over it. Well, I haven't. Pick someone else."

The idea of the Fantasy Fixes had come out of a night Reggie would never forget. And she ought to know, because she'd been trying to do so for the past six months.

"You know, I don't think we can do that this time," Danice said, leaping onto Ava's bandwagon with an unrepentant grin. "I think Ava's right. Every single one of us here has taken at least one turn so far. Ava and Corinne and I have even taken two each. It just wouldn't be right if we kept skipping over you. Why, personally, I don't think I'd be able to live with myself if we didn't make it our first and foremost priority to get you Fixed just as soon as possible."

"Maybe I'm not broken," Reggie growled, but her protests fell on deaf ears. Not that she'd expected much else. No one could talk Danice Carter out of an idea, which is why the Fantasy Fixes had gotten off the ground to begin with.

Ava had thought it up, with Danice quickly throwing her support behind it, and since the whole thing had been born on another wild and wine-filled girls' night, Corinne and even Missy had quickly jumped onto the bandwagon. At the time even Reggie hadn't fought that hard against it. Six months ago, she couldn't see the harm. Now she was considering applying for disaster relief funds.

The Fantasy Fix had exploded into being when one too many drinks had led the five women's conversation to the subject of fantasies—in particular, to sexual fantasies.

"Have you ever acted one out?" Ava had wanted to know. "One of the really steamy ones you didn't want anyone to know about?"

Danice scoffed at that. "When would I get the chance? And with who? Reggie's the only one of us with a long-term relationship. I'm lucky if I can get lucky, let alone find a guy to act out the good stuff with."

"I don't know if that makes Reggie lucky though," Corinne observed. "Sometimes it's even harder to do the fantasy thing with a real partner than it would be with someone you don't know as well. There's more at stake. Personally, if I'm going to admit I want to dress up in red leather and have some hunk call me 'mistress,' I think I'd rather do it with a stranger."

"Mistress, huh?" Missy giggled and grinned. "You go, girl. I wouldn't have pegged you for it, but I think I like this side of you. You're right though; strangers might be easier."

"Exactly," Danice agreed. "Besides, you pull out the big guns with a lover, and he's gonna want in on the fantasizing. Lovers want to get inside your head. At least if you were doing the fantasy thing with a stranger, you can do it all the way, not worry about him whining that he wants to be the emperor this time."

They had all laughed, except for Ava. She'd had that look.

"You know, Corinne," she said slowly, "I know a guy, a real hunk, who would love the opportunity to call someone 'mistress' without paying for it or doing the long-term thing. I could maybe hook you two up."

Missy laughed. "Playing matchmaker, Ava? You know, I've been looking for a nice mountain man to kidnap me and keep me in his cabin for a weekend or two. Know anyone like that?"

"I don't know about Ava, but I do," Danice chimed in. "I could fix you up with that fantasy."

"In fact," Ava murmured, beginning to smile. "I

would be willing to wager that if we put our heads together, the five of us could design a way for any four of us to fix up the other one. Make it possible for her to live her fantasies. Give her, as it were, a Fantasy Fix."

That had been the beginning of the end. A vote had revealed the five of them to be just drunk enough and just insane enough to agree to help each other find a way to live out their wildest sexual fantasies. They'd drawn up a plan, collected five fantasies from each member of the group, and plunged headfirst into round one.

By putting their heads together, the five friends found they knew an awful lot of men who fit each other's visions of a fantasy lover. After that, making the arrangements had been easy. Round one had gone off like gangbusters, with each woman taking a turn at acting out one of her five fantasies with one of the eligible bachelors in the fantasy pool. Well, each woman had taken a turn except for Reggie.

At the time the idea came together, Reggie had still been seeing Greg—had still been living with Greg, unfortunately—so she'd been exempt. They'd skipped over her, and Reggie had told herself she didn't need a fantasy lover when she had a real one sleeping by her side every night. She hadn't realized that while Greg slept by her side every night, he also fucked his receptionist in his office every afternoon.

The relationship with him hadn't made it past the beginning of round two. Their breakup had been four months ago, and while Reggie had finally reached the stage when she could admit she was better off without the scum-sucker, she still didn't quite feel ready for a Fantasy Fix. Heck, she was barely ready for a shopping fix!

Of course, try to tell that to her friends.

And she was. She was trying really, really hard. They just refused to listen.

"Get the hat," Danice instructed Missy while Corinne returned from the kitchen with a fresh bottle of white. "Who's got custody of Ms. McNeill's fantasies? Missy? You're our record keeper."

Four women looked at each other, and Reggie had the fleeting hope her fantasies had been lost to the ether. Maybe then they could just forget this whole insane idea.

"I didn't bring them," Missy admitted. "I didn't know Corinne was finished, so I didn't think we'd be drawing tonight."

Reggie started to grin.

"No matter," Ava dismissed. "Just get a pen and paper. She can draw up five new ones. Knowing our bashful, old-fashioned, and monogamous friend, her old ones probably all featured the Slimeball, anyway."

Reggie felt the first stirrings of panic. Her friends had never liked Greg—neither did Reggie these days—but that didn't mean she felt ready to hop into bed with a stranger. Even before Greg, she'd never done anything like that. In fact, he'd only been the third lover she'd ever had. She wasn't the type for one-night stands, let alone for acting out sexual fantasies. Her friends might be all *Sex and the City*, but Reggie was more *Leave It to Beaver*.

"You know, I really think—"

"That you need to make these good, girl," Danice interrupted firmly, handing Reggie a pad and a pen. "Now is your chance to live it up. Get fantasizing."

Reggie shook her head and tried to hand the pen back. "No, really. I don't have any fantasies."

"Don't lie, Regina. It's not polite," Ava said, pinning her with a hard stare. "Everyone has fantasies."

Missy returned to the group and held up the straw hat she had snagged from Reggie's hall closet. "Who's going to draw?"

"I will," Corinne offered, and set her refilled wine glass on the cocktail table. "Since I had the last Fix."

Reggie felt her already nebulous control over her own fate slipping permanently from her grasp. "No. Wait a minute, you guys. I'm not so sure this is really a good idea. I mean, I don't think I'm ready for this. Maybe I need to finish getting over this thing with Greg—"

"Trust me when I tell you, darling, the best way

to get over that asshole is to screw him right out of your memory." Trust Ava to lay it all out in black and white. She never had been one to beat around the bush. "And since I don't see you going out and picking up an assistant to help you with that, it is up to your friends to pick one up for you."

"But—"

"Plant it, Reg." Danice pushed Reggie down onto the sofa and handed her a large glass of wine. "It's your turn, and you are not backing out this time."

Reggie barely hit the cushions before Corinne took a turn with the browbeating. "No more stalling. You had your chance to veto this Fix in the beginning, just like we all did. But once you threw in your fantasies, and we started round one, you were committed."

Reggie scowled. "I ought to *be* committed."

"Actually, that's a really good point," Corinne interrupted. "She was in this beginning with round one, right? But she never got a turn. So I think"—she paused to grin at the other women— "Reggie should get a double draw. Two fantasies for the price of one, so to speak."

"Yes!" Danice's exclamation overrode Reggie's protest. "It'll be our job as the Fixers to find a way to fit the two fantasies together. Don't worry, toots. We'll find a way to make it happen for you."

"Absolutely."

"It'll be great."

"Just trust us."

Oh, God. She was doomed.

Reggie looked at the solid wall of sisterly unity in front of her, and knew resistance would prove futile. There was no getting out of this. Not with Ava leading the charge right over the edge of the cliff.

"Write!" the woman ordered, pointing imperiously at the blank paper on Reggie's lap. "We need five fantasies, Ms. McNeill, the kinkier the better."

"But—"

"No buts. Concentrate on butts." Corinne grinned. "And pecs and abs and talented hands. And maybe one or two other things."

They all laughed, and Reggie knew her reprieve had come to an ignominious end. She could never get away without listing five fantasies and throwing them—and herself—on her friends' nonexistent mercy.

"I don't see the pen moving, Reg," Missy teased her, waggling her eyebrows. "Get going. This is your chance to do all the things you weren't sure were even physically possible."

Reggie started to snap that she'd prefer the impossible, but she stopped when a thought occurred to her.

She pursed her lips and tapped the pen against the pad. "So were there any rules about these fantasies? I can't remember all the particulars we decided on. I think I was too drunk."

"Anything goes, baby." Danice grinned. "You can ask for anything you want, and if we can't get it for you, we have to pay the forfeit. One month of celibacy each."

"Which is not going to be a problem, darling. We can get you anything you want, Regina, so quit stalling and start writing."

Reggie narrowed her eyes and obeyed Ava's command. She knew she was being vindictive with the first four slips of paper she filled out, but panic had taken over and she found the insistence of her friends only added to the tension. As far as she could tell, a month of abstinence would be good for them. Maybe it would get their minds off sex for sixty consecutive seconds.

Pushing down her conscience, Reggie quickly scribbled out four fantasies, each impossible for anyone to fulfill. Not even her resourceful friends could manage to find a vampire, an alien, Bigfoot or Elvis, still alive, in shape, and fully functional.

Take that, she thought, folding the scraps of paper neatly and setting them on the table.

"Oh, you cannot tell me you don't have enough fantasies," Danice glared, planting a hand on her hip and shaking her head at Reggie. "You are twenty-seven years old, girl, and the last two, you spent chained to Groping Gregory. You got time to make up for!"

"I'm thinking," Reggie snapped back. And she

was, but unfortunately she'd just run out of *Weekly World News* headlines.

"Don't think," Ava ordered, holding out the hat. "Fantasize. Now."

Reggie racked her brain for another ten seconds and came up blank, but when even softhearted Missy started in on her to finish, she dashed off the first thing that came to mind and tossed the five folded slips of paper into the hat. The last one really *was* one of her fantasies, and her stomach knotted at the prospect of it becoming common knowledge, but the chances of it being drawn weren't good. If the gods loved her, she reassured herself, it would never see the light of day. She'd be cuddling a yeti before it ever happened.

"Fine. Do your worst," Reggie muttered, having no trouble projecting a tone of nervous resentment. "But I hope you all pay for this one day. One day soon!"

She drained her wine glass while her friends whooped their glee, then she reached for the bottle of pinot grigio and poured another.

Corinne settled down on the couch beside Reggie and patted her knee companionably. "Buck up, grasshopper. We love you, and I can guarantee that we will give you one hell of a Fix."

"That's what I'm afraid of."

Reggie had never really wanted a Fix. She'd wanted a marriage and a family and a white picket fence, but Greg had ruined all that. And what was worse, her friends would probably have had a harder time believing that was her fantasy than they would with the alien abduction scenario. For Reggie, though, sex wasn't just about sex. Sex was great, of course, but she'd never been able to treat it lightly. She wasn't wired that way. For her, sex was about having a relationship with another person and allowing herself to be vulnerable to him, and who wanted to be vulnerable to a stranger?

Reggie wanted to be in love, not in lust.

"All right, ladies." Ava stood in front of the coffee table with Reggie's hat in her hand and a wicked smile on her face. "If I may have your attention, let's get started, since our Fix for this draw is already a bit behind the rest of us. Corinne, if you'd care to do the honors? Remember, we need a double draw for Ms. McNeill."

Corinne grinned and leaned forward to reach into the hat Ava held just above their heads. "Can I get a drum roll, please?"

Danice banged her hands on the edge of the coffee table. *As if I don't already have a headache*, Reggie thought, crossing her arms and tucking her chin to her chest like a petulant two-year-old.

With a flourish, Corinne drew two slips of white paper from the inside of the hat and rubbed them together like a couple of crisp twenties before handing them off to Ava. "The envelope, ma'am."

"Thank you, Corinne, darling. Now, what do we have here?"

The other three women leaned closer while Reggie sulked into her glass.

"Let's hear it!"

"Come on, what's it say?"

"I bet it's kinky. The quiet ones are always kinky."

Ava ignored them while she read. While one carefully sculpted eyebrow arched into a perfect bow. While her lips pursed. While she whistled long and low.

"I knew it!" Corinne blurted out, punching the air in emphasis. "I told you it's the quiet ones."

"You have no idea," Ava purred, finally looking up to see Reggie turning a peculiar shade of magenta. "Why, Regina Elaina McNeill, I am shocked. You are quite the little vixen, aren't you?"

"What's it say already?"

Ava smiled. "It says that our dearest friend thought she'd be pulling a fast one on us. Sorry to disappoint you, Regina darling, but you *are* getting Fixed, whether you like it or not."

Missy frowned. "What are you talking about?"

Ava held up one piece of paper and read aloud. "Regina says she wants to be 'seduced by a sexy, mysterious vampire.'"

Corinne turned a glare on Reggie. "That is not fair, Reg! Your fantasies have to be plausible. You can't hold us responsible for not being able to find you someone who doesn't even exist!"

"Hush. Don't get your panties in a twist, Corinne, dear," Ava soothed. "You are not destined for celibacy. We will provide Reggie with what she asked for."

Danice rolled her eyes. "You had a few too many glasses of that wine, Ava. Vampires aren't real."

"I know that, and since Regina is perfectly sane—at least legally—she knows it as well. If Reggie actually wanted us to find her a genuine vampire, she would be cheating, and I know our friend would never do that. Which means we need to view her fantasy in a more creative light."

"Like how?"

"I'm so glad you asked." Ava purred her answer to Missy's question, but her gaze never wavered from Reggie's. "It just so happens I know of a certain club in the East Village that hosts a regular event on the last Friday of each month. They call it the Vampire Ball."

Corinne laughed. "So we can find Reggie a man there! Since she knows she can't have a real vampire, she'll have to accept a man who could pose as one. Ava, you're brilliant!"

"I try, dear."

"Yeah, you're very trying." Reggie scowled. "I can't believe you're going to pawn me off on some freak who is so out of touch with reality he pretends to be a vampire to get his kicks. That is so pathetic."

Ava's Cheshire cat grin turned steely. "You agreed to the enterprise, Reggie, and you submitted the fantasy. You're bound by the rules just like the rest of us, so unless you want to submit something more realistic, this is the fantasy you get."

"One of them, anyway." Bless her mediating heart, Missy stepped between the two women before they could come to blows. "What does the other fantasy say? Does she want to be abducted by aliens, or have Elvis's love child?"

Missy tried to joke about it to lighten things up, which Reggie appreciated, but when Ava shook her head and smiled wider, Reggie felt every muscle in her body tighten with fear.

"Neither," Ava purred, holding up the other slip of paper. "She doesn't want to be Bigfoot's love slave, either."

Oh, no! In that moment, Reggie knew for certain the gods had abandoned her to an ugly fate. She knew which other fantasy Ava had selected. The need to escape suddenly overwhelmed her.

"I need a drink." Reggie pushed off the floor and attempted to head into the kitchen to hide. She never made it past the end of the coffee table. Danice grabbed her by the shoulders and forced her back to a seat on the sofa.

"Ah-ah, Reg. Sit your butt back down and prepare to get Fixed."

"Come on, guys. I'm sorry for making up the vampire thing," she stammered. "Can't we just forget about it? I'll write a real fantasy this time. I promise. Let's start over. Please?"

"Not a chance. Now that we know you want to be"—Ava consulted the slips of paper—"as you say here, 'seduced and overpowered by a lover,' we are not going to let this go. Especially not when you also have this burning desire to be 'bound, spanked, and dominated' by a sexy, commanding brute."

"Oh, wow," Missy breathed, her mouth rounding into an O of surprise, and she stared at her friend through new eyes.

"Reggie, I can't believe you never mentioned this. What else have you been keeping secret from us?"

"Nothing," Reggie insisted, though it came out kind of muffled by the hands in which she had buried her flaming face. "Not a damn thing. How could I keep secrets from you people? You're worse than tabloid reporters!"

"Actually," Corinne offered, "I *am* a tabloid reporter."

Danice grinned. "Hey, it's not like you want to get back together with Gregory the Grotesque. Now we just know you're a wild thing in the bedroom. No biggie."

"Oh, not at all." Reggie drained her wine glass and refilled it, taking it with her when she curled into a ball in the corner of her sofa. "Humiliation never killed anyone. I'm sure I'll get over it in another couple of incarnations."

Missy, always the softy, wiped the smile off her face and squeezed Reggie's arm. "Hey, it's not so bad. It's not like you don't know anything embarrassing about any of us. I mean, come on. You know about my mountain man thing. You know Danice got picked up by a marine on shore leave. You know Ava auditioned for a strip show. Let's face it, honey. You're not the only girl out there with . . . sophisticated tastes."

Seeing their words were maybe beginning to get through to their blushing comrade, Corinne perched on the arm of the sofa beside Reggie and topped off the other woman's drink. "She's right, you know. Besides, we're your best friends. We'd love you even if you had secret fantasies about Dubya. We'd think you were insane, but we'd still love you."

That drew a reluctant smile.

"We would," Danice insisted. "A little kink ain't nothing to be ashamed of, girl. If your fantasies were as vanilla as the rest of you, that's when I'd start to worry."

Ava waved a hand to get their attention. "All true, of course. And, since our reluctantly cooperative friend has two fantasies that work so very well together, I think we can safely assure her that we are going to make sure they come true, and quite quickly as well. Next week happens to be the last Friday of the month, which means the five of us will be having a very interesting night in the Village. If I can propose a toast?"

The women reached for their glasses and held them aloft in anticipation.

"To our dear friend Regina," Ava said after a brief pause. "And to her very own Fantasy Fix. May they be very happy together!"

CHAPTER 2

JUST BECAUSE THE GODS HAD ABANDONED HER to a cruel fate didn't stop Reggie from praying they'd keep her from breaking her ankle.

She took as deep a breath as the black satin corset her friends had laced her into would allow, and concentrated very hard on balancing on her four-inch heels while she descended the steps into the darkened club.

Seven solid days of frantic pleading, threats, and attempted bribery had failed to sway Ava or any of the other three women from their determination to "Fix" Reggie. They insisted on making the scheduled trip to a nightclub in the heart of the East Village that had been made over for the monthly vampire event as the Mausoleum, an unrepentantly gothic piece of urban kitsch. None of them had even shown any sympathy for Reggie's pleas, except for Missy.

Even then, as softhearted as she was, Missy

refused to side with Reggie against the others. Instead she'd tried to offer reassurance.

"It's not like Ava is really going to pawn you off on a loser, Reg," Missy had said over the phone earlier. "She was just trying to get your goat for giving us such a hard time. You know what she's like. She'd kill me if she knew I told you this, but she knows a guy she's been planning to hook you up with forever, and she's having him meet us at the club. I've met him, and he's great. Now will you relax?"

The answer to that—a resounding no of a headache—began to throb behind Reggie's temples in time to the industrial-techno music that boomed through the loudspeakers. She tried her best to ignore it and stuck like glue to her friends. If she lost them, she'd never find them again in the gyrating throng of identically black-clad bodies.

Of course, that went both ways. If she could slip away unnoticed—

A hand clamped over her wrist.

"Stay close!" Ava leaned into their little huddle, but she still had to shout to make herself heard any farther than six inches away. "Let's head over to the bar and get a drink before we plan our attack."

Ava always had been perceptive, and she refused to let go of Reggie while she squeezed and shimmied her way through the crowd toward the black-lit bar at one end of the cavernous room.

She must have guessed that Reggie had already been planning to bolt.

The women squirmed their way across the dance floor like an amoeba with five pseudopodia. Getting up to the bar required the judicious use of a few elbows and an acquired immunity to insults. As the first to reach an empty inch of space, Danice yelled their drink orders, and the others closed ranks around Reggie, who promptly rolled her eyes.

"Come on, guys," she protested when they hurried to snag a tall bar table that had just been vacated. "Don't you think you're being just a little paranoid? I'm here. I came. I answered my door when you picked me up instead of refusing to buzz you in. I put on these excuses for clothes you told me to wear. I even let you plant a bag full of sex toys in my closet! I've surrendered. I'm not likely to go anywhere now."

"But we know you well enough not to trust you," Corinne pointed out, accepting a dark brown beer bottle and taking a moment to survey the crowd. "Ava was the one who thought the corset would be enough to keep you from running. But I brought a leash along just in case."

"Bite me."

"Oh, you'd like that, wouldn't you?"

"Children, please. We have more important things to do than squabble like three-year-olds. Regina looks fantastic in her corset, and I'm sure a leash won't be necessary, unless her fantasy wants her to wear one." Ava glanced discreetly at her watch. "We have exactly four hours and fifteen minutes before the party ends and Regina turns back into a pumpkin. Battle stations."

Reggie's four friends faced the four corners of the bar and started scanning for potential partners. Frowning, Reggie leaned close to Missy's ear and spoke in a low murmur, "I thought you said Ava already had someone picked out."

"She does, but she wants you to squirm a little," Missy hissed back, her eyes on the masses of men and women passing before her. "Could you at least look a little nervous? If she knows I warned you, she'll kill me."

Looking nervous would not be a problem. Reggie felt more than a little out of place surrounded by so many strangers, all of whom seemed to have a genuine fear of sunlight and rather theatrical wardrobes. She hadn't known you could see so many white faces outside of a mime convention.

With a sigh, Reggie scanned the crowd and hoped Ava's friend turned out to be significantly different from any of the men she'd noticed so far.

The crowd really wasn't her type. Most of them were too young for her, and even the ones who were her age or older somehow managed to look like children playing dress-up. How could she feel attracted to someone who put so much time and effort into pretending to be a fictional character? She had always preferred her men to have a tighter grip on reality, not that you'd know it from her track record. Take Gregory, for instance. Apparently most of the women in lower Manhattan already had.

Sipping her amaretto sour and leaning her elbows on the scarred table, Reggie figured since her friends wanted to do all the work in picking up a man for her tonight, she could indulge in a little brooding over her recent failures.

Greg epitomized her "type," which probably meant she should reevaluate the concept of types from the bottom up. He'd been confident, attractive, intelligent, and ambitious, the kind of man mothers all over the world dreamed would walk into their daughters' lives. If she hadn't died when Reggie was a kid, her mother would probably be calling daily and asking what happened to that charming Greg fellow Reggie used to bring home for holiday visits.

Lisette the Slavic Slut had happened, Reggie acknowledged, trying very hard not to picture the little blond bimbo bent over Greg's desk with her skirt hiked around her waist and her G-string tangled around her ankles. Reggie had been late for her lunch date with Greg and hadn't thought anything about walking right into his office when she saw Lisette's empty desk. She'd thought the woman had been taking a break. Instead, she'd been taking it doggy-style from Reggie's fiancé.

"Reggie! I can explain!"

Had anyone ever invented a more hackneyed reaction to that scene? She'd always credited Greg with a certain level of intelligence, but apparently she'd overestimated him. He might have been a genius when it came to portfolios and earnings ratios, but when it came to facing a shocked lover with his dick hanging out of his pants, a dark smear of lipstick on his neck, and his hands all over his administrative assistant, he possessed the approximate smarts of a seven-year-old caught throwing snowballs at the poodle next door.

"Reggie, I swear, Lisette and I were just—"

"Screwing like rabid minks on top of the latest NASDAQ reports?"

Reggie wished she'd come up with that response at the time, but all she'd been able to do was stand there with her mouth open and her breath frozen in her chest and the hand that wore his ring clenched tightly around the doorknob.

She took another sip of her drink and forced her mind away from replaying the rest of the memory. She still recalled every ugly word they'd hurled back and forth at each other, oblivious to the hallowed reputation of Sterling and Woulk Financial, Inc., but that didn't mean she wanted them echoing in her head right now. Greg's infidelity had ruined her plans for a marriage and family, her trust in the ability of men to keep their promises, and most of her last six months.

She'd be damned if she'd let him ruin her night as well.

After finishing her drink on an empty stomach—she'd been too nervous to eat dinner earlier—Reggie could almost see how Ava might have a point about this whole fix thing. Maybe a good, fantasy-fulfilling one-night stand *was* the best way to forget about Greg. And if Ava already knew the guy, Reggie could be confident he wouldn't be an axe murderer or some sort of monster. Maybe she just needed to relax and let herself go with the flow.

Reggie pushed away from the table, taking a minute to brace herself against the alcohol racing to her head, just as the DJ spun into a new tune. The song had a deep, hypnotic beat and a dark, haunting melody. Signaling for another drink, she consigned her instinctive reticence to the wind and let her body pick up the rhythm of the music. The black leather pants she'd thought would be too confining turned out to move quite well with her shimmying hips. She ignored the looks her ass attracted from a few guys at the bar and tried to locate her friends.

Danice obviously liked the beat, too, because she'd accepted an invitation to dance with a tall, burly biker and shouted she'd be right back. Reggie watched her go, envying her friend's ease in the crowded club. When the waitress set a fresh glass in front of her, Reggie raised it to her lips and turned to face the bar. She wondered if she'd be able to pick Ava's friend out of the crowd.

Not the one right in front, she decided, watching a pretty, pale boy gesture grandly to the bevy of emaciated young women who surrounded him. Ava knew Reggie well enough to realize she'd never go for an overly theatrical kid. How in the world would she take someone like that seriously? He'd pull out a pair of handcuffs, and she'd have to ask if his daddy knew where he'd gotten them. She similarly dismissed a handful of brooding punks and a couple of leather-clad biker types. Ava's taste ran to something significantly more sophisticated.

Stubbornly ignoring her headache, she started to think Ava's friend might have stood them up when her gaze hit the end of the bar and skidded to a halt.

The most perfect man she'd ever seen sat there in the shadows with a hand wrapped around a glass of amber liquid and his eyes locked directly on her face.

DMITRI VIDÂME NURSED HIS SINGLE GLASS OF Scotch and wondered if there might be enough liquid in the glass to drown himself.

Literally.

Because he was about four minutes away from burying his face in it and breathing deep. Perhaps the fumes would counteract the odor of sweaty, chemically enhanced humans with sex on their minds and cobwebs in their heads.

If it hadn't been for Graham's insistence that this "Vampire Ball" made a perfect place for a young rogue to hide in plain sight, Dmitri would never have let himself be caught within ten city blocks of the place. Such a gothic circus as this event hardly fit his normal thinking as to what constituted a good time, and frankly, the attendees who filled the Mausoleum's vast basement dance floor had begun to annoy him.

Look at them, he marveled, struggling to keep the sneer from his face. *If any of these children ever came face to face with a genuine vampire, they'd soil themselves and go running home to Mommy.*

Barely cut loose from apron strings, and the little humans thought themselves misunderstood and tormented. They thought they felt more comfortable in the dark than in the sunlight, thought they knew what it meant to be isolated and tormented.

Dmitri wanted nothing so much as to slap some sense into them.

Actually, that wasn't precisely true. Even more than a little judicious violence, he wanted to go home. A quiet evening in front of his fireplace sounded infinitely more appealing to him than another five minutes surrounded by pretentious children in "gothic" garb. Even one of the endless, politically charged meetings of the Council of

Others, which he currently headed, sounded more appealing. Considering that that body had been founded to govern the uneasy alliance of the vampires, werewolves, changelings, and other nonhuman inhabitants of New York City, looking forward to one of its meetings made quite a statement.

Dmitri swore under his breath and tossed back half of his drink in one swallow. He had let Graham, his good friend and fellow Council member, talk him into coming to this torture session. Rumors had recently reached the Council about a few young vampires who had taken to frequenting these goth events and feeding off the eager attendees. The fledglings risked exposure with their behavior, and the Council had decided they needed a stern warning.

It hardly counted as a crisis of epic proportions, and Dmitri would have been happy to let a few of Graham's Lupine packmates do the Council's dirty work, but the werewolf leader had volunteered Dmitri and himself for the job instead. Dmitri was tempted to "volunteer" Graham for the French Foreign Legion in exchange.

Neither man had spotted any of the suspected rogues during their two interminable hours at this event, and Dmitri was more than ready to go home. As soon as Graham stopped sniffing around that blowsy little blonde he was currently "questioning," Dmitri would say his goodbyes and head out. Maybe he'd stop for a bite on the way home, just to wash the taste of this place out of his mouth.

He had so many better things he could be doing, he reflected, trying to pick Graham out of the shifting crowd.

Where had he and that blonde disappeared to? The Council had been busy lately, but even diplomatic problems hadn't kept his mind occupied. He felt boredom creeping up on him and wondered if it were time for him to step down from his Council seat in favor of new pursuits. Dmitri had been born a warrior in a world where strength equaled survival and warfare had been a way of life, but progress had forced the retirement of his broadsword many years ago. These days wars were fought from a distance, with computers and satellites and aerial attacks.

Technology had taken all the fun out of the bloodshed.

Dmitri sighed and rubbed a hand over his stylishly short hair. Back in the good old days, he'd worn it long and tied it back with a leather thong before battle and the memory left him feeling suddenly old. Even older than his years. In the beginning, warfare had kept him interested, then it had been business and investing, but even that complex game had begun to lose its appeal. How would he entertain himself now, for all the years to come?

Restless, he pushed the depressing thought

from his head and tapped fingers on the scarred wooden surface of the bar, sorely tempted to just forget his goodbyes and leave Graham to his fate and his bimbo. He reached for his glass to drain the last drops of fiery whisky, and that's when he saw her.

Temptation.

She stepped up to the bar, swept along in the wake of four other women, but Dmitri could not have described a single one of them. He saw only her, with her face like a vision and her body like a gift from the gods.

The woman looked impatient and a little nervous and sadly out of place among the ridiculous throngs that surrounded her. For one thing, she had the look of a woman, rather than a child. He could see she was young, probably in her late twenties, but she wore her age comfortably, as a mature woman should. Her skin, milk white and dusted with freckles the color of honey, looked smooth and unlined.

Dmitri saw a great deal of skin, from her hairline to the generous swell of her breasts where they were cuddled and lifted by the black satin of her corset; from the graceful curve of her shoulder to the tips of her slender fingers. Her snug black leather pants and tall black boots covered everything else, hugging her curves with loving care and making his body tighten.

Lord, she is stunning.

He certainly felt stunned. He hadn't reacted to the mere sight of a woman in longer than he could remember, but he reacted to this one. Already he could feel his cock hardening beneath his trousers, filling with blood and heat, while his sense of boredom died a sharp and final death.

She stood out in stark contrast against the sea of sameness that surrounded her. She, too, had dressed all in black, but she shared nothing else with the other women in the room. Her skin had the pearlescent glow of natural fairness, and her hair had not been dyed a flat and light-absorbing black. It rippled over her shoulders and down her back in waves of burnished mahogany. When she turned her head, the light caught it and sparked dancing flames across the shiny surface. Dmitri imagined burying his hands in it, using his grip to hold her still while he drove into her body.

He wanted that body, he acknowledged, wanted to feel those pale, white curves against him, under him. Her body flowed beneath clinging black cloth and stiff metal boning in a reflection of Venus's glory. Smooth, graceful shoulders curved down to generous breasts, and the corset accentuated the way her waist nipped in waspishly beneath their enticing fullness. Her hips flared from that narrow span, round and lush and firm, and her legs, gloved by the smooth leather pants, looked round and soft and perfect for clasping around his hips, or throwing over his shoulders, or tangling firmly with his.

He sat there at the bar, staring and fantasizing and wanting her, and while he did so, he gave in to his instincts and slipped lightly inside her mind.

She didn't notice him, as wrapped up in her thoughts as she was, but he'd have been astounded if she had. Most people didn't notice his mental presence even when he didn't keep quiet, like he did now. Very few people out there had any sort of psychic talent, and even fewer knew how to use it. He didn't probe deeply enough into the woman's mind to see if she did; he just wanted to get a sense of her, to decide if more than her beautiful body intrigued him.

More than intrigued, he found himself entranced and unexpectedly entertained. This woman possessed a lively mind and a sharp-edged humor.

Look at that. He heard her voice in his head, husky and feminine and arousing. *Lord Velveteen thinks he's just the shit sitting there with those silly little stick figures fawning all over his poet shirt. Does he have any idea how ridiculous it is for a grown man to have a visible rib cage and lacy shirt cuffs?*

Oh, wait. That's right. He's a long way from a grown man.

He watched her raise a glass to her slick, painted mouth, and his eyes narrowed. He wanted those lips to part around his cock, and the violence of his lust surprised him. This woman had an unsettling effect on him.

And that one, he heard her scoff. *How ridiculous*

*does he look? He's got more mascara on than I do, and
he didn't even check for clumps. Is he crooking. His.
Finger. At me? Get real, sonny. I'm not about to answer that insulting little summons with a makeup tip,
let alone with what you're after.*

Dmitri's head whipped around, and his gaze
locked on the mascaraed Romeo. A quick mental
push sent the kid reeling back against the bar and
put the fear of God into him—or, at least, the fear
of Dmitri.

*Where is this guy Ava invited? If I have to wait
around this circus much longer, he can kiss his chances
for some nookie goodbye. I don't care how badly they
think I need this. I refuse to consider sleeping with
someone who can't even manage to show up on time
for it.*

Rage turned his vision black for a split second,
and Dmitri actually felt his fangs lengthen in anticipation of the wounds he would inflict on any
man who dared to touch her. He would show these
pretenders a real vampire's fury if a single one of
them thought to lay a hand on what Dmitri intended to claim for his own. His woman would
not be touched by any man but him.

His woman.

Dmitri registered the possessive term with
surprise and tested the phrase in his mind. In all
his considerable lifetime, he'd never felt such an
instant proprietary interest in any woman. He'd
never been tempted to conquer and claim so

quickly. But in this case, he wanted to mark the woman so the entire world would know to keep its distance.

When he saw the woman turn her gaze to him, he ruthlessly tamped down his emotions and moved his touch to the edge of her mind. He didn't think she had noticed his presence within her, but he felt it prudent to be cautious. Already, he detected a stubborn and independent streak in her. He didn't want her to struggle against him. Not yet.

He felt her gaze on him, and he met her stare with a bold one of his own. Heat arced between them, slicing through the crowd as if to remove all barriers separating them. He wanted no barriers, wanted her bared to him, body and mind, so he could sate himself with her flesh, her thoughts, and her blood.

She was perfect, and she would be his.

CHAPTER 3

LORD, BUT HE IS SCRUMPTIOUS.

Unable to keep from staring, Reggie decided even if this wasn't Ava's friend, he was the only man she wanted tying her to a bed tonight, thank you very much.

He perched on his barstool with the lazy, elegant grace of a panther, and his thick, dark hair looked as glossy as a panther's furry hide. It capped a face of arresting sensuality. She couldn't call him handsome, not with features so firm and chiseled they looked like they'd been cut from granite, but she could definitely call him yummy. In fact, she'd just adore eating him all up.

His hard features matched his body, or what she could see of it from across the room. He had the graceful, muscled physique of the big cat she'd already compared him to, with broad shoulders, long, muscular legs, and a lean, flat stomach. His dark, casual clothes suited him and drew attention to his impressive frame.

She found herself craning her head to see him better through the milling crowd. A knowing smile curved his sensual mouth, and Reggie blushed, cheeks flaming even harder when another gorgeous male specimen stopped beside her mystery man and placed a hand on his shoulder. The newcomer leaned his head down to hear what Mr. Mouthwatering had to say, and when his head turned and his eyes locked on Reggie, she knew they were talking about her.

Oh, my. Apparently the truly drop-dead gorgeous travel in packs, she thought, when she got a good look at Mr. Hunk's friend.

The second man had a body covered in lean, hard muscle, and his toffee-highlighted, chocolaty dark hair looked like it needed a good cut. His skin was darker than Mr. Oohlala's, but he had the same sort of commanding presence and authoritative stare.

She waited for the same surge of lust that had hit her the moment she saw the first mystery man, but nothing happened. Her brain appreciated that the friend made a truly appealing decoration, but she experienced no urge to tear off her clothes and fling her body against his. Shifting her gaze to Mr. Magnificent, she felt her hands reaching toward her zipper.

Across the bar, her mystery man laughed out

loud, and she heard the sound even over the din of music and conversation. She felt it, too. It vibrated in the pit of her stomach and aroused her like a caress. Her thighs clenched together.

Okay, Reg, get a grip, she instructed herself, breaking eye contact and looking around for her friends. Maybe they could distract her from her hormone attack. Danice and Corinne gyrated on the dance floor, oblivious to anything other than the music, but at least Ava and Missy were still sticking close to Reggie's side. Frankly, Ava wasn't likely to budge until the guy she'd arranged to fix Reggie up with got there.

Reggie thought she could count on Missy, too, but even as the thought crossed her mind, a group of women stopped next to their table and launched a babbling greeting for Melissa Roper, their old pal from college, here at the nightclub. Grateful for the chance to focus on something other than Mr. Take-MeNow, Reggie pasted on a smile and let Missy introduce her to the other women.

Their small table suddenly became the place to be in the crowded club. The friends seemed to breed more friends, and their numbers swelled from four to seven. Reggie stepped back to make room for yet another one of them to hug Missy hello and found herself maneuvered entirely away from the table. An elbow struck her in the small of her back, and she turned to glare at whoever hadn't watched where he was going. She scanned the crowd, but no one looked close enough to be the culprit.

Sighing, she turned back toward Missy and the college friends only to realize she'd lost their table completely. Somehow, when her back was turned, she'd been swept away in the crowd and couldn't even see where Missy and Ava had been standing.

She started to get angry before another thought struck her. If she couldn't see her friends, they couldn't see her. She could make good her escape!

Suddenly, she felt like she'd just managed a prison break. Now if she could just avoid the warden and the bloodhounds long enough to make it through the front door, she'd be a free woman.

She wasted no time. Ducking behind a tall man in purple latex, she started to weave a path through the bar toward the front entrance. She'd gotten maybe five feet before a hand closed around her elbow and pulled her to a halt.

"Surely you are not leaving yet, *malishka*?"

Reggie rocked to a halt on her four-inch heels and froze. She felt the warm hand on her skin and the dark presence beside her, but everything else disappeared. Even the throb of the music faded into the background. Reggie refused to acknowledge whether or not anything else had taken up throbbing instead.

The smoothly accented voice that spoke from slightly behind her wasn't nearly as surprising as the firm, warm hand that slid down over the smooth satin of her corset to settle with intimate possession on her hip. Her head snapped up, and she found herself looking into the intense, black eyes of the stranger from the end of the bar.

Wow. He's even yummier up close.

That was her initial reaction, followed closely by an embarrassed blush when he smiled down at her with a lazy sort of amusement, as if she'd spoken her comments aloud.

That's impossible, Regina. He's just a guy, not a Psychic Friend. So get a grip. And what is he doing with his hands on me, anyway? I know I've never seen him before. He is not the sort of thing a girl forgets.

She figured that last thought qualified her for an MU degree—Master of Understatement.

The man looked like sin walking. Easily over six feet tall, probably six two or six three, his impressive muscles were even more intimidating up close. His thick, dark hair looked black in the dim light and fell in unruly waves over his forehead. He needed a cut, and she almost wished she had a styling license just to have an excuse to run her fingers through that hair.

His eyes, so dark they appeared black, laughed down at her, though his luscious, chiseled lips remained firm in his granite-hewn face.

She opened her mouth to speak, but he tightened the hand on her hip just a little, enough to distract her from what she'd been about to say.

"I had hoped you would allow me to buy you a

drink," the dark voice rumbled again, and Reggie saw something more than amusement in Mr. YumYum's black, bedroom eyes. Under the glint of humor, his gaze was watchful and intense and blazing with heat. Reggie did not consider herself the type of girl who let strange men pick her up in bars. Still, she had enough sense to regret that while she stared up at him and unthinkingly licked her lips.

The stranger's eyes blazed hotter, and his hand on her hip shifted to bring her closer. The action managed to snap Reggie out of her daze.

She scrambled to regain her equilibrium—something she'd never had a problem with before Tall, Dark, and Sinful had shown up—and turned to face him. "I never let strange men buy me drinks. You never know which one might be the next Jack the Ripper."

His mouth quirked up at one corner. "I promise I have no fondness for dark alleys, nor for prostitutes. But if it would make you feel better, you may buy me a drink instead."

She thought that might prove to be just as dangerous. "Um, I suppose I should thank you for the offer, Mr. . . . whoever you are, but I don't think so."

She attempted to step back, to reinforce her words with some distance—a buffer zone against his enormous sex appeal—but the stranger held on tight and merely smiled at her.

"Dmitri," he murmured, that wickedly amused look she'd noticed earlier back on his face. "My name is Dmitri Vidâme. And you have not, really."

Dmitri. Well, that went with the sexy hit of Slavic in his accent, but the last name had sounded almost French.

"I haven't what?" she asked.

"Thanked me."

It took a struggle, but Reggie managed to overcome her desire to melt at the sight of his sexy, mischievous smile and forced her eyes to roll instead. "For offering to 'let' me buy you a drink? That's not the sort of offer that inspires me to thank you by inviting you back to my place and showing you my naked gratitude."

Dmitri chuckled, a rough, rumbling sound that rasped over her senses like the tongue of a great big cat. "I had not thought you should. I was merely giving you the opportunity to voice your thanks in the conventional manner. But if you prefer to do this while naked"—his eyebrows shot up, and his grin deepened—"it would be rude of me to gainsay you, no?"

Reggie blushed. Even though she'd brought up the whole naked thing, somehow the idea sounded a lot more wicked on his lips than it ever had on hers. Maybe it was the rough, gravelly sound of his voice or the faint, exotic accent, but somehow Reggie thought those were probably the least of his seductive weapons.

She cleared her throat and again tried to step back. Again his hand tightened on her hip, but this time it was joined by its mate. Both hands slid over the warm silk of her corset and settled possessively at the small of her back. He drew her even closer.

Reggie looked down to see she'd somehow been led without her notice. Dmitri had backed up until he sat at the bar again, and he pulled her to him until she stood between his spread legs, close enough to smell the earthy, spicy scent of him. She took a deep, involuntary breath, savoring his fragrance, until his chuckle broke the spell, and her eyes snapped open.

She didn't even remember when she'd closed them.

"Look, Mr. Vidâme, why don't I go back to my friends and you can go back to your friend?" She blurted out the suggestion, which just showed her nerves had gotten out of control. This man could easily turn her into a babbling idiot . . . if it wasn't already too late. "I saw him talking to you earlier—"

"Misha."

"—and I'm sure the two of you had plans for . . . huh?" She stopped, the gorgeous friend forgotten.

"You should not call me Mr. Vidâme, Regina," he instructed. "You should call me Dmitri, at the very least. Though I would prefer you call me Misha. It is a nickname. A term of endearment."

He said it as if he wanted to become dear to her.

Reggie shook her head to clear out the cobwebs she could feel forming. "Wait. How did you know my name? You couldn't have heard my friends over the music."

"Actually, I have exceptional hearing, but your friends only called you by that horrid nickname. Reggie is a name for a man, not for one so obviously a woman." His eyes roamed over her in frank appreciation. "Nor one so beautiful."

Reggie blushed at his compliment, which only made her madder. "Don't try and sweet-talk me, buster. I've had enough of that kind of crap. In fact, I've had enough of this conversation. Now take your hands off me."

Dmitri raised an eyebrow and lifted his hands from her hips, holding his palms up so she could see they no longer restrained her. "You are always free to go, Regina. If that is truly your wish."

She didn't trust the velvet purr in his voice, nor the amused expression on his face. She took a step backward.

Or, to be precise, she tried to take a step backward. She pictured herself taking a step backward. She could practically feel the impulse running down the nerve endings from her brain to her legs, but her feet remained stubbornly motionless. Since she'd already shifted her weight backward in anticipation of that step, she nearly fell on her ass.

She teetered for a moment, on the verge of an

embarrassing thump, and reached out to steady herself. Instead of catching the cool wood of the bar, her hands caught the solid warmth of Dmitri's thighs, encased in soft, black denim. As soon as she steadied herself, she snatched her hands back as if they burned.

They only tingled.

"What the hell is going on?"

Dmitri shrugged. "I did as you asked, *dushka*. I have taken my hands off you. I have told you that you are free to go." He leaned closer to her until she could feel his breath brush her skin. "You must not want to leave me."

"Bullshit," Reggie said, trying to cover her growing unease. "You've done something to me, and I want to know what the hell it is. No, actually, I don't care what you're doing, I just want you to stop it and let me go."

She braced her hands against his legs and pushed, but her feet remained stubbornly glued to the floor. Dmitri leaned forward, and she turned her head, straining to get away. One large, masculine hand touched her hip and trailed up her side, skirting the outside of her breast until it closed over her chin, gently but firmly turning her back to face him. He forced her eyes to meet his, capturing her gaze and holding it as surely as he held her feet in place. Which she knew he was doing. Somehow.

"Do you really?" he murmured, nuzzling her

cheek so a hint of stubble rasped against her skin. His other hand slid around her hip to rest in the small of her back and press her closer. His thighs tightened, and he surrounded her, held her caged and confined and unable to escape. She couldn't even tear her gaze from his. His dark eyes restrained her as securely as his hands, drew her deeper until she wondered if it would be so bad to drown in those glittering, black pools.

Do you really want me to leave you?

Helpless, seduced, she felt her head slowly shake from side to side. *No.*

Dmitri smiled again, but this time the expression appeared dangerous and male and predatory, rather than amused. *I thought not. You want to belong to me, Regina, as much as I want you to be mine.*

His voice rumbled over her, around her, until it was the only thing in her universe, the only thing other than his hands and his skin and his dark, dark eyes. Yet even as he spoke to her, she could see the play of desire and satisfaction on his lips. Lips that never moved.

Reggie froze, her eyes going wide, her lips parting, and her breath grinding to a halt. "Oh, my God," she whispered, still unable to move, but equally unable to believe she had heard this man speaking to her inside her head, had felt him holding her in place even when he ceased to touch her. "Who are you?"

His hand slid from her chin to cup her face, his fingers tangling in the soft silk of her hair. And still his eyes held hers, keeping her still and enthralled. "I have told you, *dushka*, I am Dmitri Vidâme. And I will be your lover."

CHAPTER 4

REGGIE COULDN'T REMEMBER THEIR LAST FEW minutes at the bar, but she remembered the feel of Dmitri's palm on the bare skin between her shoulder blades. She didn't remember saying goodbye to her friends, or paying for her drink, but she remembered his hands on her waist while he walked behind her and guided her through the crowd to the front door.

She didn't remember the cab ride home, but she remembered the steely strength of Dmitri's thighs beneath her as she sat on his lap and rested her head on his firm shoulder. She remembered his fingers cupping her breasts through the heavy silk of her corset, his thumbs making teasing swipes over her tight nipples.

She remembered one of those incredible hands drifting over her stomach and cupping possessively between her thighs, making her flesh tingle and throb beneath her leather pants, but she didn't remember leaving the cab and entering her apartment building.

Her memory neglected to store the ride in the elevator up to her floor, or the long walk down the empty corridor to her apartment, but she would never forget the silent, overwhelming presence of the man who walked beside her.

She couldn't recall unlocking her door, but she remembered the feel of Dmitri's body, the heat of him when he crowded close behind her, urging her into the dark room and closing the door.

She remembered nothing until he flipped the switch on her bedside lamp and her consciousness turned on as well. She came back to herself in a flash and found herself standing in the middle of her bedroom with her nipples hard and her body aching and the hot, dark depths of his eyes threatening to swallow her whole.

"Oh, my God," she said, taking a frightened step back. A surge of adrenaline made her tremble, and she locked her knees to keep from falling. "We're in my apartment. I brought you to my apartment. I don't do this kind of thing. I don't understand what's happening."

His voice caressed her as surely as a touch. "There is no need to be afraid, Regina. What you have done in the past has no relevance here. All that happens this night happens only at your wish."

She shook her head. "No. I didn't wish this up.

This is your idea. It must be." Wrapping her arms around herself, she shivered.

Or did she tremble?

"What are you doing to me?"

"Only as you wish, *dushka*," Dmitri murmured, prowling toward her in the dim light. "Only what pleases you."

She retreated from him, shaking her head. "You can't be real. This can't be real. I must have made you up, because no one could possibly do what you're doing to me."

"What am I doing to you, Regina?"

Making me want to beg for your touch.

She ignored her thought. "You're scaring me."

That sounded like a much safer response.

Dmitri moved closer, and she retreated. They danced those same steps over and over until he backed her into the smooth wood of her bedroom door, and Reggie had nowhere else to go.

He leaned close. "It is not fear that causes your heart to race, *milaya*." He reached out, making her jerk back nervously, but he just brushed a stray tendril of hair from her face and held her gaze with his. "It is not fear that makes your breath quick and your mouth dry. It is not fear that tightens your nipples and dampens your panties. It is want."

Reggie's thighs clenched. His words made her hotter than she'd been the last time she'd come, and he wasn't even touching her.

"You can't be doing this to me," she said, hoping

she could make the words true by speaking them. "This can't happen."

Dmitri chuckled, a deep, rumbling sound that resonated in her head and her heart and deep inside her womb.

"You will be amazed by all the things that can happen, *milaya*, if you will just let go and trust me."

Let go. God, when had she ever let go? Regina McNeill had been raised a good girl by good parents in a good neighborhood in southern Connecticut, and all that goodness came with rules. There had always been rules in her life, and Reggie had always followed them. Do your homework. Play nice. Look both ways. Say "please" and "thank you." Wash your hands before dinner.

All her life, Reggie had let other people make the rules and never thought to protest. Yet here she was about to break the biggest rule of them all: never take candy from strangers.

Dmitri Vidâme was like candy, a big chocolate truffle standing in front of her, looking as rich as cream and as sweet as sin. If she reached her hand out to him, what would happen? Could she have a taste and remain untouched? Unchanged? Or would he bring on an addiction she couldn't fight? He seemed prepared to offer her all the forbidden delights she'd never had the nerve to ask for.

Power and submission. Pain and pleasure. Struggle and release.

He tempted her, shamelessly. Like the serpent in the Garden.

Like the devil himself.

Reggie wanted it so badly she scared herself, and a frightened Reggie was a belligerent Reggie.

"Trust you?" she scoffed, stiffening her spine and glaring up at him. "I don't even know you! I just picked you up in a bar. You could be anyone. Or any *thing*. How am I supposed to trust you?"

God, she sounded like her parents, her aunts, her uncles, her teachers. Everyone who had ever told her to be ashamed to want certain things. Only bad girls wanted those things.

She braced herself for his anger, almost hoped for it. If he were angry, maybe she wouldn't want so badly to rip off all her clothes and jump him. Better to push him away than to risk being dragged under with him.

She was glad she could still speak her mind though. It comforted her to know no matter what this weird power he had over her, he hadn't turned her into some mindless sex drone. As long as she could still recognize herself, her fear stopped short of panic and terror.

Dmitri smiled, not an angry roar in sight. "You make excuses for yourself, Regina. Yet even as you do so, you know in your heart that the point is moot. Part of you already trusts me, or I would not be here. You would not have invited me into your home. Into your bed."

She resented the way his voice could make her ache for him. "I invited you into my bed, huh? Is that what I've done? It's funny, because I don't seem to recall saying that little thing."

"You do not have to speak for me to know your desires, *dushka*. I know precisely what you want, for it is what I want as well."

Knowing you want to tie me down and fuck me until my brain explodes is hardly comforting, buster.

Tamping down her wayward thoughts, she opened her eyes wide and batted her lashes up at him. "Really? You want an end to world hunger and a 1968 Jaguar sedan in British racing green?"

"You should be careful not to sass me too much, Regina Elaina." All at once, the three inches between their bodies became no inches, and he cupped his hands around her ass, kneading the flesh through the form-fitting leather. "I may have to punish you."

Yes, please!

Reggie cursed herself and the hot surge of desire that flared at the thought. Instead of fear, his statement aroused nothing but her nipples and her curiosity. And her body. She couldn't forget her body. No matter how hard she tried.

Her lips parted before she could stop them, and she was left to listen in horror when her tongue ran wild to tease the tiger. Had her body already taken the decision out of her hands? It certainly felt like it.

It felt like surrender.

"Oh, really?" She barely recognized her own voice for all the seductive purring. "And would you like to punish me, Dmitri?"

His eyes glinted, and his hands squeezed her ass. "As much as you would like to be punished, *katyonak*."

"What does that mean?" And could he please give her a lengthy explanation so she'd have time to think of an escape route?

"*Katyonak?*"

"Yes."

"It is an endearment. It means 'kitten.' "

Something in Reggie melted, and this time it wasn't even below her waistband. "Is that how you think of me? An innocent little kitten?"

He raised one hand to cup her face, lowered the other until his fingers slid between her ass cheeks and pressed against her leather-covered core from behind.

"An adventurous little kitten," he corrected, flicking one finger over the smooth, hot leather, "bent on mischief. Soft and sensuous and filled with curiosity, but still just a bit skittish."

With one hand on her face and his other hand cupping her through her increasingly uncomfortable leather pants, Reggie felt bound more tightly than iron shackles could have managed. This man had complete control over her body, and the look in his eyes told her he wanted it that way.

She trembled.

"Am I right, *katyonak*? Do I make you nervous?"

She trembled again, and her body shivered against his, bringing a very wicked smile to his lips. His hand pressed harder against her, and her folds spread for him, parting around the seam in the crotch of her pants. Suddenly even the thick leather seemed like no barrier at all.

He had the advantage, and he pressed it. The hand he hadn't already buried between her legs slid down from her jaw to close around her throat, not squeezing, but circling it like a collar and pressing her head gently back against the door. The position forced her spine to straighten even further than the corset alone had managed, and she stood there, pinned between his hard body and the hard wood, unable to look at anything but him. Unable to *feel* anything but him.

Wanting nothing but him.

He stared into her eyes, his thumb smoothing the skin of her vulnerable throat while his other hand began to rub the furrow between her thighs with firm, steady pressure. She felt like a toy, positioned for his pleasure, dominated and controlled beneath his hands and his eyes and his breathtaking presence.

God. How could she be so excited?

Why did she have to fight to keep from whimpering, to keep her eyes from drifting shut, to keep her thighs from parting wider to urge him closer? Should she really enjoy being treated like some sort of blow-up doll for a strange man to use?

"You have nothing in common with such inanimate objects, *milka*. A doll does not enjoy her lover's caress." His fingers slid forward, pressing the rough leather seam against her tender flesh, until he nudged her clit. Reggie bit back a moan, but she couldn't control the way her hips rolled into his touch. "Only a woman becomes so hot, so wet, so richly scented."

He inhaled deeply, breathing her in. Reggie saw the way his nostrils flared and the heat that burned in his eyes and wondered how she smelled to him.

Then she wondered what the hell she was thinking. She tensed, and nerves overwhelmed her again, no matter how wet he made her.

"That is very good, Regina," he murmured, nuzzling the sensitive hollow behind her ear. He might as well have nuzzled her clit, because his touch made her gasp and shake. "I want to make you nervous. And I want to make you wet. Before the night is over, I want to make you do many, many things you've only imagined. And that is what you want as well."

She wanted to deny it, wanted to tell him he

bored her and he should leave her alone. But his fingers slid forward and closed gently around her clit.

When he squeezed, she came.

Her body tensed and shuddered against the cold, wooden door. Her hips jerked hard against his hand, and she slicked the crotch of her leather pants with an embarrassing wetness. She stood there, dazed and breathless, held up not by her water-weak legs, but by his hand on her throat and his fingers on her spasming body.

"Isn't that what you want, Regina?"

She thought about denying it. She longed to deny it, but she knew he could feel the way her body still fluttered beneath his hand. She couldn't lie, but she didn't want to admit it either, so she kept her mouth shut and glared at him instead.

He smiled and twisted his hand until his knuckles dug into the soaking leather on either side of her sensitized clit. He flexed his fingers, and she whimpered.

"Isn't it?"

"God, yes!"

"Good girl."

All of a sudden his hands fell away from her, and she sagged boneless against the door. "What—?"

She hadn't had time to blink, but Dmitri stood several feet away, his lips curved in a hard, wicked smile. He looked so pleased with himself. If her pussy weren't still throbbing, she'd be tempted to wipe the smirk off his face.

"Patience, *dushka*," he murmured, looking amused by her mutinous expression. "You shall have what you want."

His eyes gleamed, and she could have sworn she felt his hands on her again, rubbing slowly over her swollen breasts and simultaneously cupping between her thighs, circling her wrists, and kneading her ass. If he hadn't been standing three feet away, she would have been tempted to believe he'd grown a hundred new hands. She could feel his touch everywhere. Sensory memory, she told herself. Never mind that he hadn't held her by her wrists.

"You shall have exactly what you crave, Regina, but only if you do as I say. Can you do that?"

She hesitated, wanting to say no, to scream, to run for the hills. At least, that's what her upbringing wanted to do. Her body wanted to wrap itself around him and not let go until she was too weak to move. She wasn't inclined to give her naughty bits the deciding vote.

But then her nipples chimed in, followed by her thighs, her arms, her ass, and, finally, her traitorous lips.

"Yes. I can do that."

She thought she caught a warm flash of pride

and pleasure before his expression firmed into a mask of impassive control.

"Good girl. In that case, strip off the leather and get on the bed. But leave the corset where it is."

CHAPTER 5

IT TOOK A MINUTE FOR THE COMMAND TO SINK in, but once it did, Reggie swallowed. Hard.

Strip? Now? Here?

"Strip," he repeated. "Now. Here."

He leaned against the post at the foot of her bed and watched.

Reggie bit her lip. Moment-of-truth time. Her body wanted the clothes off her back and Dmitri on her front. Her mind called her ten kinds of idiot. Her curiosity cast the deciding vote. When would she ever have this kind of opportunity again, especially with a man who made her this hot? And especially when she felt so dazed and disconnected from reality that she could say with a clear conscience that she just hadn't been thinking straight.

She couldn't back out now.

Her hands moved to the side zipper on her leather pants, but her eyes stayed on his face. Just looking at his firm, authoritative expression and his austere, compelling features sent a shiver down her spine. She couldn't read his thoughts, but her body didn't care. Her nipples tightened beneath their silk covering, and she slowly lowered the zipper.

"You might want to take the boots off first," Dmitri drawled, watching but not moving. "Unless you want to be stuck with your pants around your ankles and no place to go. Not that the image doesn't have a certain naughty-schoolgirl appeal." His eyes glinted, the only crack in his stoic demeanor. "But we'll save that particular scene for another time. Boots first."

The images sprang into her mind like an ambush. She saw herself, bare-bottomed and draped over his knees to face the consequences of her disobedience. Dmitri would be stern and unyielding, and she would be shaking and repentant, with an ass that glowed pink and warm from her spanking. A shudder raced through her.

Dmitri noticed. His eyes burned, and she felt the force of his satisfaction.

Her cheeks flushed even hotter, and she hurried to obey him. She reached down to pull off her boots and realized she had a problem.

Reggie bent to a thirty-five-degree angle before the confining corset jerked her to a halt. She was stuck, and all of a sudden she recalled a key detail of her wardrobe, like the fact that she'd put on the corset after the boots; and they could only come off in the opposite order.

She straightened up and cleared her throat. "Um, I seem to have a small problem."

Dmitri quirked an eyebrow.

"I can't untie the boots while I'm wearing the corset."

He said nothing.

Reggie suspected he knew exactly what her problem was, but she explained anyway. "I can't bend over far enough. Unless I take off the corset."

At least that got him to speak.

"Did I tell you to take off the corset?" he asked with the exaggerated patience of an adult to a slow-witted child.

He made Reggie feel like that naughty schoolgirl, and she quickly blocked out that thought before it got her in any more trouble. She shrugged. "You said to leave the corset where it is."

"Precisely."

She shifted her weight and frowned. "But I told you, I can't take the boots off while the corset is on. And I can't take the pants off until the boots come off."

He just raised his other eyebrow and waited.

"Fine then." Reggie crossed her arms over her chest and glared at him. "If I can't take the boots off, you have to find some other way to get into my pants, buster."

Reggie savored her defiance for all of three

milliseconds. Until she saw Dmitri's eyes narrow. His jaw firmed, and he pushed away from the bedpost, taking one menacing step toward her.

"I don't believe I heard you properly, Regina," he purred. This time the rasp sounded more like a threat than a rumble of pleasure. "Did you just talk back to me? Because if you did, I'm afraid you'll have to be punished for it."

For a heartbeat, she contemplated sassing him again. Not only would it give her great emotional satisfaction, but it would be the tug on the tiger's tail that likely would get her turned over his knee and spanked until she begged for mercy. And if she egged him on, she wouldn't have to take responsibility for it. She could blame him.

She quivered. Dmitri stepped in front of her until his chest pressed against her and his breath tickled her eyelashes. He clouded her mind with the feel of him. Her stomach did a back flip, and suddenly, defying him was the last thing on her mind. She wanted to please him, needed to win his approval. To earn his touch.

"I'm sorry," she whispered.

He gripped her chin in his hand, raising her eyes to meet his. "What did you say, Regina? I couldn't hear you."

She licked her lips, fought back another shudder. Every time she drew breath, she smelled him, and the earthy, spicy scent of him made her stomach clench. "I said I was sorry. I didn't mean t-to talk back to you like that."

Dmitri watched her, staring at her as if he were measuring her words and her sincerity and weighing them against her offense. His thumb stroked the tender underside of her jaw until her breath caught in her throat. He smiled.

"Better," he murmured, "but still not a proper apology. Who are you apologizing to? Me? Your bedroom? The universe?"

She chewed on her lip and frowned. "To you."

"And so you should, but I could not tell that from your apology. When you tell someone you are sorry, you should address him properly."

The look in his eyes told her he wanted something, even though she didn't know what. The feel of his hands on her, especially when one of them slid to the small of her back and pressed her hips firmly against the ridge of his erection, made her want to squirm. Her pussy ached and dripped, and her nipples hurt from beading so tightly. She needed relief, and she wondered what she would have to do to get it.

A thought occurred to her.

"Do you want me to—" She broke off and blushed. "I mean . . . are you asking me to . . . call you 'master'?"

What was the proper etiquette for this kind of situation? Emily Post needed to add a chapter or two.

His mouth curved in a slow, hot smile, and his hand slid from her chin to the nape of her neck. His fingers tangled in her hair and began to massage the hollow at the base of her skull. The feeling traveled down her spine until her thighs pressed together.

"I have already told you what I wish you to call me," he whispered. "Do you not remember?"

She nodded slowly and moistened her dry lips. "Misha."

"Yes. You will call me Misha, Regina, for you will not need so obvious a reminder of what I am to you."

Which meant he would be her master. Part of her rebelled, but other, more demanding parts rejoiced. Where had her parents gone wrong to turn her into such a pervert?

Dmitri—*Misha*—leaned forward and pressed a soft kiss to her forehead. Then he released her and resumed his position at the foot of her bed. "Now, I believe I told you to remove your boots."

Boots? What boots? Reggie looked down. *Oh. Right.*

The man could put her in a daze faster than a two-by-four to the forebrain. She shook her head and reached for her feet. And found herself right back where she had started. She might be short, but in the confining corset, her boots were still a long way out of her reach.

She straightened up and cleared her throat.

"I'm sorry, Misha, but I can't reach my boots to unlace them." She worried her bottom lip between her teeth, and then took the plunge. "Would you please help me take them off?"

She saw his approval and felt absurdly proud of herself.

"Since you asked so nicely, *dushka*, I would be happy to help you." He beckoned her to him. "Come and put your foot up on the bedrail where I can reach it. You can still bend from the hips."

She obeyed, crossing to the bed and raising her left foot to the rail beside his thigh. The position spread her legs wide, and she caught a hint of her own fragrance. She saw Dmitri inhale deeply, and she quivered.

He pushed her trouser cuff high enough to unlace her calf-length boots. His hands moved with brisk efficiency, and she couldn't wait to feel them on her again. Her heart skipped a beat when the thought finally sank in that once he removed her boots and she dropped her pants, she would be able to feel his touch on her exposed flesh. Just the thought almost sent her back over the edge.

She needed a quick distraction. "What does that word mean? The one you keep calling me."

He pulled her laces free and tapped her right thigh. She obediently switched legs, lowering the left and propping the right on the bedrail.

"*Dushka* means 'sweet' or 'sweetie.' *Milaya* and *milka* mean 'sweet little girl.'" He finished with her second boot and pushed it to the floor. His eyes met hers. "I have not yet tasted you, Regina, but already I know you will be very sweet on my tongue."

Oh, Lord. Her eyes all but rolled back in her head. The man talked a good game.

He grinned. "Now get back where you were and do as you were told. And this time, no backtalk."

Reggie took a deep breath and nodded. Her knees wobbled like rubber, so she stepped carefully back into position. She was putting on a show for him, but the idea excited rather than offended her. She wanted him to be aroused by the sight of her. She wanted her body to incite his lust. She wanted to trip him and beat him to the floor.

She toed her boots off, trying not to imagine the feel of his tongue against her overheated flesh. If her imagination didn't cut it out, she wouldn't even last until they got around to the actual sex. She'd burst into flame the moment he laid a hand on her.

Even his gaze threatened to singe her. She felt it like a wave of heat traveling up the length of her legs and coming to rest at the curve of her hip, right at her zipper. Quickly, she slid the metal tab down and hooked her thumbs in the waistband of her pants. She started to push the heavy material down, but a burst of nerves stopped her. She couldn't believe she was really doing this, stripping herself naked for a man she'd just met. Maybe she should just—

He growled.

He didn't speak, didn't tsk his tongue, didn't clear his throat. He growled like a predator, and she thought his lips curved in something just short of a snarl.

Maybe she should just take off her pants.

Squelching the nerves and the temptation to turn tail and run—mostly because she figured he'd just chase her—she slid the leather over her hips and down her thighs as far as she was able without bending over. Stepping out of the confining material with as much grace as she could muster, she kicked it aside and found herself all but naked in front of him.

Unable to postpone it any longer, she lifted her gaze to his.

If black could burn, his eyes burned in that moment. His gaze started at her toes and slid up along the length of her bare legs, tickling her skin like a caress. The heat made her shiver, and she imagined how her nerves would riot when he finally touched her.

She watched his eyes, wanted his hands, but when his gaze reached the vee of her legs and the flare of her hip, it cooled and made her shiver.

"Take off the panties," he ordered, his voice rougher than before. Deeper. "And don't wear them again. They get in my way, and I want you always available to me. Do you understand?"

She nodded. She could hardly deny it when

his words sent a rush of moisture flooding from her. She ignored the pounding of her heart and stripped off the damp, green thong.

"Yes, Misha."

"Good. Now get on the bed. This is the second time I've had to tell you."

And don't make me tell you again.

His voice had been neutral, but Reggie caught the subtext. He wanted obedience. The weird thing was, she wanted to give it.

Swiftly, though a little jerky with nerves, she crossed the few steps to the bed and crawled onto the velvety chenille spread. She knelt there, perched awkwardly on her heels, unsure of what to do next. Her hands fluttered, wanting to cover her naked pubis, wanting to touch him. In the end, she forced them to her sides.

Dmitri watched from the foot of the bed, his dark eyes glowing in the dim light, his expression bland. He was driving her crazy. His nonchalance had built the tension inside her to a breaking point. With every breath, her nipples ached and her pussy throbbed and her palms itched with the need to feel him against her.

She wanted him to talk to her, to touch her, to take her. He needed to do something before she lost her mind, even if that meant throwing her down and screwing her senseless without an iota of foreplay. For God's sake, the entire night with him had been foreplay. She wanted *now*play.

He stepped around to the side of the bed and stood in front of her. "Face me," he ordered, "and open your legs."

She bit her lip and obeyed, but there was no way she could meet his gaze while she did. She looked down instead, and her vision became filled with the sight of her own pale thighs and the dark valley between them. Her body leaked like a faucet, and she could see little drops of her juices beaded in the close-cropped curls between her legs.

"Wider."

Trembling, her breath coming faster, she obeyed, shifting her weight to maintain her balance while she spread herself open before him.

He extended his hand and laid one long finger against the skin at the inside of her knee. While she watched, he drew it slowly up the inside of her thigh until his fingers tangled in her damp curls. He rubbed, and she stopped breathing.

One finger tapped firmly against her inner thigh.

"Wider."

She opened wider, spreading inch by inch until he finally stopped tapping. She could have pressed the soles of her feet together, and the muscles in her groin and thighs trembled to hold the position.

God, she felt so exposed. Her shiver had nothing to do with being cold.

She couldn't meet his gaze, couldn't look away from the sight of her own body, spread lewdly wide and naked for his pleasure. She felt the cool air against her hot flesh, saw the deep red of her labia and the dark, fiery brown of her curls.

And she saw his hand, large and strong and possessive upon her.

"Very nice," he murmured while his fingertips twirled and tangled in her curls. "I am pleased to see you know how to behave yourself, *dushka*."

His fingers flexed, pulling the short strands of hair and tugging little pinpricks of pain from her skin. The sweet, sharp sensations made her pussy clench and forced a moan from her throat.

Her eyes drifted shut until his free hand raised her chin and he ordered her to look at him.

"You look very pretty like this, Regina." His hand left her chin and smoothed over her until her skin faded to silk and his palm rested in the valley of her tightly corseted waist. "But do you know why a woman in a corset is really so appealing to a man?"

His voice sounded casual, even indifferent, but the feel of his lean fingers petting her mound made Reggie quiver. She couldn't concentrate. She could barely remember the question, but he clearly waited for an answer.

"Because—" It came out as a squeak, and she cleared her throat to start again. "Because it exaggerates her figure?"

Her hips rocked forward, trying to force his fingers lower. They were so close to her clit, but she didn't want them close. She wanted them *on*.

He evaded her.

"Not really," he murmured. "Yes, the corset enhances her figure, but no more than a good bra and a tight pair of jeans. No, there are other reasons. Deeper reasons."

Reggie bit back a moan. The only deeper she cared about in that moment was the deeper caress of his fingers. If he expected her to be able to follow his conversation when his fingertips rested less than two inches from her swollen and needy clit, he was insane.

His fingers began to wander, bypassing her clit and sinking down the curve of her pubis to brush delicately over her slick, flushed lips, and she knew she was insane. The man was driving her crazy. She sucked in her breath with a hiss and canted her hips higher. He only lightened his touch.

"A man sees two irresistible things in a corseted woman."

His fingers teased her sensitive tissues while his tone sounded like a professor at the lectern. She wanted to kill him.

Right after she tossed him down and raped him.

"First, the restriction on her movement makes it impossible to run from him," he continued, seemingly oblivious to her violent thoughts. "It places her at his mercy, appeals to his primitive instincts. It makes him feel powerful in comparison."

How Dmitri could not feel powerful when his tormenting fingers decided whether she would live or die, Reggie couldn't understand. If he gained more control over her, he would have to force the breath in and out of her lungs. The man was killing her.

A split second later, his hand shifted, and Reggie knew she'd been right. He'd killed her. His exploring fingers halted and withdrew. She whimpered a protest, but her whimper became a scream when his finger returned, parting her wet folds and plunging deep inside.

Dmitri was a large man with large hands, and the extent of her arousal combined with the swelling of her inner tissue to make that one finger feel as large as a penis. Her body felt stretched and full and achy.

"And second . . ."

He's still talking. How the hell can he talk? Oh, God!

His free hand slid around to her bottom, pushing her hips forward and rocking her pelvis against his hand. Her clit bumped his wrist, and she gasped.

Her breathing grew harsh, and he leaned forward, speaking into her ear until she felt his words as much as heard them. "Second, it reminds him that a woman's body is at its most beautiful when it is bound and shaped by his hands."

She couldn't help herself. She shuddered, her entire body racked by it, flooding Dmitri's hand with moisture. She came on a long, high whimper, her body clenching around his invading finger. She couldn't believe it—one finger and she came like a porn star. What would happen when he actually took off his clothes and got around to taking her?

Her hands released their death grip on the bedspread and reached up to touch his broad, muscular chest.

"Please, Misha," she panted. Struggling to catch her breath. "Won't you take your clothes off? I want to see you. I want to touch you."

"Maybe later, if you continue to be a good girl," he said dismissively, removing her hands and placing them flat against the bed beside her hips. "For now, we will continue as I wish. Stay still, and close your eyes."

She closed her eyes and tried not to move, but when his hand slid from between her legs and he stepped away, she whimpered and reached for him. She felt bereft without his touch and his overwhelming presence beside her. The air felt empty where he had stood.

"Hush, *dushka*."

Easy for him to say.

She drew in shallow, shaky breaths and listened hard. She wanted to know what he was doing. Her mind swam with the possibilities, but he moved silently, giving her no clues.

He seemed gone for hours while she knelt there on the bed, panting and exposed like some lewd offering to a pagan god. Her nerves tingled, but before she could register awareness of his return, he slipped his hand into her hair and tugged, tumbling her back onto the mattress in a blur of satin and skin. Her arms were dragged above her head, wrapped with a soft, silky cord, and bound to something solid and immovable. A second later, his weight shifted, and she felt her thighs pulled apart, her ankles roped with the same type of cord and tied securely to the bedposts.

He accomplished it all so quickly she didn't have time to gasp a protest before she found herself secured spread-eagle to her bed. She just lay there, her head spinning, until the rasp of a zipper knocked her straight back into reality.

Her eyes flew open. "What was that?"

Dmitri chuckled. "Clearly not what you thought," he teased, holding up a half-open duffel bag so she could see it. He cast a pointed look to the button fly of his jeans. "Though even if it had been, would that have been a reason for disobeying my commands?"

Her eyes snapped closed, and she shook her head. "No, Misha."

"I thought not." His fingertip brushed the crescent of her lowered eyelashes. "You must try harder if you wish to be a good girl, *milaya*."

She heard him rummaging through the bag

and stiffened when she realized he hadn't brought it with him. Her stomach turned a slow somersault when she remembered the bag of tricks her friends had left at her apartment. Her bossy, interfering friends.

Oh, God.

She gave a surreptitious tug at her bindings, but they held fast. The cord Dmitri had used might feel soft against her skin, but it held fast, as did his knots. Clearly, the man knew what he was doing.

Reggie couldn't decide if his talent for this kind of game meant she should start screaming and hope for nosy neighbors, or bend her knees, wiggle her ass, and shout, "Come and get me, big boy!"

In the end, she just lay still and listened to her heart pound. And tried to ignore the images crashing through her mind. Images of herself, bound and helpless while this dark, mysterious stranger positioned her and took her and slowly drove her out of her mind.

After endless, agonizing minutes, she caught the muffled thump of the bag against the hardwood floor and felt the dip of the mattress when he moved onto the bed beside her.

"You can open your eyes now."

Reggie did, and wasted no time in scanning the bed and nightstand for whatever implements of destruction he had removed from the duffel. From her limited perspective—the bindings prevented her from lifting anything more than her head—she couldn't see a thing. Wary, she turned back to Dmitri. He looked amused.

"If I wanted you to see what I was doing, I wouldn't have made you close your eyes, would I?" His mouth curved in a little smile, and he ran his fingers across her collarbone, skimming them down her side until they curled around her thigh in a brief, disarmingly affectionate squeeze. "Now I want you to see what I'm doing."

She saw.

She saw those beautiful, powerful hands of his reach up to the bodice of her corset. She saw them shift the heavy layers of silk away from her breast, exposing a hard little nipple. It tightened further in the cool air, and she flinched when the backs of his fingers brushed against it while he folded the fabric under itself and tucked it out of the way. He repeated the action on the other side, making her nipples ache and her breath catch. When he finished, the corset supported her lush breasts, holding them high and full above her, completely exposed to his eyes and his hands.

She saw them offered up to him, pale and swollen and pouting for his touch, but when his thumb and forefinger closed over one erect peak, she stopped seeing. All she could do was feel.

Dmitri pinched, his touch firm but gentle. Reggie sighed and shifted restlessly. Against her aroused bud, the pressure felt like a caress. She needed more. Her eyes began to drift shut.

"No," he growled. "Look at me."

She struggled to obey.

"You liked that."

He seemed to wait for an answer, so she forced herself to nod.

"But it wasn't enough for you."

God, did he have to point out what a pervert she was? She blushed, but shook her head.

"Then I should not repeat it." He withdrew his hand, and her heart sank.

"No, please," she gasped, arching her back to offer her breasts up to him. "Please, Misha. Do it again."

She felt his silence, counted his pause in her racing heartbeats. His hand slid back to her nipple, and he repeated the pinch with the exact same amount of pressure. "Like that?"

"No," she moaned, shaking her head. "I want . . . more. Please, Misha." Her voice dropped to a whisper. "Please. Harder."

He removed his hand altogether. "I don't think so. If you cannot be clear with me, I must assume you do not really want this."

The loss of his touch made her chest tighten in fear. "Please don't leave me like this," she whispered, on the verge of tears. "Please, Misha."

"Please, what?" His tone sounded polite, but bored, and she knew he wouldn't cut her any slack.

She wanted to slap his face and walk away, but tied to her own bed, neither was an option. Besides, she wanted him inside her so desperately she was prepared to negotiate.

Hell, she was prepared to surrender.

She licked her dry lips, took a deep breath. "Misha, would you please pinch my nipple harder?"

She heard his silence, felt him stretch it out for long minutes. He knew he tortured her, and she knew he did it on purpose.

"I don't think so," he said abruptly. "I think we need to remind you of your position."

Embarrassment and anger opened Reggie's eyes, and she jerked hard against her bindings, scowling furiously up at him. "What? Somehow being tied half-naked to my bed isn't a good enough reminder?"

She knew she sounded snippy, but damn it, he'd made her beg and then he'd refused her. It almost killed her mood.

"Clearly not." He turned his back and reached down to the duffel he'd left on the floor. "You must not take your position very seriously, or you wouldn't still be talking back to me, would you?"

He shook his head and clucked his tongue in admonishment. "No, I think before we go any further, you need a crash course in remembering both your place and your manners."

Her scowl didn't budge, not until he straightened up and turned to face her. At that point, her expression slid right into something less like defiance and more like shock. Bordering on panic.

In his left hand, Dmitri held an impressively sized dildo. In his right, he grasped a black leather flogger with tails as long as his forearm. Above them both, his expression remained polite and impassive.

"Now then, I think we're ready to get started."

CHAPTER 6

"MISHA? MAYBE WE COULD TALK ABOUT THIS first . . ."

Dmitri stepped close to the side of the bed until he looked directly down at her. "What do we need to talk about, Regina?"

Damn it. His use of her name failed to reassure her. What had happened to the endearments? She scrambled to regroup. "I just thought . . . well, this isn't . . . quite what I was expecting. When I pictured this moment."

"On the contrary," he corrected her, "this is precisely what you were expecting. This is how you envisioned submitting to a man, is it not?"

Reggie frowned. He spoke as if he knew that for sure, as if he'd read her mind again. And here she'd been doing so well pretending that hadn't happened.

God, what are you thinking? It couldn't have hap-

pened. Things like that just don't happen! This is not an episode of Ghost Whisperer.

"No it isn't," she protested, ignoring her niggling conscience. A situation like this called for judicious lying. Perhaps even through her teeth. "I thought it would be—"

"Exactly as I have presented it to you," he finished firmly, cutting straight through her excuses. He set the toys down on the nightstand and sat beside her, cupping her cheek in one hand. "Do not lie to me, *dushka*. Not about anything. I will not tolerate it."

"How do you know I'm lying?" She didn't really want an answer, but she didn't want to head back to the scary territory they'd just left either.

"I know your thoughts, *milaya*. You have a very strong mind. Oh, do not be missish or act as if this shocks you," he said when she tried to look disbelieving. "You knew this at the bar, and yet you still let me bring you home. You feel as drawn to me as I feel to you."

Right. Like she would admit to that one. The last thing this man needed was more ammunition against her. He already had her so hot, she felt as if she were melting from the inside out.

"I'll admit I noticed something weird before now, and I can't deny I'm attracted to you, since I did let you get me naked and tie me up," she conceded. "But I still don't know how you can claim to read my mind. That kind of thing is impossible."

"It is quite possible, as you well know." He sounded impatient. "Shall I prove to you how possible it truly is, Regina Elaina?"

Oh, shit. No one ever added her middle name unless she was in really big trouble.

Reggie backpedaled hastily, which was quite a trick, considering her feet were still tied to the bedposts.

"That's not necessary. I'm sure—" She broke off when she saw his expression.

He stared at her, his eyes narrowed, his lips firmed into a thin line.

She braced herself for a wave of anger. Somehow she had the feeling Dmitri's temper could be explosive, but nothing detonated. Instead, she found herself fascinated by the changing expressions that played across his face.

When stern discipline shifted to hunger, followed by amused satisfaction, she decided anger might be a better choice.

"Oh, Regina, you naughty girl," he purred, leaning close and bracing his arms on either side of her. He lowered his face until his breath tickled her skin. "Don't you know it's dangerous to taunt a hungry man?"

She swallowed hard, her eyes wide and wary while she stared into his eyes, only inches from hers. He couldn't possibly know what she had been imagining.

"I will never let another touch you, *milaya*, but I can give you what you dream of. Would you like me to fulfill your darkest fantasies, Regina?"

She started to shake her head, but when the first touch rasped against her skin, she froze. Her eyes opened impossibly wide, and her lips parted on a soundless gasp. She could see his arms had not moved. His hands remained planted on the mattress on either side of her head, supporting his weight as he leaned over her, yet she felt a dozen hot, eager hands caressing her naked flesh.

Firm fingers tightened around her puckered nipples, pinching and tugging the rosy flesh. Hands slid up her thighs, over the round warmth of her belly. More hands invaded her body, pressing into the heat between her spread thighs, parting her slick folds and penetrating her. She felt one finger enter her, then two, then three, stretching her uncomfortably wide while her lover remained unmoving above her.

The phantom hands multiplied, touching every inch of her skin at once. They kneaded her ass, stroked and probed along the secret cleft, parted her round cheeks and rubbed erotic circles around her rosebud.

Unseen fingers pumped steadily into her dripping pussy, and Reggie cried out. She felt like a dozen lovers caressed her, each demanding a response from her overwhelmed senses. But the only lover she could see remained hard and motionless above her, his black eyes blazing while he watched her shiver on the brink of orgasm.

Fear welled up in her. She couldn't understand what he was doing to her, how he could make her feel these things, and all at once she wanted nothing more than to get away from him and from the power he wielded over her.

"No!" she shouted, trying to twist away from the invisible hands, but they were everywhere, and the silk ropes held her pinned for their exploration.

She squeezed her eyes shut. *They're not real!* she told herself, desperately willing her senses to ignore what her mind couldn't accept. *It's a trick. No one is touching you. No one is here but Dmitri. It's a trick. Ignore it, and it will stop.* But it didn't stop.

The fingers inside her thrust faster, the thumb on her clit rubbed harder, tighter circles, and she began to cry.

"Stop," she whimpered. "Please stop."

The hands froze, not withdrawing, but going completely still. Dmitri's breath stirred the hair beside her ear, but all she could hear was the throbbing beat of her own heart and the ragged sound of her breath sawing in and out of her lungs.

She heard his voice rumbling so close to her ear his lips brushed the sensitive lobe.

"Why should I stop?" he asked, soft and low

and purring. "This is what you imagine, late at night, when you stroke your own needy flesh. This is what you feel in your mind when you rub your little clit and try to fill yourself with your own little fingers. Why not let me give you what you want, Regina?"

"Because you scare me!" she shouted at him, not caring that he could have heard her if she'd only breathed the words. He was that close. But she was crying, and her own fear made her angry.

She opened her eyes and turned her head to glare at him, ignoring the tears that clumped her lashes and blurred her vision.

"Do you want to hear me say it, Misha?" she demanded. "Fine, I'll say it. I'm chickening out. I'm a wimp, a wuss, a coward, who never should have gotten myself into this situation to begin with. I'm terrified! Is that what you want to hear? I'm not ready. I can't handle this. Clearly I'm not ready to give in to someone else's control, no matter how sexy I find you."

She sniffled, hating that she couldn't wipe away her tears, that he could see her crying and vulnerable. He still didn't move.

"Now, if you'll just untie me, I'll go make an appointment with a shrink and you can get the hell out of my apartment. Happy?"

"I am becoming much more so." Dmitri answered her rant and her glare with a smile and a tender kiss on the tip of her nose. He sat up, and the phantom hands disappeared. "I told you I wanted you to be completely honest with me, Regina. That includes telling me about your desires and your fears in equal measure."

"You never said that. You told me not to lie. You never mentioned complete honesty."

"Then clearly I should have. I do want your complete honesty, *dushka,* with yourself as well as with me. It is not shameful to fantasize about things you do not actually desire to have, but I will not tolerate it if you lie to me. Do you understand?"

Reggie nodded and shifted restlessly. He still hadn't made a move to free her.

"Well, what are you waiting for?" she demanded. "Now that I've spoiled all your fun, aren't you going to untie me and get going?"

For the first time, Reggie heard him laugh. It sounded rich and dark and utterly sinful, like good chocolate.

Did I just compare his laugh to a food product? After he invaded my mind and made me cry? God, I really do need that shrink . . .

"You spoiled nothing for me, *milka.* And I didn't say I am finished with you yet."

Her eyes widened. "Uh, wait a second, buddy. In this country, when we say, 'Stop now and untie me,' the implied subtext there is, 'Or I will call the police and see your sorry ass rot in jail for rape.' Maybe I should have explained that to you earlier."

Dmitri just flashed her his wicked grin. "Oh, I

can read your subtext perfectly well. Now close your pretty mouth for me, hmm?"

"Argh!"

As exclamations went, it wasn't particularly eloquent, but Reggie thought it summed up her frustration nicely. She tried to think up something more descriptive and withering to shout at Dmitri's back when he leaned down to retrieve something else from the duffel bag. After the last incident, she expected an iron maiden, or maybe a cattle prod (So what if they would never have fit! She was having a moment of hysteria, here!). Instead, when Dmitri sat up, he held two richly colored silk scarves in his hands.

"Isn't it a little late for those?" she asked, not caring if enough venom dripped from her tongue to put an asp to shame. "In case you hadn't noticed, I'm already tied up."

"Oh, I noticed." He stood to get a better view and looked down at her with an expression of purely male satisfaction etched on his face. "You are a glorious sight, *nenagyladnaya*, you on whom I could never tire of looking. But you are still not in the right frame of mind for our time together. I believe this will help."

Reggie would have glared up at him, but apparently Dmitri's adjustment to their little scene involved using one of the silk scarves to blindfold her. The dark, paisley-printed cloth cut off her vision entirely, though Dmitri carefully examined

the position of the layered material along her brow
and her cheeks and beside her nose to be sure no
gaps or holes allowed light to seep beneath.

"There. How is that, *milka*?"

"Just peachy."

Dmitri chuckled. "Good. Then be a good girl
and lie perfectly still for me."

"Well, since I can't reach the phone to dial 911,
I guess I don't have much choice, do I?"

Reggie was all set to work up a bloody scream
the instant she felt the touch of the leather flogger
against her skin. Instead, what came out of her
mouth ranked somewhere between a whimper and
a gasp of pure surprise. Rather than the sting of
harsh leather, Reggie's skin jumped at the feel of
soft, silky feathers caressing her stomach.

You always have a choice, milaya.

The words whispered through her, less a sound
than a knowing, and Reggie groaned. *Damn it,
he's doing it again.*

The feather tickled her stomach below the hem
of the corset, dipped into the crease between hip
and thigh, and swirled in teasing circles down toward her parted legs, half an inch at a time. *How
can I be doing it again when I have barely started?*

I don't know how you're doing it in the first place!

Her abdominal muscles clenched against the
sensations racing through them, and Reggie shook
her head to clear it. The idea of being tied down
and at the mercy of a strange man freaked her out

quite enough. Being tied down and at the mercy of a strange man with supernatural abilities might just be too much for her to handle.

You can handle more than you think, dushka. *And you will.*

The feathery touch withdrew long enough to let her take a breath, but not long enough that she could brace herself before it returned, this time stroking softly against the underside of her breast. It felt different this time, though. Before, the sensation had been like a ghosting on her skin, gone without a trace, so if she had been alone (and not tied up), she would have wondered if she'd imagined it. This time the feathers, though just as soft, seemed to leave an echo of their touch on the skin beneath her left breast even as they moved on to the right.

"What are you doing?" she gasped, her back arching involuntarily to press her skin against the phantom touch.

He didn't answer—at least, not verbally. But the very next thing to pierce her consciousness was the warm, damp glide of his tongue along the skin where the feather had dusted.

"Oh! What—?" She broke off at the feel of the feathers tickling her mouth. When they pulled away, she instinctively licked her lips. She felt the fine grit of dust for a split second before the texture melted against her tongue, leaving her with the warm, sweet taste of honey in her mouth.

It is almost as sweet as your skin, milka. *But I think you taste even better on your own.*

His tongue flicked out in a last, brief caress to the heavy curve of her right breast. All at once, he lowered his head and drew one taut, dusky nipple deep into his mouth.

"Ah," she groaned, while the meaning of her life distilled down to that one moment and the sensation of Dmitri sucking at her breast.

His mouth felt like a furnace against her skin, and he drew on her flesh with strong, rhythmic pulls. She tried to reach down to him, to cradle his head in her hands, but she only succeeded in tugging hard at the silken ropes that bound her.

Frustrated, she groaned even louder and arched closer to him. His mouth felt wonderful—better than wonderful—but the attention to her breasts only made the flesh between her legs throb in time to his sucking.

His teeth closed around her nipple in warning. *Perfectly still,* milaya. *Be a good girl for me.*

"Misha," she began, her voice faintly pleading. "Please . . ."

Aren't I pleasing you? Even in her mind she could hear the amused note in his words, and she scowled.

"Tease."

Dmitri chuckled, pulling his mouth from her breast with a hollow pop. He left her only long enough to trace a path across her chest to her other nipple. He latched on with evident greed, and Reggie moaned, her hands clenching and releasing uselessly above her head.

Am I teasing you, dushka?

One strong, long-fingered hand began to attend to her abandoned nipple, caressing the nubby areola before taking the swollen tip between finger and thumb and pinching a little less than gently.

"O-oh!"

She felt his mouth leave her aching breast, felt the loss of his heat when he drew back from her. Yet his fingers continued to play with her puckered nipple, pinching and rolling the swollen nub.

Even with the blindfold on, she sensed his eyes on her. His gaze itself touched her, caressed her like another hand. She felt it on her face and her breast, and she shivered.

"You like that," he murmured aloud this time, more an observation than a question, but she couldn't muffle her breathless whimper of response.

His fingers tightened further, sending sharp stingers of pleasure-pain along that unique pathway of sensation that ran from her breasts to the very core of her.

"Yes!" She gasped it, fighting against her bonds, fighting to feel more of him. "Please, Misha, more."

"So polite," he murmured. "Such a good little girl you sound, *milaya*. Are you really a good little girl?"

Reggie could barely remember her name and he expected her to answer questions?

"Anything. Whatever you want, Misha. Just, please. More."

If anything, his fingers softened around her nipple, making her whimper in frustration. He was doing it again. He had made her so hot, and now he was pulling away!

That thought echoed in her head for about three milliseconds before it—and every other conscious thought she had managed to come by—flew out of her head, pushed aside by the sensation of his long, thick finger parting her soft folds and penetrating her.

It felt so good, so much better than the phantom hands he'd touched her with before. This time the touch felt real and solid and hot against her wet tissues. She couldn't help it. A low keening cry burst from her lips, and her hips jerked sharply upward to envelop his invading digit as deeply as possible.

"Misha!"

His hand smacked her sharply on the flank. She heard the cracking sound of it before she felt the impact, but the sting sent her hips pressing back to the mattress.

"Ow!"

"I told you twice not to move, Regina."

His voice sounded firm and forbidding, but somehow Reggie didn't feel frightened. In fact, even with his rough pinch of her nipples and the firm spank he'd just given her, Reggie still wasn't afraid.

Because you trust me, dushka. *As you should.* His words sounded tender and patient, definitely a contrast with his last spoken commands and with his outward manner. Reggie hadn't thought it was trust she felt when he'd pointed that silicone baseball bat of a dildo her way, and it certainly hadn't been what she'd felt when he'd overwhelmed her with that magic-hands trick.

A moment of panic, he dismissed. *Natural, really. You were not ready to experience that forbidden fantasy of yours. And the toys were not what you wanted.* He flicked his thumb against her firm little clit to make her gasp, and inserted a second finger into her slick heat. *This is what you wanted.*

The width of the two digits stretched her, reminding her of how long it had been since she'd had sex. She felt full and somehow more spread and exposed than being tied mostly naked to the bedposts had already managed.

"This is what you want, isn't it, *dushka*?"

She couldn't think clearly. She couldn't even tell the difference between his voice in her head and in her ears. It didn't matter anymore. The only thing that mattered was that he keep touching her. That he take her.

"Isn't it, Regina?"

He punctuated the repeated question with a

twist of his wrist, sending his fingers even deeper inside her, rubbing against her slick, sensitive inner flesh.

"Yes!"

She hoped that was the right answer, because it was probably the most coherent reply she could manage.

"Yes, what, Regina?"

Oh, God, don't make me think! Make me come! Can't think—can't . . . Ah! Uhn . . . more . . .

His fingers pinched her nipple tightly and lifted, tugging hard at the beaded peak. A flash of pain tried to register in her hazed mind, but it blended with the pleasure and became just another level of the sensation that overwhelmed her. She moaned.

"Yes, what, Regina?" His fingers pumped inside her pussy, the way made slick and smooth by her wetness. Crooking his index finger, he scraped the nail carefully against her inner wall. "Yes, you want this?"

"Yes. This! God, Misha—" Her head flew back against the pillow, her muscles clenched and straining with the pleasure. "Anything. Anything you want, Misha. Please!"

She was too far gone to sense his presence when he leaned close to her, but she felt his breath whisper against her ear.

"And if I want you to beg, *dushka*?"

His purring rumble shot through her, combining with the erotic imagery of his words to make her jerk and tremble beneath him.

"Yes, please," she whispered, her voice becoming as husky and intense as his. "I'll beg. I'll do anything, Misha. Anything you want. But please, please make love to me."

She arched her back, pressing her nipple into his palm and her hips into his hand, pushing herself against his fingers. Her muscles clenched, squeezing as if it were his cock filling her.

"Misha, please take me."

All at once, she felt his weight lever away from her, and she couldn't suppress a distressed whimper.

Hush.

Before she worked up a full-fledged protest, she felt his hands on the silk that covered her eyes. The scarf loosened and fell away, and Reggie blinked against the soft light of her bedside lamp. Her vision focused enough to make out Dmitri's hard, muscular chest, and her eyes were closing again when he lowered his mouth to hers.

It was the first time he had kissed her, and Reggie knew the moment would be frozen in her mind for a very long time. He wasted no time courting her mouth, offered no deference to the newness of the experience. He devoured her, his lips covering hers, teeth nipping, tongue invading. He kissed as if he would swallow her, take her inside himself, as she prepared to take him inside of her.

The kiss made her resent her bonds. She wished fervently her arms were free to wrap around his broad shoulders, that she could run her fingers through his soft, dark hair. She wished her legs were free to wrap around his waist and urge him inside her.

Please, Dmitri. I can't wait anymore. Please come inside me now.

He responded before she finished the thought. She felt the blunt, round head of his penis press through her slit and lodge against her aching entrance.

She heard his voice in her mind. *Open for me,* milka. *Open wide for me in welcome.*

And then she heard nothing.

In that moment, her cunt became her entire existence. Her world centered on the soft, wet channel between her legs and the thick, hard invader that demanded entrance.

She felt that first-time hesitation, the heightened tension and the sense of wonder at the ability of her body to stretch apart for a man, to take him inside of her and give him pleasure. She felt the sensation of stretching and the brief doubt about whether or not her body would accommodate his. With Dmitri, she felt right to wonder.

His body pressed hard against her opening and Reggie froze, waiting for the burning sensation to ease. She felt an internal pop when the head breached her entrance and expected the dulling of sensation that usually followed. Instead, her body stretched further when Dmitri began to force his length even deeper.

The shaft of his cock felt hot and smooth and thick as it tunneled inside her, at least as thick as the head. Instead of the stretching sensation easing, it grew even more intense with every inch he pressed inside her.

Reggie whimpered and shifted her hips, looking for a break from the intensity of the sensation, but Dmitri grew ruthless. His hands reached down to grasp her hips, forcing her high and hard against him. He held her so tightly she knew his fingertips would leave bruises where they dug into her flesh.

"Uhn! I can't . . . I— Ah! Dmitri, please. No more!" Her head tossed wildly against the pillow, her eyes clenched shut, her brow furrowed in distress. She tugged against the cords around her wrists as if she could climb up and away from him. She would die if he stopped, but she didn't know if she could bear for him to continue.

"Yes. More. Look at me." He rasped the words through gritted teeth.

Reggie struggled to obey. She pulled harder at the silk cords to distract herself while she tried to force her eyelids to lift. When she had managed slits, she caught sight of Dmitri above her and almost snapped them closed again. His eyes burned with heat and lust, and his normally harsh features might have been carved from dark granite.

"Take me," he growled, shoving another inch into her distressed passage. "Take all of me."

Reggie gasped, squirming beneath him, using her grip on the cords to try to pull herself away from him. "I can't! Misha, please."

He only gripped her hips tighter and thrust deeper. "All of me."

And with one mighty lunge, he buried his entire length inside her.

She screamed.

She felt as if he had split her in two. He felt so huge, so much bigger than anything she'd ever experienced, and so much harder. His cock stretched her until she thought she couldn't stand it, and his hard hips pressed into hers and forced her pelvis flat against the mattress. When he started thrusting, he would kill her.

He started thrusting.

Instead of ripping her apart like she'd feared, the intense pleasure-pain of the friction set off a chain reaction inside her. Her body clenched around his cock, her muscles clenched against the cords, and her nipples clenched into painfully tight buds where they rubbed against his broad chest.

Instead of trying to draw away, she threw herself at him, flinging her hips up to meet his thrusts, bucking wildly beneath him, while sounds she'd never heard before escaped her lips. She moaned, she panted, she squealed, and through it all, she begged him to take her harder.

"More! Misha, please. Harder!"

He grunted and complied eagerly. His weight lowered onto her, pinning her to the mattress and holding her in place for his thrusts. His arms slipped beneath hers and clamped onto her shoulders, pressing her body hard into his pounding thrusts.

Her entire body spasmed. Her neck bowed, shoving her head back into her pillow. Her body arched beneath him, trying to fuse them together so she would never be empty again.

He moved in a blur of motion, racing with her toward orgasm. Her body fluttered around his, and he groaned. He lowered his head, and she felt his forehead press against her chest. A thin sheen of moisture slicked both their skins, and they rubbed together so hotly she knew they would spark at any moment.

Harder and harder he thrust, faster and faster until she couldn't hope to keep pace. She stopped moving and, instead, braced her feet against the mattress and held her hips high and hard against his. His thrusts became shorter and faster, and he rubbed hard against her clit with every motion. The tension coiled inside her, and she choked on her own breath. Her inner muscles clamped down hard until he had to force himself free of her grasping muscles.

"Come for me," he grunted. "Now."

With a shriek, she obeyed. Her mind went blank, and she swore her heart stopped. Frankly, she couldn't have cared less.

The pleasure ripped through her, as brutal as their mating itself, wringing her of all feeling until she collapsed limp beneath him.

Three short, hard thrusts later he followed, shouting his pleasure to the ceiling while he pumped her full of his seed.

Reggie lay motionless, waiting for awareness and sensation to return to her well-used body.

My God. I think I'm dead, she mused, too tired to get worked up about it. *He fucked me to death.*

Not yet, milaya, he chuckled. *But there's always next time.*

CHAPTER 7

DMITRI LAY ON HIS SIDE, WATCHING REGINA sleep. After their first intense mating, he had quickly untied her bonds and removed her confining corset. Nude and exhausted, she had cuddled close, settling her soft, warm frame against his side and slipping into sleep as easily as a toddler.

That had been hours ago, and ignoring his renewed hunger for her had become almost impossible.

He brushed a silky tendril of hair off her cheek, rubbing his knuckles against the velvet-smooth surface of her skin. He'd never seen anything so beautiful as his Regina, naked and bound, or naked and orgasmic, or naked and asleep, with her knees curled up toward her chest and her hands pillowed beneath her cheek.

He felt an intense sense of satisfaction at having made her his. While the hunt had been brief, he felt none of the boredom that usually followed close on the heels of a conquest. Instead of feeling sated with her, he'd found possessing her only whetted his appetite. Hence, the enormous erection he sported at that very moment.

Shifting closer to her, Dmitri curled around Regina's body and wrapped his arm about her, resting his palm flat against her pelvis. He pressed her back against his hips until his erection nestled between her cheeks.

She murmured something unintelligible and shifted against him. Finding a comfortable spot, she drifted back to sleep.

Dmitri savored the feel of her body in his arms. He nuzzled his face against her neck, breathing deeply of her scent. She smelled of honey and musk and desire, the warmth of her skin carrying the scent to his appreciative nose. Good enough to eat, and Dmitri suddenly felt very hungry.

His tongue traced the shell of her ear, teased the small hollow below, and she rewarded him with a sleepy murmur of pleasure. His arms wrapped more tightly around her, the hand on her stomach tilting her pelvis back against him while he lifted her leg in his other hand and draped her thigh on top of his.

She sighed and tilted her head slightly to give him better access while he nibbled his way down her throat to the warm, scented curve where her neck met her shoulder.

"Misha."

She whispered his name in her sleep, and he growled, a low, possessive rumble of triumph and lust. He had to have her again.

His hand slid from her thigh up to cup around her breast. He squeezed the soft weight, pinching his fingers around the nipple and causing it to harden into a rosy nub. She murmured and pressed back against him.

He arched her hips further, canting them up until he could nudge against her entrance. His hand slid down, combing through her neatly trimmed curls to delve between her soft thighs. Her folds parted softly for him, and he tested her readiness with the tips of his first two fingers. She dripped with desire, more than ready for his possession. He shifted his hand up until it cupped over her lower stomach, only the tip of the middle finger still parting her and pressing against the focus of her arousal.

He pinched her nipple hard between thumb and finger, simultaneously pressing down on her clit and breaching her tender entrance with his erection.

He knew the instant when she woke, felt her tense around him and whimper, her passage clenching while its abraded walls tried to relax enough to admit him. He watched her face carefully, searching for signs of real distress. Her brow furrowed, though her eyes never opened, and she bit her lower lip, her skin flushing delicately. She made no move to stop him, so he continued, patiently but inexorably forcing his way in to the hilt. She moaned.

"Easy, *dushka*," he whispered, kissing the side of her neck and rubbing small circles around her clit. "You can take me. Slowly, slowly. That's my girl."

When he slowed to a stop, her body rippled around him and then eased, hugging his cock in a silky, wet embrace.

"Misha," she sighed.

He kissed her temple and touched his tongue to the dark curve of her lashes resting against her cheek. He cupped her breast and her hips closer against him and began to move.

He eased in and out of her with long, smooth strokes, loving the way she clasped about him, the tightness of her body like a virgin's surrounding him. He knew it had been several months since she'd broken up with some little insect of a man who polluted her mind like an oil spill, and from reading her thoughts, he knew they had ceased to be intimate long before the relationship ended. Judging by the way she closed so tightly around him, he guessed she had taken no other man to her bed since.

The thought gave him a savage sense of satisfaction. He hated that Regina had ever taken another man into her body, but now he would make sure he was the last who would ever feel her warm, eager welcome.

Concentrating on the pleasure she gave him, Dmitri quickened his thrusts, urging his cock more forcefully into her. She whimpered, reaching one arm back to curl around his neck, holding him close to her. She turned her head and parted her lips, rooting blindly for his kiss.

He took her mouth as he took her body, with gentle force, ruthless control, and an overwhelming sense of inevitability. He adored the taste of her, sweet and warm and spicy, like honey and cinnamon and the unique flavor that was Regina. He teased her tongue and tickled the roof of her mouth, urging her to play with him. She responded eagerly, sucking at his tongue, drawing him deeply within her, just as she drew his body into her tight heat. Dmitri groaned low in his throat, the sound like a growl, and thrust his hips harder against her.

Reggie tore her mouth away from his and turned her face to muffle her moans of pleasure in her pillow. Dmitri pulled it out from under her and scowled.

"No," he rumbled, sliding his hands to her hips and rolling her onto her belly. "You will not hide the sounds of your pleasure from me. I will hear every breath and every moan I wring from you. Do you understand?"

Reggie braced her hands against the mattress and moaned, tilting her hips to try and take more of him. "Yes, Misha," she whimpered. "I understand."

He grunted a response, grabbed her pillow and his, and lifted her hips to slide the support beneath her. The pillows tilted her hips up toward him, and Dmitri's eyes narrowed in satisfaction at the sight of her bottom elevated for his possession.

He thrust faster into her, draping his weight along her back to pin her to the mattress. His next deep thrust bumped hard against her cervix, and Reggie's control snapped. She came, moaning and bucking beneath him.

Dmitri grabbed hard onto her hips and rode out her pleasure, his face buried in the curve of her shoulder. He could hear her pulse beating frantically just beneath her skin, could smell her excitement and her pleasure and the rich scent of her life, warm and vital.

Hunger stirred in him, and he groaned. He had struggled with his desire to taste her during their first, furious mating, but now it surged to life with twice the insistence. He needed to mark her, to take her life force inside of him until she could never part from him again.

Resolute, he slowed his movements inside her just enough to allow him to focus his thoughts on hers. He entered her mind much more gently than he entered her body, less sure of his welcome. She didn't seem to notice, too wrapped up in her physical senses to attend to the others. It made things much easier for him while he drew a gentle veil over her consciousness. He wanted her to remain tangled in the moment, but not to remember what he was about to do.

When he felt sure she knew nothing else but the feel of his body inside hers, he draped his hard frame over her back and quickened his rhythm, pressing his hips harder against her.

Her spasms drove him wild, and he gave in to his need. With his hips hammering into her with animal savagery, he opened his lips against the tender skin at the seam of her shoulder and sank his fangs into her sweet, pale flesh. He fed, oblivious to all but the taste of her blood in his mouth, the feel of her skin and her flesh and her hot, tight body.

He drew from her like a starving man. The taste of her filled him, overwhelmed him. Sweeter than the honey, hotter than her passion, her blood nourished him like nothing ever had. He felt drunk on her essence. She intoxicated him like vodka, only sweeter. Clearer. More pure. He feared he would never have enough of her, and the thought pierced the fog of his lust. He drew back, his body clenching above hers while her taste overwhelmed him.

He came on a roar, the cry filling the room and echoing off the walls. He pumped into her until he emptied himself and collapsed on top of her, struggling to catch his breath.

She was glorious.

When he regained control of his muscles, Dmitri

brushed her hair away from the damp skin of her neck and kissed the spot he'd bitten with reverent tenderness. She remained motionless, and he knew the veil over his actions had held. He murmured her name.

"Regina."

She sighed and shifted, but made no response. She'd fallen back to sleep.

Dmitri chuckled, unsure if he should be flattered or insulted. Gently disengaging their bodies, he scowled at the loss of her wet heat surrounding him. If he could simply stay inside her for the rest of eternity, Dmitri figured he would live a very happy life.

A glance at the clock told him dawn would come soon, and he sighed. He knew he had to leave her. He could think of nothing more appealing than remaining in her bed and holding her for the rest of the night and all of the next day, but she would not find it easy to adjust to his lifestyle, and he knew crowding her too quickly would likely send her running from him.

He would never allow that to happen.

He sat up in her bed and stretched muscles that ached pleasantly from his exertion. He should leave her before the sight of her tempted him to further exercise.

He kissed her tenderly on the cheek, grinning when she grumbled in her sleep and curled away from him. He had worn her out, and she obviously refused to let him interrupt her sleep for sex yet again.

He had no plans to wake her, no matter how his libido urged him to do so. He would let her sleep for now. He could afford such generosity, because he knew it would not be long before he saw her again.

Brushing her tangled hair off her cheek, he let his hand cup the side of her face while he gazed down at her and slipped his mind into hers. He double-checked his veil and found no trace of memory lingering to tell her what he was or that he had fed from her while they made love. All she would remember was passion and pleasure.

He had to resist the urge to give the pleasure memories an extra boost, just to be safe. Instead, he gave her the thought that he desired her as much as she desired him, that he could not wait to see her again. He molded the thought until it took the proportion of memory, and he could be certain she would heed it. He kissed her once more and stood.

He took a few moments to straighten up, pulling the disarranged sheets back onto the mattress and smoothing them down, tucking Regina inside. He wound up the cords and the blindfold he'd used on her and put away all the other accoutrements of their encounter. If he hadn't known Reggie's friends had provided her with these things, he'd have gotten a very different impression of her, he thought, grinning. Reading her mind definitely made things easier.

When the room looked tidy, he pulled on his jeans, draped his shirt over his shoulder, and carried his boots into her living room. He snooped just enough to find one of her business cards, which he pocketed before he finished dressing and let himself quietly out of her apartment. Now that he knew where she worked, he would be able to keep tabs on her during the week while he dedicated his attention to clearing a path for their relationship.

It grated at him, the thought of the snail's pace he would have to endure while he worked to overcome her natural suspicions of him. He hated the time it would take, wanted to make her officially his now, but he would have things settled so no one could doubt Regina belonged to him—not even Regina.

CHAPTER 8

REGGIE WOKE SATURDAY MORNING WITH A song in her heart and an ache between her thighs.

Eyelids snapping open, she flew into a sitting position in the middle of her big bed and surveyed the room around her. It looked like he'd never been there.

She blinked, but everything appeared perfectly normal. The room was neat and bright in the light flooding through the two casement windows. She didn't know what she'd been expecting to see, given that they'd confined their activities to the bed the entire time, but there should have been something. Surely the most amazing night of her life would leave her with some kind of reminder?

Then she stretched, and she discovered exactly where the reminder came from; it lurked in her muscles—every single one of them.

She ached from her neck down, remnants of the bondage as much as the enthusiastic sex. Bringing her arms back to her sides, she rolled her shoulders to loosen the tight muscles and absently rubbed her wrists. They bore no marks, no sign of the ropes that had held her still and spread for Dmitri, but she could still feel the twisted silk against her skin.

She did find marks on her hips, though, dusky impressions that showed where his fingers had bitten into her flesh while he held her still for his pleasure. And hers.

God, what a night!

With a heartfelt sigh, Reggie swung her legs over the side of the bed, stood, and failed to suppress a wince. She hobbled, as bowlegged as a drunken cowboy, into the adjoining bathroom and turned the shower on hot.

Once the pelting water had loosened the worst of her knotted muscles, she shampooed her hair and lathered a loofah with her favorite citrus-scented soap. The familiar fragrance brought memory flooding back.

I love your scent, milaya. *Like honey and musk and warm, wet woman.*

Even in the heat of the shower, the memory made her shiver. She wondered what would happen when she actually saw him again. The man would be lucky if she didn't trip him and beat him to the floor . . .

She froze, dripping lather onto the tile. *Would* she ever see Misha again?

Oddly enough, Reggie had every confidence that she would. Despite the fact that she'd woken up alone in her bed with not a hair out of place and not a scrap of evidence to prove Dmitri Vidâme even existed, she didn't doubt for a second that he would come back to her.

Her mind tried to analyze it, recalling that she didn't know where he lived, what he did, or even if Dmitri was his real name, but she didn't care. She knew with an unshakable faith that her time with Dmitri had been more than a one-night stand.

Operating on autopilot, her mind otherwise occupied, she finished up her shower, wrapped herself in a bath sheet, and headed into the kitchen. She was starving. Apparently, being ravaged within an inch of her life by a mysterious man with psychic powers could really work up an appetite.

Not that she planned to think much about the psychic thing. *One step at a time, Reg.*

She rummaged around for some food while the coffee brewed. Cereal wouldn't cut it this morning. Her hands were full of two eggs and a carton of milk when the phone rang, and of course, by the time she managed to set them down without cracking the eggs, her machine had picked up. Reggie reached for the receiver, but yanked her hand back when she heard the voice on the answering machine's speaker.

"Reggie, it's Ava. If you're there, pick up." Pause. "I'm going to assume that you're exhausted and still asleep, but if I don't hear from you by this afternoon, I'm going to call the police. Call me."

The machine clicked and beeped when the call ended, and the recording stopped. Reggie groaned and groaned again when she saw the rapidly blinking light indicating she had more messages waiting. Bracing herself, she pushed play. All of the messages were from Ava.

Beep. "You better have a damn good reason for sneaking out of the club, Regina Elaina McNeill!" Ava must have called on her cell last night, because Reggie could hear the noise of the club in the background. "Just wait until I get my hands on you!"

Beep. "All right, you get slightly less painful revenge. Missy just said she saw you leave with someone gorgeous. Of course, we have no way of knowing he's not a serial killer until you *call and let us know you're okay*!"

Beep. "The club's closing in a few and no call. Where are you? You'd better be okay, or I'll kill you myself."

Beep. "We checked with the bartender, since no one has heard from you, and he said you left with a man named Dmitri, who he guaranteed was not a psycho axe maniac. He'd better be right, and you'd better call as soon as you wake up."

Reggie rolled her eyes at the machine and hit

the delete button. She knew her friends only wanted to make sure she was okay, but their attitude rankled, especially after they had gotten her into the situation to begin with. If not for their Fix plan, Reggie would never have gone to that club, let alone have left with a total stranger. Godlike sex appeal or no.

She glanced over at the clock and did some quick calculations. Saturday at eleven meant Missy would be at the park with her niece and nephew and would check her cell for messages in precisely half an hour, just before she took the kids out for lunch. Telling herself "prudent" sounded better than "cowardly," Reggie dismissed the idea of calling Ava and dialed Missy's cell. When the message ended and the voice mail program beeped at her, Reggie spoke.

"Hi, it's me. I got a bunch of messages from Ava on my machine. I just wanted to let everyone know I'm fine. I had a great time last night, but I've got a ton of chores to catch up on today, so I might not talk to y'all until Monday. Give Nicky and Beth hugs for me. Bye."

After she hung up the phone, she pushed Ava from her mind and focused on the really important things. Like food.

An hour later, fortified with an omelet and coffee, and decently dressed in a pair of faded jeans and a knit top, Reggie made good on her lie and got down to cleaning her apartment. Not being a total slob or an unmarried man, she found it went quickly.

When the phone rang an hour later, she almost missed it over the dull roar of the vacuum cleaner. As it was, she barely got to the receiver before the machine picked up.

"Hello?" She knew she sounded breathless, but that's what happened when someone called on cleaning day. They'd have to deal.

"Reggie?"

Okay, what higher power have I pissed off this week? Reggie wondered while she sank to the arm of the chair beside her and took a deep breath. "Hello, Greg."

"I was hoping I'd catch you at home. How've you been?"

You mean, since I caught you debriefing your administrative assistant on your lunch hour? Or can you not debrief someone who's wearing a thong?

"Just fine, thanks."

"That's fabulous news. I've been thinking about you a lot lately, you know."

Reggie pulled the phone away from her ear for a second and stared at it incredulously. Was he honestly using his AM radio voice on her? The one he generally reserved for kissing the asses of his biggest clients, and for charming young secretaries out of their panties?

What gives?

"Listen," she heard him schmooze as she returned the receiver to her ear. "I know you probably aren't all that thrilled with me these days—"

Gee, do you think, Einstein? "Don't be silly."

"But I'd really like to see you. I feel terrible about the way we left things. Really terrible." His voice dripped with counterfeit sincerity. "Do you think there's any chance you might consider meeting me for a drink somewhere?"

Whoa. That brought her up short. Gutless Greg the Wunderjerk wanted to see her again? For what? Did he really think she wanted to hear his lame explanations all over again? Did he think it would make the slightest bit of difference if he finally apologized? If he begged for forgiveness? If he got down on his hands and knees and groveled before her feet like the immoral dog he was?

Okay, so maybe that last bit would help. She sure enjoyed the imagery. "When did you have in mind?"

"Tonight?"

Reggie scowled. What? Just because she didn't have other plans on a Saturday night was no reason for him to assume her life was as pathetic as it was.

As it had been.

Greg spoke into the silence of her hesitation. "Unless you already have plans."

"Well, I do have something planned," she lied, her tone purposely cool and bored, "but I might be able to spare you twenty minutes or so if you could make it early enough. Say, seven-thirty? Let me check my calendar."

She made a big production of flipping through the calendar she kept beside the phone, hoping the sound of the pages turning would carry over the phone lines. She scrolled her finger down the list of errands she'd recorded there and tried to sound breezy.

"Yes, I think I could squeeze you in around seven-thirty, but I have to—"

The words caught in her throat when her finger reached the bottom of the page and slid across the unfamiliar handwriting. Written in bold strokes across the white, lined page, she read, "Captain Jack's, eight P.M. Wear the red."

Dmitri. She didn't need to recognize his handwriting to know who had written himself so matter-of-factly into her schedule. Into her life.

"Seven-thirty is perfect," Greg said, shaking her out of her stupor. His voice sounded excited and sleazy all at the same time. Which really should have surprised her less. "I could meet you at that place right down the street from you. Captain Morgan's?"

"Captain Jack's," she corrected, dazed.

"Right, that one. I'll see you there at seven-thirty." He paused. "Thanks for agreeing to this, Reg. I appreciate you making the time to talk to me after what happened."

Reggie muttered something even she didn't understand and hung up the phone with numb fingers. Her mind had already evicted Gregory and busied itself with unpacking Dmitri's suitcases and tucking his slippers under her bed. Apparently her gut feeling in the shower had been right. She would be seeing Dmitri again, and sooner than she'd thought. Like tonight.

Wear the red.

Feeling uneasy, as if someone watched her from the corner, Reggie dropped the vacuum and headed for her closet. Reaching inside, she rummaged into the very back and pulled out a sealed garment bag. Her hands ripped open the dark plastic covering and smoothed over the velvet material of the dress it concealed.

Short, tight, and unrepentantly crimson, it was a dress she hadn't ever actually worn. She'd bought it for the holidays last year, planned to wear it to spice things up with Greg, but that was B.L.—before Lisette. Instead, she'd had it cleaned unnecessarily and sealed it away in the back of her closet like another bad memory. She'd forgotten she owned it, until Dmitri reminded her.

Wear the red.

He meant this dress; she didn't own any others in red. With her auburn hair, she tended to think the color clashed, so she avoided it as a general rule. The contents of this garment bag were the exception. But how had he known about it? The bag had been sealed and still hidden where she'd last put it.

The man reads your mind, and you wonder how he knew you owned a red dress? she asked herself, then answered with a frustrated, *I was trying not to think about the mind-reading thing.*

Collapsing onto the bed beside the red dress, Reggie groaned. She used to live a nice, ordinary life. Honest. She worked at an ad firm, she hung out with her friends, she had dated a financial analyst, and she had never let anyone tie her up. But then her boyfriend turned out to be a cheating scum sucker, her friends lost their minds and turned into sex-yentas from hell, and she hooked up with a man who read her mind and persuaded her to reenact the Pornographic Perils of Pauline.

At least the job's still normal.

"Yeah, I'm the one who's losing it." She sighed, finally admitting it out loud. She should probably resign herself to life in a padded cell.

Nothing so drastic. Perhaps merely velvet-lined handcuffs.

The purring voice inside her head sounded so familiar and so impossible, Reggie offered the only logical response. She screamed.

Hush, milaya, *or someone will think you are being murdered.*

His voice, impossible as it sounded, laughed at her from inside her mind, and Reggie wondered how this was meant to convince her of her sanity?

Though perhaps they will just think your companion from last night is visiting you again.

"Very funny," Reggie snapped, glaring into the thin air that Dmitri most definitely did *not* occupy. "Where are you, and why are you trying to turn my life into an episode of *The Twilight Zone*?"

He chuckled. It felt like her brain vibrated.

I am at home, milaya. And I am here with you. Have you missed me?

"Not as much as my sanity."

You are not crazy, Regina, just a bit too focused on what you believe to be real and imaginary. I will enjoy opening your eyes to new . . . possibilities.

"Will you stop that? Enough with the double entendre. Or was that a triple entendre?"

It was a promise.

Reggie rolled her eyes, jumped up off the bed, faced thin air—since Misha was still not anywhere near her—and growled, "That's it, buddy. Get out of my head and stay out! We are going to lay this down in person, using noises and vocal cords and all sorts of wacky social conventions. Whatever you had planned for tonight can wait until you give me some answers. Now, go away!"

He left with a chuckle, but leave he did. Reggie experienced the removal of his presence from her mind like a physical withdrawal and clenched her teeth against the instinctive urge to call him back.

"Jerk." She snarled the insult and, lacking a certain arrogant Russian to clobber, slammed her closet door shut. "That tears it. Men are just pigs. All men. Every single sleazy, sex-obsessed, lesbian-fantasy-perpetuating, sports-show-watching, big-breast-ogling, secretary-screwing one of them!"

CHAPTER 9

FOR THE FIRST TIME IN SEVERAL HUNDRED years, Dmitri Vidâme had trouble sleeping, and he knew exactly where to lay the blame.

He had returned to his home as usual, just before sunrise, intending to ensconce himself in his study for a few hours of work at clearing some business off his desk. He'd spent forty-five minutes shuffling papers and staring into space before admitting defeat. There was no way he could concentrate this day. Not after the night he'd just experienced.

Regina Elaina McNeill.

His distraction. His obsession.

His mate.

Who would ever have thought he would find her? Here, now, after all this time.

In spite of the pretty stories humans liked to tell each other about his kind, Dmitri was neither the victim of a curse, nor a tortured soul. He needed no woman to return light and joy to his life, nor did he require love to keep him from turning to evil as he aged. He had not been evil in his mortal life; he would not become so now.

Dmitri, son of Rurik, had been born in the city of Novgorod in the year 1199 to a Slavic mother and a Viking father. Though his sire's fortune had been made in trade, Dmitri had been raised to be a warrior, cutting his teeth and sharpening his blade on the steady stream of Mongol invaders who had overrun his homeland. He had fought countless wars, earned wealth and land of his own, and won the title of prince among his people before he turned twenty-five. As far away as the eastern steppes, men spoke of him as both fierce and just, and speculated that he must have made a pact with the devil to survive hale and whole into his thirtieth year at a time when a man of forty wore the mantle of an elder.

There had been no devil, of course, merely a love of fresh food, cleanliness, and exercise long before the surgeons general got around to recommending them. It wasn't until a beautiful serf offered him a gift in exchange for her freedom that Dmitri truly became immortal. To this day, he considered the exchange a fair bargain.

It had taken a decade or two for Dmitri to adjust to his new life, but never had he regretted his choice. The adaptability that had made him so feared on the battlefield had stood him in good stead while he learned that vampires were not so different from humans, really. Oh, they drank blood, to be sure, and their strength and speed were unmatched by humans, nearly rivaling that of some of the more powerful shapeshifters. Vampires could read the minds of most humans and perform small tricks very similar to hypnosis, the way he had done to keep Regina near him in the bar last night. But mind control was something else altogether, both difficult and unethical, and to be honest, he had no wish to control Regina's mind. He took too much delight in her wit and her stubborn streak of independence. Controlling her body beneath him in bed was more than enough for Dmitri. Provided he gained the right to do so often enough to suit him.

To own the truth, Dmitri did not require a mate. Over the long centuries since his birth, he'd never lacked for female companionship. Female bodies held no secrets for him, and he'd never felt so captivated by a woman that he could imagine her in his life for longer than a few brief encounters. Never had he wanted a woman so badly.

But by God, he wanted this one.

Leaning back in his worn leather desk chair, Dmitri folded his arms behind his head and gave his mind free rein to travel where it wanted, knowing exactly where it would head: to tumbled curls the color of smoldering embers, to skin as smooth and rich as vanilla cream, to the tight clasp of a body perfectly molded to accept him.

Regina.

Just the memory of her stirred his desire to life, want curling in the pit of his belly like a hungry serpent ready for its feeding. Before the beast had a chance to hiss, the phone rang, dragging Dmitri back to reality with a frown.

"What?"

"Did I wake you? I was trying to catch you before you went to sleep."

"Had I been asleep, I would not have answered the phone. What do you want?"

"Well, I was going to give you some news," Graham said, sounding amused and arch on the other end of the line. "But now I think I'd rather ask how a man who ditched his friend at a club in favor of leaving with a heavily stacked redhead with a mouth that could raise the dead could possibly sound so cranky on the morning after. What happened? Did she turn out to be a lesbian?"

Dmitri sighed and pinched the bridge of his nose. "What is your news, Graham?"

"I asked first."

"And I ignored you," Dmitri growled, "which a man who did not lick his own testicles for recreation would have taken as a hint."

"You're just jealous."

"Your news, Lupine."

Graham heaved a theatrical sigh. "Fine. I can take a hint. You don't want to talk about Miss Rack-tastic 2000. Does that mean you'll pass me her number?"

The growl lowered slightly in volume and raised considerably in menace.

"Oo-kay. I'll mark that as a 'no.' But don't think I'm going to let this slide," the shifter warned. "This is the first woman I've ever seen you go possessive over, and I've known you since the day my father told Mom she smelled nice in her new miniskirt."

Dmitri gritted his teeth. "I'm not getting any younger, Winter."

"But you're not getting any older either, Mr. Grumpy Fangs." Graham's voice grew briefly muffled, as if he were clamping the phone between his shoulder and his ear to free up his hands. "All right. Here it is. After you and . . . well, after you left the club last night, I ran into one last person I thought it might be interesting to interview."

Relieved at the change of subject, Dmitri picked up his pen and scooted closer to the desk. "Who?"

"Some kid named Charles. He didn't give me his last name, and I didn't want to spook him by asking."

"Did he seem skittish?"

"You might say that. Personally, I'd say 'paranoid.' But then, I don't have your experience in diplomacy."

Dmitri raised an eyebrow. The Lupine might be Alpha of his pack, but he was only in his thirties. He didn't have Dmitri's experience in anything. "What made you think the human was paranoid?"

"First, the fact that he wasn't human, and he'd been *not* human for such a short time, the skin behind his ears was still dripping."

"Vampire?"

"Yup."

Dmitri frowned. He couldn't be expected to know every vampire in Manhattan (there were hundreds of them, after all), but something about this story made the back of his neck itch. "Did you ask who had made him?"

"Sure. And after I explained what being made meant in your circles, he told me he didn't know. He said he'd just woken up on Monday feeling really, really thirsty."

Swearing, Dmitri turned to his computer and flipped on the monitor. Maybe the rumors about rogue vampires operating in Manhattan had some substance behind them after all. "I want you to e-mail everything you found out from him so that I have it in writing. Did you get his address? Some other way for us to get in touch with him again?"

"Just an e-mail address," Graham answered. "For some reason I seemed to make the kid nervous. It was like he didn't want me to know where he lived."

Dmitri just grunted.

"Of course, since I didn't have a pen and paper, the kid was kind enough to use the napkin he'd been holding to write the address down for me." Now the Lupine sounded smug. "Did I mention he was just barely turned? In fact, he's so new, he still smells. Maybe enough to track him."

Finally, some good news. Lupines had an amazing sense of smell, so good that they ranked as the best trackers in the world, better than anything else on two legs. Or even on four. While most vampires didn't produce an odor that the shifters could track, it took a while for the scent of the mortal human to fade, anywhere from a few days to a few weeks. In the case of the mysterious "Charles," his recent turning might work to their advantage.

"I'll try to trace the e-mail address," Dmitri said, scribbling down the information as Graham recited it. "Doing that's always a tricky bet, though. I might have to ask you to tail him anyway."

"How long before you know? He smelled last night, and his scent is still on the napkin, but there's no telling how fast it will fade. If we wait too long, tracking him won't be an option."

"Give me the day."

"Won't you be sleeping?"

"I can get started and leave anything I find for Justin to follow up on. He does things to my computer that make it embarrassing for me to even speak the word 'Internet.'"

Justin Abar had been Dmitri's personal assistant for the past ten years, during the entirety of which, the young man had remained twenty-three years old. As a human servant to a vampire as powerful as Dmitri, he enjoyed the benefits of a flexible schedule, a ridiculously generous salary, and an exemption from aging. In exchange, he helped keep his employer's life running smoothly, acted on Dmitri's behalf during daylight hours, donated blood from time to time, and remained absolutely dedicated and trustworthy.

He was also a computer hacker par excellence.

"Okay," Graham said. "I'll give you a call around midnight to see where we are. Anything beyond that, and I'm going to start feeling nervous."

Agreeing, Dmitri hung up the phone and turned his annoyed scowl on his computer. Now, instead of spending the last few hours before he slept thinking about the woman he planned to make his own, he was going to have to waste time tracking down a baby vamp and his rogue maker.

Well, he decided, pushing away the irritation to focus on the matter at hand, better to start now and get it over with. He had written himself into Regina's calendar before leaving her apartment a couple of hours ago and he did not plan to miss that engagement, Council business or no.

CHAPTER 10

STARING AT THE CONTENTS OF HER CLOSET, clad only in a towel and her ratty bathrobe, with a glass of milk in her hand, Reggie planned her attack. The crucial first stage involved walking into the bar tonight and making Greg swallow his tongue. Then she would think about asking someone to perform the Heimlich maneuver. Maybe. But only if she was feeling generous. And only if it didn't conflict with whatever plans Dmitri had made for the evening.

She surveyed her arsenal with a critical eye. Part of her wanted to ignore the red dress just because Dmitri had ordered her to wear it, but when she flipped through her wardrobe, she thought it might be her only viable alternative. Plus, she figured after the little performance she'd put on in her mirror, buttering up the man who wanted to make her pay might not be a bad idea.

Still, her contrary nature sent her searching

through her closet one last time. Her usual collection of man-magnet dresses didn't pack enough punch, not to mention that Greg had seen almost everything she owned. If only she'd reacted to the breakup by shopping, she'd be set, but instead, she'd holed up in her apartment like a hermit. Now, she was paying the price.

Her right hand reached out to flip through hangers, discarding potential outfits while her left hand brought the glass to her lips for a healthy swallow of milk. Although Reggie didn't consider herself a big drinker, she'd considered having a glass of wine tonight for a little liquid courage. But the more she thought about the evening ahead, the more she decided her stomach needed soothing at least as much as her nerves.

"Boring. Boring. Seen it. Ugh." Mumbling a running commentary on her rejections, Reggie finally reached the end of the closet. She'd left herself with only one choice.

"Damn it." Frowning, she perched on the end of the bed and glowered at the open closet door, as if she could intimidate it into creating new and exciting outfits for her to wear. It didn't happen. She ran her gaze down the entire closet rod one more time, trying to see if she'd missed anything, or if any ideas popped into her head for new ways to combine garments into breathtakingly sexy outfits. No luck. The only things she saw were her own boring old clothes and the red velvet dress that could make a porn star proud. Salvation eluded her.

Reggie drained her glass in disgust and set it aside. Fate decreed she should wear the red dress, and she knew how to give in gracefully. Sort of.

She pulled the dress out of the closet and hooked it over the back of the door. When she stripped away the plastic, the rich sheen of silk velvet caught the light and seemed to breathe. Her hand went out to touch it, drawn by the luxurious promise of the fabric. She'd paid a fortune for the thing, more than she wanted to remember, but in that moment, she decided it had been worth every penny.

Her skin looked pearly-pale where it touched the material, set off against the backdrop of crimson velvet. Instead of washing her out, the color refined her skin to a shade of rich, warm cream that looked smooth enough to spread on a scone . . . or a set of silk sheets. No wonder Dmitri wanted her to wear it.

Of course, he also might have been influenced by the fact that the garment just missed being a size too small. If the saleswoman hadn't assured Reggie that the designer intended a snug fit, she'd have tried on a larger size. As it was, she remembered the material fitting her almost as closely as her skin, where it covered her skin, anyway. The abbreviated bodice sat off the shoulder and drew the eye to her breasts while the hemline fought for an equal share of attention by falling somewhere just long of indecent exposure.

Carrying it with her to the full-length mirror on the door, Reggie held it up against her body, smoothing a hand across the luxurious cloth. She had to give Dmitri credit; he had fabulous taste. Stripping out of her robe, she pulled on her bra and thigh-high stockings before she gave in and shimmied her way into the tight dress.

She sighed at the feel of the heavy velvet against her skin when she finally wrapped the gorgeous garment around her. She struggled for a minute with the zipper until it slid up its full height to just below her shoulder blades. Then she stepped back and surveyed the results in the full-length mirror.

"Damn. It's perfect."

AT PRECISELY 7:25, REGGIE STEPPED THROUGH the door of Captain Jack's nightclub and took a deep breath. Well, as deep as she could without tumbling out of the low-cut dress and giving the inhabitants of the bar a better show than the strip club two blocks east. She felt the weight of appreciative male glances sliding over her, even though she normally remained oblivious to that kind of attention. Tonight, she felt it, and it felt fabulous.

She knew she looked better than she had in a long time, maybe better than she ever had. The dress presented her lush curves like an offering, pushing her generous breasts together and raising them until they seemed in danger of spilling from the neckline. The snug fit accentuated the small-ness of her waist and hugged the curve of her hip until all eyes were drawn by the contrast. Her skin seemed to glow against the crimson velvet and the auburn silk of her hair, which she'd allowed to tumble in unruly waves down her back. Her legs were encased in the sheer, black, thigh-highs whose tops just barely managed to stay hidden under her hem, and her dainty feet disappeared into a pair of matching crinkle-patent red stiletto heels.

All in all, Reggie looked like sex on a stick, and she wasn't the only person in the bar who thought so. Too bad Dmitri wasn't early enough to see her grand entrance.

"Reggie! What are you doing here?"

She automatically turned at the sound of her name, but when she saw who had called out, she swore quietly and creatively. Corinne and Danice sat at one of the small, round tables near the edge of the bar, and they waved her over with enthusi-asm. Of all the rotten luck!

"Girl, after those messages Ava left you, I thought you'd be avoiding all of us like the plague. But look at you!" Danice pulled back and gave her friend a comprehensive going-over. "You are hot!"

"Absolutely. What inspired you?" Corinne's

eyes widened. "Are you meeting the guy from last night again? Where is he? Can we meet him?"

Reggie shifted.

"Tell us every dirty little detail," Danice demanded. "I never even got a look at the lucky man, but I heard a rumor he makes 'gorgeous' sound like an insult."

Reggie struggled for some way to weasel out of answering questions and was preparing to yell "Fire!" at the top of her lungs when a hand fell on her shoulder.

"Reggie, thanks so much for agreeing to meet me." All three women turned at the sound of Greg's voice. He ignored Reggie's friends and took her by the elbow. "I got us a quiet table by the wall where we can talk."

Reggie froze and wondered which higher power she could have offended enough to land her in this situation.

Of all the bars in all the clubs in all the world, my friends just had to choose this one tonight.

The situation achieved an extra level of ironic pain due to the fact that the women seated beside her hated Greg with a passion, even more than Reggie had ever been able to bring herself to hate him. It spoke for their loyalty, but not for a pleasant meeting.

"Oh, have you learned to keep it in your pants long enough to have conversations these days,

Gregory?" Danice smirked, not even attempting to hide her contempt.

"Gregory has always been good at talking, Nicie," Corinne said. Around Greg, even journalistically impartial Corinne turned brittle and cutting. "It was telling the truth that he had a problem with."

"Ladies." Greg nodded civilly to Reggie's friends, which was enough to make his ex-fiancée do a double take.

The last time Reggie's friends and her jerk had run into each other, it had been trash talk at twenty paces. Greg had made it clear while they were still dating that he despised her friends and had no intention of pretending to be nice to them. Why should he have changed his tune now?

Now that she thought about it, Reggie noticed that more than one thing about Gregory had changed. His elegantly tailored suit looked familiar, but he seemed to wear it better these days. The subtle pin-striping set off the blue of his eyes, making them appear brighter and more intense than Reggie remembered. He looked somehow healthier, too, as if he'd just come back from a long vacation, refreshed and rejuvenated.

He even looked taller somehow.

"I hope you'll excuse us," he continued, his voice sounding deeper and smoother than before. More compelling. "But Reggie has graciously agreed to speak with me about an important private matter, and it's so rude to keep a lady standing. Sweetheart, I've saved a table for us at the back of the bar. Shall we?"

Reggie risked a quick look at her friends and registered their "Lucy, you got some 'splainin' to do!" expressions. They'd just have to wait until later, though, because she was not about to pass up the opportunity to have Gregory Martin groveling at her feet in a public place. There were some things to which a girl simply did not say no.

She murmured her agreement, cast her friends an "I'll tell you later" glance, and let Greg guide her to their table with a hand in the small of her back. She kept her head high and her shoulders straight and added an extra swing to her hips when their path through the crowd forced her to walk in front of him. Let the twit salivate, because she had better people to do than him these days.

It was kind of funny, though; Reggie found it difficult to focus on Greg, in spite of his possessive touch and the low patter of conversation he kept up as they moved through the bar. Instead she felt the almost tactile sensation of someone's gaze upon her. She looked around, expecting to see Dmitri poised somewhere in the shadows. He wasn't there, but she still could have sworn his fingers slipped beneath her hair and caressed the back of her neck.

She brushed the sensation off as imagination, at least until she felt the distinct pressure of a hand pat her ass and squeeze the cheek affectionately. She jumped about eight inches and looked around, but no one was remotely close enough to have touched her. She scowled, and a shiver raced through her.

Gregory noticed her tremble when he pulled out her chair, and he frowned. "Are you cold?"

"Not at all," she said. She looked warily around her again before slipping into the chair and pulling her attention back to the man in front of her. She smiled coyly and fluttered her lashes at him. "In fact, it's kind of hot in here. Don't you agree?"

Greg offered her his smoothest smile. "I wouldn't have a few minutes ago, but that was before I saw you in that dress. Reggie, you look stunning."

She smiled and thanked him prettily, grim satisfaction stirring within her as she let her lousy, cheating ex reach across the table and cover her hand with his. The moment felt a bit surreal. Not just because the opportunity for revenge had come so unexpectedly, but because she had expected to get more satisfaction out of it.

"You're even more beautiful than I remember," Greg continued, watching her with his intensely blue eyes as he raised her hand to his lips. His mouth brushed slowly across her knuckles. "What could I have been thinking to let you get away from me?"

"I used to wonder that myself," Reggie said, leaning toward him flirtatiously even as her conscience let out a fierce protest. She wasn't doing anything wrong, and the jerk deserved to suffer. "I guess I just assumed you hadn't been thinking at all."

Greg winced and still managed to look attractive. Seriously, shouldn't that have tipped her off about him before she wasted two years on the jerk?

"I deserved that," he said, squeezing her hand gently. "I didn't treat you the way you deserved, Reggie. And I want you to know that I regret it."

Reggie raised an eyebrow. "You do, do you?"

It was becoming a struggle not to let her confusion show on her face. Sure, when she'd picked up the phone that afternoon, a secret part of her had hoped that Greg's call signaled a desire on his part to grovel at her feet and beg her forgiveness. Which she would, naturally, coldly withhold while she crushed him beneath the heels of her very fetching Beverly Feldmans.

The problem was that she'd known all along that it was a fantasy. Even when they'd been together, she'd never heard Greg apologize to her. Yet here she was, sitting across a tiny bar table from her cheating ex-fiancé, who was honestly begging her forgiveness and being surprisingly attentive to her every word and action. More attentive, in fact, than he'd been during the last nine months of their relationship.

Greg's attention had fixed on her like a starving man fixed on the display in a bakery window. He hadn't looked at her with that much hunger since the first time they'd had sex. Heck, even then he'd been more full of himself than fascinated by her charms. The chance for revenge was too good to pass up.

Experimentally, Reggie trailed the fingers of her free hand along the top of her bodice, calling attention to the way it cupped her breasts and emphasized her generous curves.

"So, Gregory," she purred, trying to make her voice seductive rather than hoarse, which was how she thought she sounded, "why don't you tell me why you wanted to see me? After all this time."

She brought her hand up to where her shoulder and neck curved together and brushed her fingers back and forth across her bare skin. Greg had always loved her shoulders. All that tennis she'd played in high school, he'd said. Either way, it appeared his attraction to that particular part of her body hadn't waned. If anything, it seemed stronger than ever. His eyes had locked on her fingers like an automated missile targeting system. He looked almost hypnotized.

The satisfaction of seeing the man who'd cheated on her all but drool at the sight of her gave Reggie a deep sense of satisfaction.

This could almost be fun!

Fun for whom, dushka? a voice murmured inside her head. *Perhaps I did not make our relationship clear to you last night?*

A whisper of warm breath stirred against Reggie's ear and a warm, rough tongue reached out to toy with her earlobe. She spun around so fast she almost fell off her chair. No one stood close enough to whisper to her, let alone to touch her. No one other than Greg.

Of course, Reggie had begun to suspect that distance didn't mean all that much to Dmitri Vidâme.

Careful, dushka. *You would not want to injure yourself by being careless*, he chided.

Damn it, Misha, she fumed. *You can't just sneak up on people like this. It's rude! And it's rude to carry on a conversation with someone who can't see you.*

Oh, is it? he purred. *As rude as meeting another man on the same evening that you and your lover have plans to spend time together?*

She felt a phantom hand slide up her thigh and tease the sensitive point where the lace of her stocking met her bare skin. And yet the only man close enough to touch her was Gregory, who had clasped her fingers in his two, very visible hands atop the table.

Is it as rude as that, Regina?

Dmitri, not now. She shifted, figuring if his hands weren't really there, they couldn't affect her unless she allowed it. She would just pretend she didn't feel a thing. *Your note said we were going to meet at eight. I've still got twenty minutes.*

"Are you all right, Reggie?" Greg frowned, his eyes narrowing as he squeezed her hand just a little too tightly. "You seem . . . distracted somehow."

"I'm sorry." Reggie forced a smile. "I, um, I didn't sleep well last night, and I guess it's left me a little scatterbrained. I don't mean to ignore you."

What she did mean to ignore was the way the imaginary fingers between her thighs had begun to stroke higher and higher up the soft expanse of her inner thigh, teasing and tantalizing in a way that reminded her exactly why she hadn't gotten much sleep the night before.

A deep voice chuckled against her ear. *I guarantee, dushka, that when you sit beside me, you will not notice any other distractions.*

"No. No, it's all right." Greg sighed, his voice yanking her mind away from Dmitri's phantom touch and back to reality. "It's no more than I deserve, really. But I've got to be honest. Leaving you was a mistake, Reggie, and I know that now. I miss you, and I couldn't keep going without seeing you again. Without asking you if you would consider giving me a second chance."

Three things happened simultaneously in that moment: Reggie's mind went blank, Dmitri's presence blinked out of her mind like a light bulb burning out, and the bar's live band began to run through their sound check by playing an earsplitting version of a 1980s death metal hit.

Greg swore. Or at least, Reggie assumed he did. She saw his lips move, and judging by his expression, whatever had come out of them hadn't been pleasant.

Pulling her to her feet, he leaned closer to her and shouted directly into her ear. "This is ridiculous! Come outside with me! We can't talk with all this racket!"

He didn't wait for a reply, just used his grip on her hand to drag Reggie in his wake through the crowd. She tried to tug her hand free, but Greg's grip was surprisingly strong. He must have started working out more since they broke up.

Instead of bringing her toward the bar's entrance, Greg forged a path toward the back door, shoving it open and hustling her into the rear alley before she could launch a suitable protest. The night air was chilly and damp, and the narrow space between the bar and the building next door looked dark and deserted. Not exactly someplace she would have chosen for a rendezvous with an old flame. But then, Greg had always been a little oblivious to that kind of thing.

Reggie wrapped her free arm around herself as a shiver shook her. Suddenly, she really wanted to go back inside. Or even to the coffee shop on the corner. Anywhere but here, alone with Greg.

She turned to him with what she hoped was a pacifying smile and put a little more effort into trying to tug her hand free. "Look, Greg, I don't want to be a bitch, b—"

"It's too late for that, Reg," her ex growled as he shoved her hard against the cold brick of the alley wall and pinned her there with the weight of his body.

Reggie gaped. She couldn't think of anything else to do. He'd literally shocked her senseless. Not in all the years she'd known him had Gregory Martin displayed any sort of penchant for violence. He'd never hit her, never shoved her; heck, the man even whined when he snagged a fingernail on her sweater. So why was he suddenly looming over her with a bad-movie-villain grin on his face and his blue eyes glowing a color Reggie could almost have sworn was tinged with red?

She fought back the first stirrings of fear this man had ever caused her. Then she got annoyed that she was feeling somehow afraid of a wuss like Greg.

"Greg, let me go!" She wedged her hands between them and shoved hard against his chest. "You're being an asshole right now, and I've got to tell you, if this is supposed to be how you win me back, you're going to have to try a new strategy!"

Greg didn't even budge. He just leaned closer until his breath brushed against her cheek, smelling of mint and copper and something else that made her skin crawl.

"I don't have to win you back, Reggie," he whispered. "Do you know why?"

Fear sped through her and made a sharp left turn toward panic. Reggie began to struggle in earnest. "Because it's a moot point since you can't get it up with anyone who actually has taste and morals?"

He grabbed her by the arms and pinned them to the wall behind her, leaning into her until she shrank back, revulsion making her want to melt into the wall to escape him. She could feel his fingers digging into her skin. They would leave bruises, she realized, and the thought turned her stomach. If he left bruises, she would have to look at them and remember where they had come from.

God! She thought she might be sick.

She turned her head, looking for a breath of air not tainted by the scent of his breath and the cologne he always wore. When they were together, she had thought he smelled good enough to eat. Now his odor made her think of something left to rot too long in the summer sun.

Cursing her sexy yet insubstantial heels, Reggie tried to get a leg between his so she could knee him in the balls. He had deserved it even before tonight, but now she hoped she shoved them clear out his eye sockets.

Damn it! She didn't remember Greg being this strong. When had he gotten this strong?

"Ah-ah," he scolded, grunting when her knee connected with his thigh. "You shouldn't antagonize me, Reg. Things have changed since you last saw me. I'm not the kind of guy you want to insult anymore."

"It's not a want, Greg; it's a psychological compulsion."

Sucking in a deep breath, Reggie gathered her strength and made one desperate lunge toward him. She didn't care if she butted him in the cheek with her skull, stabbed him in the eye with her nose, or sank her teeth into any skin close enough for her to bite. She would do whatever she had to if it made him let go long enough for her to run.

She caught him under the chin with the side of her forehead. The impact made her teeth rattle in her skull and left her dazed for half a second, but Greg didn't even flinch, let alone loosen his grip. He had her trapped and a wave of dizziness hit as Reggie began to think she just might not be able to get away.

What the hell was happening? How had she gotten here? Of all the ways she had expected this evening to go, being raped and murdered by her ex-fiancé in an alley behind a crowded bar had not appeared on the agenda.

Reggie lived an ordinary life, so how on earth

had she been picked to meet such an extraordinary end?

"You used to be so sweet, Reggie," the jerk breathed, raising her hands over her head so he could pin them with a single one of his own. When she tested that grip, she found it just as firm as if he'd been using both hands. "It's a shame you had to turn into such a raving bitch."

Greg lifted a free hand and brushed the weight of her disheveled hair behind her left shoulder, leaving her neck and throat bare to the cold night air. It took all of Reggie's strength not to whimper. Especially when his gaze fixed on the tender skin, and the gleam in his eyes seemed to grow even redder.

"But then again," he whispered, and Reggie closed her eyes so she wouldn't have to see him lower his head, wouldn't have to see him turn such an intimate position into something foul and corrupt. "Then again, I've learned these past few months that sometimes the bitches taste even better than the Barbies."

God, this couldn't be happening.

Reggie's head began to spin. The world receded, going dark and out of touch around her. She felt hot and cold and sick to her stomach, like she might pass out or vomit or run screaming into the night. Every muscle in her body tensed as she felt the stir of hot, rancid breath against her flesh, felt

the rough yank of his hand in her hair tugging
her head to the side, felt the humidity of his
parted lips as Greg opened his mouth . . .

. . . and screamed.

CHAPTER 11

DMITRI DIDN'T TAKE MUCH TIME TO PLAN OUT his attack. The minute he turned into the alley and saw the man with his hands on Regina, he sprang like a hungry predator.

One hand lashed out, grabbing the bastard by the arm and wrenching hard enough to dislocate the shoulder and snap the humerus in one motion. Belatedly, he clamped his other hand over the man's mouth to cut off the screaming. In that moment, he wanted nothing so much as to break the bastard's neck and leave him where he fell, surrounded by the garbage he resembled. Not only had this man been the one who had caused his Regina so much pain in her past, but he had *dared* to touch her again after Dmitri had claimed her as his own. He deserved to die.

But Regina did not deserve to witness it.

Cursing, he tossed the man aside, sending him crashing into the dumpster at the end of the alley.

He spared Regina a glance long enough to determine that she had no visible injuries before fixing his attention back on her attacker. He could feel his own lips curve in a snarl, and saw fear flash across Gregory Martin's expression before it was quickly suppressed. In its place, the human mustered a snarl that made Dmitri look twice and curse.

Fangs. The man had been turned. Someone had made Regina's former fiancé into a vampire.

"This is none of your business, old man," the man hissed, his useless left arm dangling unevenly by his side. "You need to leave before it's too late."

Out of the corner of his eye, Dmitri saw Regina waver, then slide down the wall to sit with her back against the bricks. He wanted to scold her for not taking better care. The pavement was damp from the recent rainy weather, and it was too cold for her to risk her health with such behavior. Then again, from the look on her face, he doubted she could have continued to stand even if he had commanded it. For a moment she stared straight at him, her gaze dazed and unfocused, before her eyes fluttered shut and she slipped into unconsciousness. His instinct was to rush to her side, but he knew she would be safe now that he was there to watch over her. And he had more pressing matters to attend to.

"Too late for what?" he demanded, turning back to Martin and baring an impressive set of fangs of his own. "For you to abuse someone weaker than you for your own amusement? Tell me, were you planning to drain her? Or just have a little snack while you practiced your technique for abusing women?"

"Like I said, it's none of your damned business."

"Listen to me, fledgling." Dmitri took a menacing step forward, his fists clenching at his sides. He wished fervently that they were around this pathetic idiot's throat instead. "Your maker seems to have neglected a significant portion of your education, so permit me to tutor you in a few very important facts."

He stalked deeper into the alley, every step bringing him closer to the fool who had dared to attack Regina. *His* Regina.

Maybe he wouldn't strangle Martin after all. Ripping the beating heart from the bastard's chest would prove even more satisfying.

"First of all, the vampires of this city obey certain rules, the most important of which is that we do not kill humans, and we do not feed from unwilling donors."

Dmitri glided forward, noting with satisfaction that Martin had begun to ease away from him, his arrogant expression taking on a wary cast.

"Second," Dmitri continued, "that rule and all the others that govern us are laid down by the Council of Others. What the Council says is the law, and you will respect it as such."

"Our kind can't be dictated to like children," Martin sneered, even as he continued to back away from the very real danger before him. "We're not humans; we're hunters. Mortals are nothing but cattle for us to feed on."

Dmitri beat back an instinctive snarl. He'd heard this kind of argument before, and he remained unconvinced. What men like Martin tended to forget was that all vampires had been human at one time, and looking down on one's own origins was a good way for a warrior to make enemies. And to lose his head.

What struck Dmitri as curious, though, was that it usually took a few centuries for a vampire to grow as arrogant as this one had managed in the few short months since he'd been turned. In Regina's memories of their relationship, the man had been clearly human.

"An interesting theory," Dmitri murmured, backing the other man slowly and steadily into the blind end of the alley. "I don't suppose you'd care to tell me who taught you this interesting philosophy?"

"I don't need to explain myself to you."

"Oh, I think you do."

Martin continued to back up, sidling toward the side of the alley as he realized he'd been leading himself into a trap. "Why?"

"Because I am Dmitri Vidâme, head of the Council of Others," he rumbled, gathering his muscles for the strike. "I make the rules for our kind in this city. And if the Council won't take you in hand for your indiscriminate feeding, I'll kill you myself for laying your hands on my woman."

Perhaps he should have dispensed with the warning.

Instead of quaking in his heels as Dmitri had anticipated, Martin widened his eyes just before he launched himself forward, not in an attack, but in a desperate bid for escape. Because Dmitri had failed to give the younger credit for thinking of such a bold move, the gambit took him by surprise, and he instinctively pivoted to avoid being hit as the fledgling barreled past and out the end of the alley.

Instinct had Dmitri taking the first steps to follow before a faint noise caught his attention and brought him instantly back to Regina's side.

He gathered her carefully into his arms, lifting her against his chest as if she weighed no more than a snowflake. To him, she did not. Cradling her limp form, he brushed a kiss against her temple and watched as her eyelids fluttered but remained closed.

"Hush, *milaya*," he murmured, accompanying the words with a gentle touch to her mind, easing her from unconsciousness into sleep. "You are safe. You will always be safe now, because you are mine. And I shall treasure you for all time."

Regina sighed and nestled her head more

closely against his shoulder. "Misha," she whispered, and he felt something inside him soften in acknowledgment.

"Yes, *dushka*. It's time to go home." He kissed her again and headed for the mouth of the alley. "Rest. Sleep. And when you wake, I shall be with you."

He meant the words as a promise. He fully intended to look after her for as long as she needed him. But in the meantime, while she slept he intended to make a few phone calls and try to dig up some information on his latest discovery. Not only were there rogues in the city feeding on unknowing victims all around the club scene, but it looked like at least one vampire in Manhattan had decided to begin turning mortals without permission. When the Council found out, they would not be pleased.

Pouring on a burst of speed, Dmitri used his abilities to cover the short distance to Regina's apartment building in little more than an instant. He wanted to get her inside where it was safe and settle her down for the night before he began dialing those numbers. He had a sneaking suspicion that one or two of his calls could turn out to be rather loud.

CHAPTER 12

"YOU'VE GOT TO BE KIDDING ME."

"Do I sound as if this is a jest?"

Graham groaned. "D, the idea that a few of your fledglings were running around sucking on club kids like juice boxes was bad enough. Now you're telling me that some rogue is out there randomly turning out untrained vamps like they were so many Amway reps? The Council doesn't pay me enough for this shit."

"The Council doesn't pay you at all," Dmitri pointed out. "Its operations are strictly volunteer supported."

He took care to keep his voice down and the telephone close to his mouth, but he still kept one eye on the door to Regina's bedroom in case she stirred. She'd already been asleep for more than half an hour and he couldn't be sure how much longer she would remain unconscious.

"Yeah, and don't think I haven't clued in to

how ridiculous that is," the Lupine griped. "No one should have to put up with this kind of idiocy without some sort of compensation coming their way."

"Think of the prestige."

"Think of shoving it up your ass."

Dmitri sighed. "While I appreciate your sentiment, I do not have the time to listen to your complaints at the moment, my friend. I need you to help me track down this fledgling. Without him, we have no way of discovering his maker."

"Yeah, I get that part. But what about the other thing I'm already 'helping' you with? You want me to give up on the kid from the club and just do this instead?"

Dmitri bit back a curse. He'd almost forgotten about their lead on the rogues, and that wasn't like him. He never left anything unfinished, and he didn't plan to start now. A glance at his watch told him it was only a little after nine, though it felt much later. Justin wasn't due to contact him with an update until eleven-thirty, but he didn't want Graham waiting for that information before beginning to follow the trail of Regina's ex-fiancé.

"Do not give it up, but pass it along to someone else. Put your best tracker on it, and then concentrate on this Martin fellow. He shouldn't be that difficult to find. Not only is he a fledgling, but he's an arrogant one at that."

"Right. I'll give the kid's napkin to Logan. If anyone can still pick up a scent on it, it'll be him."

Dmitri grunted his assent. Logan Hunter was Graham's beta, the second in command of the Silverback Clan of Lupines. Having Logan on the case was nearly as good as Graham doing it himself, and when it came to trailing scent, the beta might even have an edge over his pack leader. "Tell Logan to expect a call from Justin before morning. I will instruct Justin to contact Logan directly on anything involving the boy from the club. If we turn up anything on Martin on our end, I will pass it along to you myself."

"Roger. Keep your cell handy. I'll buzz you with anything important."

Dmitri flipped his cell phone shut and slipped it into the inner pocket of his suit jacket. Then he folded the jacket over the back of the sofa, stripped off his tie, and draped it on top. Unbuttoning his cuffs, he rolled up his sleeves as he entered the bedroom.

Regina lay where he'd left her, curled up in the center of her bed, a tempting splash of scarlet against the white and pale sage of her quilted coverlet. Her hair tumbled around her shoulders and spread across the pillows like a mantle of silk. Above the neckline of her gown, her skin flowed fair and smooth and flawless. It looked unmarked, but Dmitri needed to be sure.

Carefully, he settled on the mattress beside her

hip and leaned in. The scent of her rose to fill his senses, warm citrus and sweet woman. Desire flared. He didn't even need to touch her to want her, barely had to see her. She affected him as no other woman ever had, and the idea that he could have lost her tonight made him murderous.

Regina sighed in her sleep and shifted, her head turning to expose both sides of her throat. Dmitri examined the skin there carefully but found no marks. He had reached the alley in time.

Lifting a hand, he brushed a tangled curl away from his woman's cheek and watched her nuzzle instinctively into his touch. Awake, she might fear their relationship was moving too fast, but asleep her heart and body recognized her mate.

Bozhe! God! To lose her would have destroyed him.

Dmitri saw his hand tremble at the thought and withdrew, curling his traitorous fingers into a fist to still the motion. Regina, thankfully, slept on undisturbed.

It tested a man, he acknowledged ruefully, leaning forward and bracing his elbows on his thighs. After nine centuries of relationships that came and went like the seasons, to look at one woman and know she was the last . . .

Well, that could take a little getting used to.

It wasn't the thought of monogamy that gave Dmitri pause; he'd always preferred to indulge in one relationship at a time, to concentrate on one partner until it came time to move on. He enjoyed the special kind of intimacy bred from familiarity, knowing how to touch, when to savor. And women, he had found, tended to show their appreciation to a devoted lover in ingenious and enthusiastic ways, so who was he to complain?

With a lover like Regina, *how* could he complain? She welcomed him like springtime. Every time he touched her, he could feel her heart race, hear her breath catch, see the way she leaned toward him like a flower toward the sun. Everything he asked for, she gave. She flowed beneath his hands like a river of honey, warm and sweet, and clasped him to her as if she feared he would leave her. As if he would ever want to try.

When he had first touched her mind in the bar, he had wondered if he had wished her into being. It seemed rare enough to find a woman so lush and beautiful in this time of females shaped like quarterstaffs; but to see her deepest desires and know they melded so perfectly with his—well, that made him wonder why the gods had decided to smile upon him now, after all these years.

Dmitri was a hard man, a warrior, dominant not just by nature but because of the life he had lived. He had grown to manhood in a time when women could be plundered like villages, and though he had never taken an unwilling female to his bed, he had a medieval warlord's view of their sex. Women were smaller, weaker, softer; they were made to serve a man at table and in bed, and in exchange, men assumed the duty to protect and provide for them.

Not to say he expected Regina to follow ten steps behind him, or to attend him at his bath—though the idea had possibilities Dmitri thought she might enjoy exploring—he had lived long enough to mellow with time. Part of the reason why Dmitri had lived so long was that he had learned to adapt to the world that changed constantly around him. He knew modern women wanted to be seen as individuals with the same rights and abilities as men, and he had no trouble acknowledging that. It pleased him greatly, though, to know that while Regina could stand on her own two feet everywhere else, she craved for him to bend her over his knee in their bedchamber. He looked on that truth as the gift it was and knew his responsibility was never to abuse the power she so willingly gave him.

Dmitri would protect his mate with his life.

Which meant that when Graham located Gregory Martin, Dmitri would require more from the fledgling than the name of his maker. Dmitri intended to make that bastard pay for every ounce of fear or pain he had ever caused Regina. For every hurt Martin had caused her, Dmitri intended to inflict one in trade, but the scars *he* left would be visible to all with eyes to see the ruin Dmitri left behind him.

Jaw clenching, Dmitri pushed the thought away and turned his attention back to Regina. The hour was still early and he had matters he wished to discuss with his young and rebellious mate. Matters such as what she had meant by accepting a date with another man after Dmitri had claimed her as his own. Once she awoke, he would put the question to her and see how prettily she could be convinced to tender her apologies.

REGGIE WOKE SLOWLY FROM A DREAM IN which her former fiancé had re-proposed to her, turned into a Welsh corgi, and explained to her that instead of rings, they would be exchanging flea collars during their wedding ceremony.

Talk about Freudian symbolism.

Eyes still closed, Reggie yawned and stretched, the movement aborted when she felt her clothes tighten around her.

Why on earth was she still dressed if she'd gone to bed?

"I had begun to wonder how long you would sleep."

The deep familiar voice finished Reggie's waking-up process in a hurry. Forcing her eyes open, she bolted upright to find Dmitri perched on the side of her bed, watching her with those fathomless black eyes.

"What are you doing here?" she demanded. A thought occurred to her, and she frowned. "What am *I* doing here? I thought we were supposed to meet at Captain Jack's."

Dmitri didn't answer, but within the space of a few seconds, he no longer had to. Memory came flooding back to her, jumbled and confused, but just barely recognizable. She recalled dressing up, leaving early to meet with Greg, talking in the bar . . . then things started to get a little hazy.

She thought there had been noise—a lot of noise. A band. People talking and laughing. Someone screaming. She remembered fear, low and tight in her belly, and a smell, like rotted meat and wet pavement. None of it made any sense.

"What happened?" she asked, pushing her tumbled hair back and frowning at Dmitri. "I remember going to the bar. I went early, even, but I don't remember when you arrived, and I don't remember how I got home. Did you bring me?"

"I did," Dmitri acknowledged. "Would you like me to remind you? Or would you prefer to hear the story about what I found when I arrived at the place where we had arranged our meeting? How I found my date in the arms of another man? A man who used to be her lover."

His black eyes watched her intently, and Reggie had to work hard not to squirm under his gaze. Honestly, when she'd agreed to meet with Greg before her scheduled date with Misha, she hadn't expected her ex to try so hard to win her back. Sure, she'd been looking forward to his apologies, maybe even a little groveling on his part, but she'd fully intended to shoot him down, so she didn't see what right Misha had to get upset with her.

At least, that's the reasoning she tried to hang on to. Beneath it, though, a secret part of her acknowledged that she'd known how he would react to the idea. In fact, that part of her had pushed her into the meeting for precisely that reason. It had wanted to test him, to see how seriously he viewed the chemistry between them. Had it been a one-night-stand that he wanted to turn into a twofer? Or had it meant something to him? Something like the beginning of a relationship?

It looked like she'd definitely sparked a reaction.

She tried for a dismissive tone. "It wasn't like that at all. You're making it sound like I was trying to hook up with someone else. Greg asked if he could talk to me for a few minutes before our date, and I agreed. I made it very clear that I was meeting with someone else at eight though. It's not like I offered him a quickie before you got there."

Judging by the flare of anger in Misha's dark eyes, she wondered if he was about to demonstrate the literal meaning of the word "backfire" for her.

"I never accused you of such, *katyonak,* but you can rest assured that if I thought that to be your plan, we would be having this discussion with you bent over my knee and your skirts up around your waist. I will not tolerate infidelity in my woman."

" 'Your woman'?" Reggie repeated, blinking in astonishment. "Where the heck did that title come from? We had one date, Misha, and yeah, it involved some pretty entertaining sex, but where I come from, one good boink does not a relationship make."

Dmitri's expression went from arrogant to amused in the space of a heartbeat. " 'Boink'? What an . . . ah . . . original term. But I am not sure I caught the proper meaning. Perhaps you could demonstrate for me."

He leaned forward and Reggie scrambled off the bed, holding out both hands as if to ward him off. Right, like that would work.

"Don't try to distract me," she warned. "You know exactly what I meant, and I'm not going to let you derail this discussion with sex. Clearly, there are a few things here that we need to talk about. For instance, exactly when did I become 'your woman,' huh?"

Dmitri shrugged. "It was true from the first moment I saw you. As for when I realized it, I do not see that it matters. The timing cannot change the reality."

"It matters to me, bucko." Reggie crossed her arms over her chest and glared at him. "I don't recall agreeing to anything long term, and I think it would have stuck with me if you'd asked me to go steady!"

The amused look returned, accompanied by a subtle quirk of his lips. "You would have preferred if I had asked you to wear my class ring? Or perhaps given you my athletic jacket?"

She looked at him incredulously. "Where do you think we are? Rydell High in 1957? I would have *preferred* if we had maybe had a conversation. You know, gotten to know more about each other than how to get each other off."

"I would prefer that you not speak so crudely, Regina," Dmitri frowned. "It ill becomes you. In addition, I find your argument a poor one. I think we know much about each other, certainly enough to recognize that you belong to me."

Sweet Jesus, the man was thicker than molasses. Reggie prayed for patience.

"First of all," she began, struggling to keep her voice even and reasonable, "I think we exchanged maybe two dozen words before the clothes started to come off; and second, we've only known each other for maybe eight hours, total. That's hardly a solid basis for a relationship. Also"—she held up a hand when he would have interrupted—"any relationship that I'm going to agree to be in is going to involve *mutual* belonging. I'm not a possession, and I won't be referred to as one."

Dmitri seemed to relax at that, offering her a regal nod. "Forgive me, *dushka*. I did not intend to imply that I viewed you as anything less than an intelligent woman. I am afraid that my speech can seem a bit . . . old-fashioned at times. Please know that it is not a reflection of my feelings."

Something inside Reggie relaxed, and she let out a breath that she hadn't realized she'd been holding. "Good. I enjoyed what we did together, Misha"—she blushed—"but I don't want you to think that I plan to obey your every whim outside of the bedroom. The fact that I like, well, that I like you to be dominant in bed—that doesn't mean I'll put up with being treated like some kind of slave. Sex games are one thing, but real life is something else entirely."

"I understand, *milka*." He stood and reached out, pulling her gently into his arms. "I can assure you that I have no desire to turn you into a mindless toy. I enjoy your fire far too much for that."

"Good."

Reggie uncrossed her arms and wrapped them around him. Her head fit so perfectly against his chest that she couldn't resist laying it there. She felt him rest his chin on top of her head and enjoyed the feeling of being surrounded by him. He was such a large man that standing beside him made her feel small and delicate and protected.

It made her feel cherished.

He let the silence stretch out for a few minutes before his deep voice rumbled in her ear. "I still want to hear it, *dushka*."

"Hear what?"

"I want to hear you acknowledge that you are mine." He pulled back just far enough to fix her with a stern gaze.

Reggie returned it with a raised eyebrow and pursed lips. "I think I just finished telling you that I'm not going to get involved with anyone who sees me as a possession."

"And I do not. But that does not mean I do not wish to possess you."

"What if I want to possess you instead?"

He flashed her a grin, warm and wicked and laced with something more that Reggie couldn't quite define.

"*Dushka*," he murmured, lowering his mouth to hers. "You already do."

CHAPTER 13

"WELL, WELL, WHAT HAVE WE HERE?"

So wrapped up in the taste and feel of Regina in his arms, Dmitri hadn't even heard anyone approach. As soon as the voice sounded, he spun to face the intruder, putting himself between his woman and any possible threat. When he saw who stood before him, he only relaxed a little.

The interruption had come from Ava, a figure he'd seen much of when he sifted through his Regina's thoughts. She stood in the doorway to Regina's bedroom wearing a scarlet trenchcoat over a black cowl-neck sweater, with a look of pure poison in her dark, almond-shaped eyes.

"Reggie, darling, aren't you going to introduce me to your new friend?" Ava's voice, low and melodic, and her expression, a sweet, warm smile, gave Reggie the creeps. Dmitri could read his lover's unease in her mind and her body.

"Ava, what the heck are you doing here?" Reggie demanded, stepping out from behind Dmitri to frown at her friend. He could feel her flush of embarrassment, as well as her confusion. "Is something the matter? What's wrong?"

"Nothing is wrong, darling, I just stopped by to say hello." Ava's voice sounded smoother than silk and sharper than steel. "I met up with Corinne and Danice at Captain Jack's a few minutes ago, and they mentioned that you'd been there with Greg, but that you disappeared without bothering to say goodbye. Since that didn't sound like you, I became a little concerned and used my emergency key to check on you. I didn't realize you'd have company." She looked pointedly at Dmitri.

So pointedly, in fact, that he felt tempted to check himself for stab wounds.

Stool pigeons, he heard Reggie think just before she offered her friend a forced smile. "That was sweet, Av, but unnecessary." Regina took his hand and made the introductions. "Ava, this is Dmitri Vidâme. Misha, this is my friend Ava Markham."

"A pleasure," Dmitri murmured, taking Ava's hand in his and bowing slightly over it. The dark-haired woman's eyes narrowed at the gesture.

"I'm sure it is," she said, her tone dismissive. "It appears you've made quite an impression on our friend, considering you met her for the first time last night."

Dmitri's mouth quirked. Even without reading her mind, he could sense the protectiveness that radiated off Ava's slim frame. Reggie's friend had cool, faintly exotic dark looks that radiated confidence, sex, and money. She stood at least five ten in her Italian heels, and he knew her black sheath dress would bear an exclusive designer label. Ava was the sort of woman Dmitri would have been attracted to in the past, strong and aggressive and passionate, but he had recently discovered a decided preference for soft, cuddly redheads with submissive streaks.

"I am the one who was impressed, Ms. Markham. I am sure you realize your friend is a remarkable woman."

Reggie stepped forward as if to remind them of her presence.

"And she has a brain cell or two to rub together, not to mention a tongue in her head," she snapped, glaring at the two of them. "What is wrong with you people? I feel like I just stepped into the middle of an Olympic fencing match."

"Nothing's wrong, Reggie," Ava said, pursing her lips and raising her chin. "I'm simply surprised to find you here, alone in your apartment, with a man you only met last night at a club you don't usually frequent. It's not like you to pick up strangers. You usually have better sense."

Dmitri stifled a chuckle. "I've found Regina has perfect sense. As well as many other . . . intriguing qualities."

Unable to resist, he settled his hand low and far

back on Reggie's hip and squeezed, just for the entertainment value of Ava's reaction. She didn't disappoint him.

"She used to have perfect sense," Ava bit out, her dark eyes frosting over while she glared at Dmitri's hand. "But I'm seeing precious little of it at the moment."

Dmitri felt Regina stiffen under his hand.

"What's that supposed to mean?" Regina demanded, crossing her arms over her chest and glaring at her friend.

"It means there is something seriously wrong with you, Reg." Ava matched her glare for glare.

Dmitri could read the concern beneath the angry attack, but he didn't think Regina cared about the motivation.

"There is nothing wrong with me, Ava. And even if there were, it would be none of your business. I'm a grown woman. I can take care of myself."

"Then prove it by not ditching an old boyfriend at a bar, ignoring your very concerned friends, and inviting some cretin into your apartment to paw you like you're a piece of meat!"

Dmitri hadn't planned to come between the two women—he hadn't lived this long by doing something so stupid—but neither would he stand by and watch Ava insult his Regina. He stiffened at her words and touched her mind, looking for an entrance.

"Dmitri is not pawing me, but even if he were, what business is that of yours?" Regina countered. "Maybe I like being pawed! Maybe I don't care what you think about me or the men I date!"

Man, Dmitri corrected, sending the thought firmly into Reggie's mind, briefly dividing his attention between the two women. *You date only one man, Regina. Me.*

He saw Regina roll her eyes, and he bit back a grin, turning his attention once more to Ava. She had a surprisingly strong mind with some impressive natural shielding. He probed quickly for a weak spot, but it didn't take long for him to realize he couldn't just slip quietly into her mind in the space of a few seconds. She required more force than that, which meant that his best strategy might be to retreat.

Dmitri turned away from Ava and squeezed Regina's hip gently. "Do not be so hard on your friend, *dushka,*" he murmured. "She seems to be concerned about you. I believe she means well."

"I don't care what she meant, Misha. She has no business letting herself into my apartment and criticizing my taste in men just because she didn't get to have a hand in choosing one for me. In fact, I really think it's time she left."

Ava nearly screamed. "And *I* think you're out of your mind! Listen to yourself, will you? You sound like the sort of empty-headed twit you've always hated. You've known this man for twenty-four hours and already you're letting him control you as if you can't think for yourself! What is your problem?"

Regina ignored her friend and walked calmly toward the door without glancing back. Dmitri let Ava stalk after her, then followed at a safe distance. He could hear the argument continue, but he didn't listen very carefully. He was too busy thinking about this latest problem and juggling it with the others he already had on his plate. An irate friend of his mate might not rank as highly as a rogue vampire making unauthorized fledglings and setting them loose on the city without training, but it definitely had the potential to cause him trouble of a more personal nature.

Yes, he would have to do something about this Ava woman. Perhaps a strong warning would be sufficient.

Just before Ava left the apartment through the door Regina was very clearly showing her, she looked back over her shoulder at the place where Dmitri watched from the shadows by the bedroom door. Very consciously, he let his mask of polite control slip and showed her a glimpse of the things he kept inside.

He didn't think she'd confront him again.

REGGIE NEVER DID GET AROUND TO LECTURING Dmitri on his mental snooping or his dictatorial tendencies. Three minutes after she had closed the door behind her friend, he had her stripped, spread, and draped facedown over the side of her mattress while he tortured her with teasing, shallow thrusts of his fingers into her wet heat. At that point, telling him she didn't like it when he tried to control her seemed a bit hypocritical. She almost hated herself for the way he could make her pant.

"Misha!" She gasped his name like a magic word and braced her hands against the bed, shoving her hips back against him. The hand that rested in the small of her back and held her in place pressed firmly to keep her still.

What do you want, dushka?

She heard his voice, no matter how hard she tried to block him out. She could surround her thoughts with mental barbed wire, but somehow Dmitri could cut right through it and never feel a scratch. Her defenses became meaningless around him, and the thought terrified her. What if Ava had been right? Could she just lie back and let Dmitri turn her into a mindless little sex toy?

He pulled his hand free of her clinging heat, and she whimpered.

Tell me, milaya. I want to hear you tell me.

He wanted to make her beg, and part of Reggie screamed in protest, but the demanding flesh between her legs drowned out the rebellion.

"You, Misha. I want you."

Her whisper became a shocked hiss and then a moan of pleasure when Dmitri rewarded her confession with the hot stroke of his tongue between her thighs. She trembled and had to lock her knees to keep herself upright. Dmitri had slipped to kneel behind her, and he clamped his hands on her hips, pinning them firmly to the bed while he drove her slowly out of her mind.

You taste so sweet, dushka. *Sweet and spicy and delicious.*

It felt a thousand times more intense than his phantom touch at the bar, and it almost killed her to hear him speaking in his black-magic voice while his tongue lapped wantonly at her pussy and drew tight little circles around her clit. Her breath came in helpless pants. She arched her back uncontrollably, tilting her hips to give him better access to her aching flesh.

That's right. Such a good girl, he crooned to her, his hands slipping from her hips to her thighs, gripping them and forcing them wider apart. His tongue pressed her more firmly, and he kept his hands clamped just above her knees, holding her open as securely as a spreader bar.

Reggie pressed her forehead to the mattress and squeezed her eyes shut. She wanted to get closer, wanted to get away. His mouth fed at her, drank her sweetness, and pressed her faster and faster toward her climax. He seemed to sense exactly the moment when his teasing licks became unbearable, and his tongue pressed harder against her. He nuzzled lower and found her clit.

Greeting the swollen nub with a quick flick of his tongue, he drew it gently between his teeth and suckled. The sensation robbed her of the ability to reason, the ability to stand. Her body went limp and trembled. Dmitri gripped her legs and braced his shoulders against the back of her knees, pinning her upright against the bed.

She tried to beg him to fuck her, to come inside her and ride her hard, but she couldn't speak. All she could do was moan and gasp and pray for mercy. He gave her none.

He nipped lightly at her clit, sending a bolt of pleasure-pain coursing through her. She screamed, the sound little more than a shrill exhalation of air.

Tell me, dushka.

She couldn't speak, could barely think, but Dmitri would hear her. *I need you to fuck me. Please fuck me, Misha!*

He nipped her again, soothed the sting with his clever tongue. *No. Tell me who you belong to. Tell me you are mine. Tell me no other man will touch you.*

Yes! God, yes! No one else. I'm yours. I belong to you, Misha!

Dmitri growled his satisfaction and thrust three long fingers deep into her grasping cunt. It was all Reggie needed.

She came, her entire body clenched and trembling. Her back arched, and her hips pressed high against him and her mind went blank and empty. She knew nothing but Dmitri and the pleasure that coursed through her. She didn't even know the sharp sting of his fangs or his harsh growl of pleasure when her blood mingled with her juices and slid sweetly down his throat.

CHAPTER 14

REGGIE WOKE THE NEXT MORNING ALREADY brooding.

Dmitri had kept her way too busy last night for her to think about the things Ava had said at the bar, but she remembered them now. In fact, they were the first thoughts in her head when her eyes opened and squinted against the late morning sunshine. When he wasn't there to cloud her thoughts with lust, Reggie could admit she did seem to act differently around Dmitri. Somehow he brought things out of her she'd been trying really hard to pretend weren't inside her to begin with.

Reggie considered herself a strong, independent woman. She supported herself, thought for herself, acted for herself. She believed women should have the same rights and opportunities as men and should never allow themselves to be treated as if they didn't. If pressed, she would have called herself a modern feminist, a woman who appreciated men, but didn't need them to complete her or guide her or tell her what to do.

So why did it feel so good when Dmitri took control? It freaked her out that his assumption of command and dictatorial tendencies made her feel so safe and cherished. She should be railing against his attitude, not sighing with contentment when he took charge and arranged her and her life to suit him. When she felt his body against hers, it all made perfect sense, but now, in the bright light of day, she had to think Ava might have a point. Maybe she should be suspicious of Dmitri's autocratic personality.

She mulled it over while she dragged herself out of bed and pulled on her bathrobe. Once again, her muscles ached in a graphic reminder of the previous night, though this time she could add lack of sleep to her problem. Not only had Dmitri's demanding appetite kept her up way past her bedtime, but once he had let her sleep, she'd drifted into some really disturbing dreams.

She'd imagined they were back at the Mausoleum, only this time they danced together, completely naked, on the crowded dance floor. The dream had been so real she'd felt the texture of his skin against hers, the cool surface of the wooden floor beneath her feet.

In her dream he surrounded and overwhelmed her, a lot like he did in real life. They had swayed to a slow, hypnotic rhythm, while the people around them continued to mosh to the frantic, industrial music she couldn't hear. They had ignored everyone else, totally wrapped up in each other while they danced. But the dancing had changed, and in the metamorphic way of dreams, in the next instant he had been pressing inside her.

They made love there on the dance floor. She'd felt Misha's hands slide down to cup her ass and lift her, and she'd wrapped her legs around his waist and lowered herself onto his waiting cock.

No one in the dream paid any attention while Reggie and Dmitri made love in their midst. The club patrons had swirled around the couple in a sea of heat and color, but all Reggie had really been able to focus on had been Misha's deep, black eyes. She'd stared into them while he thrust in and out of her until she'd gotten dizzy and hot and trembled on the edge of orgasm. In her dream, she'd continued to stare until he opened his mouth, and she could see his canine teeth elongate and sharpen until they'd become fangs. When he lowered his head and sank his teeth into her throat, the hot, piercing pain had tumbled her over the edge, and she'd come, her cunt greedily drinking his semen while his mouth greedily consumed her blood.

The dream had faded slowly, just like the orgasm, but the images lingered with her all night. Even after she woke, she could still feel his mouth drawing at her throat and his teeth holding her in place while he fed.

That's what she got for going to goth clubs and fantasizing about vampires, she scolded herself, heading into the kitchen for breakfast. A shrink would probably love a transcript of that dream, but Reggie chalked it up to a late night, exhausting sex, and the lingering tension from her confrontation with Ava. Apparently her subconscious thought there might be some truth to her friend's accusation that Dmitri's control of her might be unhealthy instead of just unbelievable.

She popped a bagel into the toaster and was measuring grounds into the coffeemaker when someone banged vigorously on her front door. Frowning, she slid the automatic drip basket into place, pushed the button, and crossed to the door. Checking the peephole, she sighed and leaned her forehead against the cool wood. The Inquisition had arrived.

She opened the door and stepped aside to let her friends into the living room. She was on her way to the bedroom before the door closed behind them. "Coffee is on, and there are bagels in the freezer. If I'm getting the third degree, I'm damned well not going to do it naked."

"But I'm betting you ended up naked last night!" Danice's quip and the sound of laughter followed her all the way down the hall.

When she reemerged from the bedroom, still

barefoot but now dressed in worn jeans and a red knit top, her apartment smelled like a Jewish deli and sounded like a Chippendales review.

Her friends had nixed the tiny kitchen and spread out coffee, fruit, and bagels on her coffee table. Someone had dug out butter, cream cheese, and two flavors of jam, and Missy was just setting down a skillet full of scrambled eggs when she looked up and caught sight of Reggie. "Somebody looks well-exercised." She grinned.

Corinne placed a serving of eggs on a plate, added half the bagel Reggie had toasted, and handed it to her. "Sit. Eat. Talk."

"With my mouth full?"

"Don't be smart with us, Miss Thang," Danice warned. "You have a story to tell us and we are not going away until we hear it."

Reggie wasn't sure she wanted to talk about Dmitri right now. Heaving a theatrical sigh, she took a seat in an armchair and balanced the plate on her lap. "Once upon a time—"

She ducked just before a slice of orange would have bounced off her forehead.

"Try again, Reg. And this time skip straight to the hot monkey sex."

Corinne's order defeated the smart-ass strategy, but Reggie didn't want to share the details of the previous two nights with her friends, especially not with Ava. No matter how close they all were, she couldn't feel comfortable with painting them a picture of the most erotic experiences of her life.

And she still didn't want to open up the discussion with Ava about her actions around Dmitri. Instead of answering, she shrugged and pushed the eggs around on her plate. "That's pretty much it. We had hot monkey sex. He went home."

A chorus of groans and grumbles echoed through the apartment.

"A less than rousing tale." Ava leaned against the arm of her chair, directly opposite Reggie's, and cradled a coffee mug in her manicured hands. "We've all spoken about seeing you and your Dmitri together the last two days. I believe we were looking for a bit more detail about your . . . relationship, Regina dear—names, positions, dimensions."

Did two nights of amazing sex equal a relationship?

The others laughed, and Reggie blushed as red as her shirt, but she still managed a respectably convincing scowl. "If you want details, call a nine hundred number."

"Why should we do that when we have you right here? For free, rather than five ninety-nine a minute."

"But I'm not here to satisfy your prurient interests."

"Of course you are." Ava sipped her coffee and eyed Reggie over the rim. Her gaze locked on the side of Reggie's neck, and her eyes narrowed. "What's that on your neck, Regina?"

"What's what?"

Reggie's hand went reflexively to the spot that captured Ava's interest, but she didn't feel anything.

"Well, that's what I call evidence." Danice wanted to see and jumped up to brush Reggie's hand away. She stared at her friend's neck so long and so intently that Corinne laughed.

"What are you looking for?"

"Fang marks," Danice answered, grinning. "I wanted to see if Reggie maybe landed herself a real vampire."

Reggie blushed when she remembered her dream. "Don't be a jerk," she muttered, pushing her friend away.

"Looks like a garden-variety hickey to me," Missy said. "Not exactly sophisticated, but I'm sure it added to the moment. Right, Reg?"

Reggie shifted uncomfortably and clamped her hand over the bruise. She'd noticed the mark yesterday morning when she dressed, which was odd, because she couldn't remember when Dmitri had marked her. She still might have to tell him to lay off the vampire act, especially after her dream. "Well, that's why we went there, right? I was supposed to get a Fix with a vampire-type guy. I did, and it's done. Who's up next?"

"Not so fast, Reg," Danice said, raising an eyebrow and crossing her arms over her chest. "You aren't getting off that easy. Part of the Fix is sharing the news with your friends, and providing a full evaluation. We still want details."

"I don't think Regina has to tell us anything she doesn't want to," Ava broke in. She surprised Reggie with her defense, but at that point, Reggie would have been glad for help from Genghis Khan and the Mongol hordes.

"Thanks, A—"

"Because I don't think Reggie's adventure counts as her Fix. She still needs to take care of that."

Reggie went pale. "What? But you can't Fix me. I mean, I already had a Fix. I mean, Dmitri was—"

"Not part of the game," Ava declared. "I had someone set up to take care of the two Fixes you submitted, Regina, but you didn't stick around to meet him. Therefore, you missed your Fix."

"I didn't miss anything! Dmitri and I—"

"I don't care if your new friend wore a black cape, plastic fangs, and made you call him 'master.' He wasn't your Fix, so he doesn't count."

Reggie's shirt paled beside her flaming cheeks.

"Oh, my God! He did!" Danice shot to her feet and did a little victory dance in front of the sofa. "Reggie's man fulfilled both her fantasies, and we didn't even get involved. You go, girl!"

Her appetite gone, Reggie set her plate down on the table and checked to see if there was room under it for her to hide.

"Wow, Reg. That is so cool! None of us were able to get our fantasies without a little help. And here you go and blow us out of the water." Missy grinned and gave her a thumbs-up sign. "I guess you didn't need our help after all."

"Let's not be hasty, Melissa." Ava set aside her empty cup. "Reggie may have gotten a couple of her fantasies fulfilled, but it wasn't an official Fix. We've all had dates outside of the Fixes, and it doesn't matter what happens on them. It's only the arranged Fixes that count. After all, we can't check with Dmitri, so how do we know Reggie isn't lying about the S and M just to get us off her back?"

Reggie saw the others taking Ava seriously and tried to cut in, but the other woman bulldozed right over her.

"I won't say it's impossible Reggie could be telling the truth," Ava continued, "but we have no way to know for sure. So I move we throw out these fantasies and start over. Reggie gets an all-new Fix."

Reggie stared at her, astounded and terrified. "Oh, no!"

"You know, Ava may be right," Danice agreed, grinning. "Must be your lucky day, girl, because you're up again."

"Right. Can't have you missing another turn," Corinne said.

"Look, guys," Reggie began, trying to reason with them, even while the idea of sex with any man other than Dmitri made her stomach churn. "I appreciate what you're trying to do here, but it's really not necessary. Dmitri would—"

"Dmitri would what?" Ava asked, her voice soft but far from gentle. "You said Dmitri didn't control you, Regina. Was that true?"

"Yes, but I'm . . . involved with him. I can't do this. Ava, you said it yourself last week. I'm monogamous. Now that I'm involved, I can't just sleep with someone else."

Ava looked determined. "Two fucks do not make an involvement, Reggie. I don't care how good this guy was in bed. Unless you ended your date in Vegas in front of a JP, you're not exclusively involved. You never even said when you're seeing him again."

Reggie scowled. On the one hand she wanted to deck Ava, but there was the corner of unease inside of her that wondered if maybe her friend was right. Maybe she was letting Dmitri control her. Maybe she should strike a blow for independence while she still could.

She ignored the way her insides recoiled at the idea.

"Fine," she snapped. "Give me some paper, and I'll give you a new batch of fantasies."

"Oh, no." Ava's eyes glinted. "After last time, I don't trust you. I had Missy bring along your original fantasies. We'll draw from those."

Reggie stared at the papers in Ava's hand for a minute, then glanced up at her friends. They watched her expectantly.

"I still think—"

"Don't think, Regina. Just sit there and be a good girl while we Fix you."

Reggie let her head fall against the chair back, and she squeezed her eyes shut. After Dmitri, she wasn't sure any of her old fantasies still applied. It felt as if he'd fulfilled them all.

God, I'm like an addict, she thought, frightened by how deeply Dmitri affected her. I think I might really need to do this. I've never acted this way about a man in my life. And I don't even really know him . . .

"My, my, but you are an adventurous girl, Regina McNeill."

Reggie heard the satisfaction in Ava's voice and decided she didn't want to know what had been drawn. "I'm sure that a very lucky man I know is going to love your night out together. In fact, I think both of you might come to view the opera in a whole new light."

The memory of that fantasy flooded her mind with erotic imagery, and Reggie buried her face in her hands with a groan.

CHAPTER 15

FOR THE FIRST TIME IN HER LIFE, REGGIE experienced Monday morning with a sense of profound gratitude and relief. She could hardly wait to get to her office and discover the deluge of paperwork and crises that awaited her. At least maybe then she'd be able to think about something other than Dmitri and the stupid Fantasy Fix.

As it turned out, she couldn't. Oh, she had a hell of a day. The small ad agency where she worked had gotten word on Friday that they'd landed a major new account with an up-and-coming electronics retailer, and on Monday morning, Reggie found out she'd been assigned to manage their first project, putting together a new logo and corporate look. The sales and management team were high on the success, and the art department was reeling under their impossible new deadline. That left Reggie to smooth all the ruffled feathers and coax a miracle out of her design team.

But even while she fielded phone calls, reviewed meeting notes, composed e-mails, and even talked a temperamental graphic artist out of quitting on the spot, her mind kept straying back to Dmitri. She felt a little like a new junkie who'd only just discovered her high and couldn't get the memory of it out of her mind. Only, in Reggie's case, the memories were also in her mouth, on her skin, and hovering in the air around her.

She had barely slept last night, too caught up in her discovery that Dmitri's scent had lingered in her bed. She wrapped herself up in the sheets that bore his distinctive, intoxicating fragrance and wrapped her arms around the pillow he'd lain on. Her pussy had throbbed and ached and felt empty after two nights of erotic excess, but she hadn't wanted to chance Dmitri watching her again while she made herself come. She'd had to lace her fingers together around the pillow she held to keep them from straying between her legs.

In any other situation, she would have been embarrassed by her obsession, but she hadn't been able to help herself. She'd felt she would go crazy if she couldn't have at least the scent and the memory of him to wrap around her. She'd fallen asleep with the echo of his hands stroking against her skin.

And she'd woken up terrified.

She'd never in her life acted like this with a man. Even in her few and failed relationships, she'd seen her lovers as partners, as men she would share her life with. They had complimented her, but she'd been complete without them. With Dmitri, his absence from her life, even for one night, had been hell. She'd missed him like an amputated limb, with the same ache and disbelief and the phantom feel of his presence. She needed him, and the thought scared the crap out of her.

"Yoohoo! Earth to Regina."

Reggie snapped back to reality with an audible pop and tuned in to Sherry's voice while the other woman tried to get her attention. "Sorry, Sher. What's up?"

The administrative assistant, whom Reggie shared with the two other project managers, rolled her eyes. "I hope you had a nice mental vacation there, because Banks is saying he needs to see the Alien Entertainment annual report draft five minutes ago."

Reggie sighed, pushed her chair over to the metal filing cabinet beside her desk, and pulled out the appropriate folder. Charles Banks always wanted something five minutes ago, but since he owned the agency, she figured she could humor him.

"Here." She handed the thick folder to Sherry. "Tell him the photography is in the lab as we speak. Mike promised we'd have it by three."

"Cool. Thanks." Sherry turned to leave, remembered something and paused in the doorway. "Oh,

I almost forgot. You've got a call on line four. Some guy."

"What does he want?" The last thing Reggie needed to deal with was an unknown artist hawking his talents.

"I asked, but he said it was personal business."

Dmitri.

For one fabulous moment, the idea made her heart race and her stomach jump. Then reality set in, and she realized he had no way of knowing where she worked and so no way of getting her number. Giving disappointment and relief a chance to slow down her pulse, she took a deep breath and prepared her standard "Send us a portfolio and we'll get back to you" speech.

"Hello? This is Regina."

"Hi, Regina. This is Marc Abrahms. Ava Markham gave me your number."

Yikes, he must be the Fix. "Oh. Um, hi."

"Listen, I know you're at work, so I won't keep you," he said. Well, he gets some points for manners, at least. "But Ava mentioned you're an opera fan, and I was able to wrangle a private box for *Turandot* on Thursday night. I hoped you might join me."

Join you; fuck you. Why quibble over semantics? At least he was being delicate about the whole thing, even if that didn't keep Reggie's face from turning a peculiar shade of magenta. He could have just gotten right down to the bottom line and asked how many condoms to bring. "Um, well . . ."

"Ava's told me a lot about you," he offered in his pleasant, mellow voice.

Yeah, like the fact that I'm a guaranteed score.

"I'm really looking forward to meeting you in person."

I'll bet. His comment only made her blush harder, but there really was no graceful way out of the situation. Tightening her grip on the receiver, Reggie took a deep breath and said, "Sure. Thursday sounds fine."

"Great." He actually did sound happy that she'd accepted. After what Ava must have told him, did he think she had a choice? "If I pick you up at six, we can have dinner before the show. Does that sound all right?"

Reggie nodded, realized he couldn't see her, and hastened to reassure him. "That's perfect. I'll look forward to it." *Like a root canal.*

"Me too. It was nice talking to you, Regina. Take care."

Reggie hung up the phone with a knot the size of Brooklyn twisting her stomach. The last thing she wanted was to spend Thursday night with a stranger, but she needed to exert her independence, to show herself she didn't need Dmitri, no matter how her mind and heart and body screamed for him.

She wasn't altogether sure she could bring herself to act out the opera fantasy with this Marc person. In fact, the more she thought about it, the more the idea made her uncomfortable. Her skin almost crawled, and the hair on the back of her neck stood on end. Her unease was that strong.

Shifting in her chair, she neatly penciled the date with Marc onto her desktop calendar. As if she were likely to forget it.

She waited for her discomfort to ease, but if anything, writing down the date only made her illogical sense of foreboding worse. Reasoning with herself didn't seem to help, since even her conscious mind couldn't quite shake the idea that seeing any man other than Dmitri counted as some sort of betrayal, as if she were cheating on him.

"Ugh! Don't be ridiculous," she muttered to herself, tossing down her pencil and reaching for the stack of ad proofs she had to review. "I didn't promise Dmitri a damned thing, and he didn't even have the decency to call after he disappeared in the middle of the night again. This is not cheating. Get rational, Reg."

But there was nothing rational about the feeling telling her that although her speech might be logical, it was also very, very wrong.

THE TASTE OF HER HAUNTED HIM. IF HE COULD have dreamed of it, he would have, but instead he staved off sleep as long as possible in order to preserve her flavor on his tongue. Dmitri knew he would never have enough of her.

He had dragged himself from her bed that second night, his head spinning and his cock aching. She intoxicated him, and he knew he would never be able to let her go. Regina was his mate, the one woman he could spend an eternity with and never grow bored.

The knowledge astounded him and echoed through him when he slipped into his rest just before dawn. She filled his last thoughts until he slept, and her image appeared to him the instant he fought back to awareness. His Regina. His woman. His mate.

He thought of her when he left his bed and made his way downstairs to his study. Not going to her immediately became an exercise in discipline. His fangs and his cock stretched and hardened at the thought of her, but he'd spent most of the weekend wrapped up in her, and even vampires had work to do. Besides, if he cleared off his desk tonight, Regina would have time to recover from his demands of the last two nights and would be rested and ready for him again soon.

Settling behind his desk, he logged on to his computer and got down to business. Over the course of his long life, he had developed a talent for financial matters, and with little else to occupy him through the years, he began to look on business as a game. Like chess, it all boiled down to strategy and to warfare, two concepts with which Dmitri felt very comfortable. He substituted corporations and mergers for pawns and checks and moved everything along according to his plans and to his whims. It had made him an extremely wealthy man.

Tonight he used business as a distraction. It kept him from butting yet again into Regina's mind, a habit he knew she hated, but which gave him so much pleasure. He adored listening to her thoughts, appreciated her sharp sense of humor and the overwhelming core of honor and love underlying everything about her. She fascinated him, and he was not a man given to easy fascinations.

Already he had let his discipline slide for her. For two days, she had been all he thought about, and tonight he had discovered the results of his inattention since that first meeting. Any man who commanded an empire as large as that of Vidâme International could not afford to take unexpected vacations. He'd had a lot to do in order to catch up. He had even done a little advance planning in order to free up more time to spend with Regina.

Thankfully, while he had paused a few times to stretch, he had not felt the need to eat. The blood he had taken from Regina the night before sustained him longer than any ever had, and he savored the additional proof she was meant to be his mate. She could sustain him indefinitely, nourishing both body and soul.

Though his energy flagged a few hours after dawn, the time when he normally would have been fading into sleep, he worked until he had completed all his pressing business. A short nap and his mate's blood refreshed him well enough that he woke again a couple of hours before sunset and finished the last of his correspondence in little more than thirty minutes. Finally, desk and conscience clear, he gave in to temptation and reached out to her.

He kept his touch light this time, knowing his intrusion had angered her the other day. He slipped into the edge of her mind, keeping his presence veiled from her while he simply sat back and savored the contact. At least until he discovered what she'd been up to that morning.

With ruthless precision, Dmitri caught the edge of her memory and reviewed her conversation with her friends, as well as the phone call she'd taken at her office just an hour ago. When he discovered the result of those conversations, his expression hardened, and he removed himself from her mind, taking one last piece of information with him when he went.

Regina had agreed to a date with another man.

I will kill him, he decided. *I will kill him while she watches, and then I will throw his body to the jackals and lock her in the tower of the castle I will purchase*

*on a remote island in the North Sea, and I will take her
so often that she will never forget the consequences of
dating other men.*

And as for Ms. Markham, he reflected grimly,
his earlier warning had clearly been insufficient
to teach her not to meddle. If she thought he
would stand for anyone coming between him and
his mate, she was very sadly mistaken, and Dmitri
would be more than happy to illustrate for her the
error of her ways.

Grabbing the telephone, he dialed information,
requested a number, and waited while he was automatically connected.

"Thank you for calling M, the Agency. How
can we help you?"

"Ava Markham. Please."

"Who should I say is calling?"

"Dmitri Vidâme."

"One moment, please."

Dmitri drummed his fingers and reviewed two
or three dozen ways to strangle his mate's interfering friend. He'd reached number thirty when
the hold music clicked off.

"Mr. Vidâme?"

Dmitri scowled. The voice belonged to the same
woman who had answered his call, not to Ava. "Is
there some problem?"

"I'm afraid Ms. Markham is unavailable."

"And I am afraid she will have to *make* herself
available," he gritted out. "Get her. Now."

Surprisingly, the receptionist did not quail at his command. Her voice firmed as she said, "Ms. Markham is unavailable *to you*. I suggest you not waste time calling back."

The line clicked in his ear, leaving Dmitri staring at the receiver in disbelief. How dare she refuse his call?! Of course he hadn't planned to make it pleasant for her, but she should at least have had the decency to listen to him harangue her before refusing to listen.

Replacing the receiver in the cradle with restrained force, Dmitri narrowed his eyes and set his jaw. "So you want to play it this way, do you?" he murmured. "Well, remember, Ms. Markham, that you made this choice." Putting a tight leash on his fury, Dmitri exhaled a long, slow breath and reached once more for Regina's mind. Because he had no real connection to Ava, he doubted he would be able to find her in the sea of consciousnesses that peopled Manhattan. The only way to get to her without being in her presence would be to track her using her link to Regina. He just hoped the women had a close enough friendship for her to leave that kind of mark in his mate's unconscious mind.

He touched Regina's mind lightly, taking care to keep his anger behind a thick mental barrier and his psychic presence unobtrusive. His luck held well enough that work had her thoroughly distracted. He could feel her irritation at someone, knew she resented the fact that it was after six and it would be at least another hour before she could leave, because someone else apparently hadn't understood the meaning of the word "deadline." He made note of the offender's name, then delved deeper.

Several feminine paths called to him, each one twined with the others so tightly it took a moment for him to sort them out. He had to double- and triple-check her memories before he got them straightened out.

The brash, intelligent, passionate one who said all the things Reggie was afraid to voice, that was Danice. Nicie, his mate called her.

Another felt calmer, lived more in her head, and a very stubborn head it was. She stood no nonsense and had the kind of biting curiosity that would often get her in trouble, but equally often lead her to the truth she relentlessly sought. Corinne.

The softest path, that was Melissa. Missy. She was all kind words and warm hugs, and Dmitri would have dismissed her as a piece of pretty fluff—pleasant but empty—had he not detected a strong core of steel beneath the surface. She would never be the one to start a war, he realized, but after all the others around her had fallen or surrendered, this woman would be the one who outlasted the enemy. Her mind stirred his respect as he set her path aside and reached for the last.

Ava.

This path stood out from all the others, equally strong, but rough and snarled, as if it could never quite tame itself enough to fully entwine with the others. The woman it led to, it indicated, was cool and collected, prickly and possessive. She would kill or die to save her friends, but she would never quite open herself to them fully. This was a mind apart, and as Dmitri grabbed hold and began to follow it, his respect for the woman it led to grew. When he finally slipped inside her unconscious, he marveled at the complexity he found before he set down to business.

At another time, her mind would have fascinated him. He'd observed at the bar the other night how much more Ava resembled the women he'd involved himself with in the past than the mate he had recently chosen. Now he could see the truth of that observation mentally, as well as physically. Regina's friend possessed a brilliant, creative mind and the iron-willed determination of a military dictator. No one had ever managed to dig up so much information on him in such a short period of time. Her acumen impressed even him, and he made a mental note to include her agency among his investments.

Monday had been a very good day for Ava, Dmitri learned. She'd stolen a very hot new model away from one of her competitors and signed him up to her agency. She'd negotiated a multimillion-dollar deal with a notoriously stingy parfumeur that her models would be the exclusive reps for his new ad campaign, and she'd heard from Marc Abrahms that Reggie had agreed to their date.

She had also found out some very interesting things about Regina's new friend, things Dmitri knew were not secret but that very few people before her had fit together so well. She had learned that Dmitri Vidâme owned a billion-dollar corporation called Vidâme International that had its fingers in an awful lot of pies. That he had no recorded family, even though his ancestors had supposedly lived in New York since the early eighteenth century. Every little thing she had found out made her more suspicious about him, and she was determined to uncover all his secrets before he could hurt her friend.

Her intentions were noble, Dmitri acknowledged, but that did not mean he intended to let her continue her meddling. If anyone were going to protect Regina from now on, it would be him.

He almost hated to shatter Ava's happy little illusions, but she meddled in affairs that were none of her concern. She needed to learn a lesson, and he would be the one to teach it.

While he sorted through her mind, the unfamiliar feel of her made him realize how profoundly his life had changed in only two short days. In his lifetime, Dmitri had touched thousands of female minds, some simple, some wonderfully creative, but each one had held his interest, even if only for a few moments.

Now, everything felt changed. Knowing the thoughts of another woman only deepened his hunger for Regina. Ava, as complex and beautiful as she might be, left him cold, while Regina set him on fire.

He hurried about his task, anxious to get it over with so he could focus his attention back on his new mate, who would still require a good amount of skill and finesse before she grew accustomed to the idea of being his.

When he slipped from Ava's thoughts thirty minutes later, he found himself exhausted. Tampering with the woman's mind had required more effort than he'd anticipated, and he felt he might not have been as thorough as he would have liked, but he'd laid the groundwork. Ava Markham's suspicions of him had been set on the back burner, and she would find her business concerns took precedence over everything else in her life for at least the next few days. He figured that should give him enough time to secure things with Regina, and once she admitted her bond to him, he knew not even Ava could come between them. And just to be sure she stayed away until he had Reggie tamed, he would have Graham and his pack keep her under watch. The werewolves did a mean stakeout.

His phone rang almost on cue.

"Vidâme," he answered automatically.

"Huh. I guess the rumors that you screwed yourself into an early grave were off the mark. I'd started to wonder."

"Good of you. I'm sure that's why you called."

Graham laughed. "Well, I did want to ask if your snack was as tasty as she looked, but somehow I don't think you're going to tell me."

"Lupines are renowned for their acute instincts . . ."

"That's what I thought." The werewolf chuckled. "I'm assuming you spent last night with your little hors d'oeuvre again since I didn't see you at the club."

Graham owned a private club on the Upper East Side called Vircolac. Dmitri had been a member for longer than Graham had been alive, but then, the club had been founded in the eighteenth century. Graham had acquired it the old-fashioned way. He'd inherited it.

"Why is it that you persist in referring to humans as menu items?" Dmitri asked, ignoring his friend's unspoken question. "It's a little creepy."

"Creepy? You're the one who uses them for food, and I get called creepy?"

"And you use them for entertainment. Does that mean I should refer to them as tennis balls when I'm speaking to you? Or do you prefer Frisbees?"

"Touché. Clearly your lady friend has made an impression on you."

"She is my mate."

Silence.

"Have you told anyone?" Graham sounded cautious and slightly stunned.

"No. There hasn't been time."

"Yeah, I can see that." He paused again, and Dmitri could hear when the thought occurred to him. "Have you told her?"

Dmitri laughed. "I'm surprised you thought to ask."

"Well, humans tend to have . . . interesting reactions to the whole vampire thing, let alone to a proposal of marriage from one. Most of them don't know a thing about you guys. How did she take it?"

This time Dmitri paused. "I don't know yet."

"Then you haven't told her. Which means you haven't turned her either."

"No. And I'm not planning to do it unless she asks."

"Ohhh-kay, if you say so." Skepticism laced the werewolf's voice. "Can I buy a ticket to be there when you break the news?"

"Smart-ass. You should be careful around me, or I will have to sic her friends on you."

Graham scoffed. "What? Will a bunch of nasty human women kick me in the shins or something?"

Dmitri grinned and told his friend the story of the Fantasy Fix. The information he'd gleaned from

Regina's mind still managed to amaze him. He'd never known human women with imaginations quite that vivid. He described the basic nature of the arrangement, how he and Regina had met, and paused for Graham's reaction.

"Wow. Her friends sound . . . entertaining. If I met a human female so adventurous, I might break my rule about dating them."

Dmitri's grin turned wicked. "I could set you up with one of them."

"Bite your tongue, fang. I was joking. I don't do humans."

But Dmitri did. He had done one extremely intriguing human several times the night before, and he could barely control his impatience to do her again.

"Well, I can respect your decision not to date them, but I will have to ask you to at least associate with them briefly," Dmitri said. "You actually called at the perfect time. I have a favor I need to ask of you. There is a woman who—"

"Whatever you need, you know it's yours, brother," Graham interrupted. "But before you get to that, you need to let me tell you why I called. It's important."

Dmitri sat up straight, all worries about Ava pushed immediately aside. "You have news on the human?"

"Yeah, and you're going to want to brace yourself for this." All hint of teasing had left the

Lupine's voice, his grim tone making Dmitri sit up straight in his chair.

"What have you found?"

"Your girl's ex. And if you want a look at him before the homicide detectives find him, you'd better get a move on."

Dmitri uttered a pungent curse in a dialect that hadn't been used west of the Velikaya in more than five hundred years. "Where?"

Graham rattled off an address. "I've got a team on the way to try and delay the police, but they won't be able to hold them long. You've got thirty minutes—max. I'll be there in fifteen."

"Make it ten."

ANYONE LOOKING IN ON THE SCENE IN THE abandoned tenement building on the western edge of Washington Heights would likely have taken comfort in the thorough job being done by the investigators who swarmed the first floor. They might have felt a touch less comforted, however, had they realized that instead of New York's finest combing for evidence, these investigators belonged to New York's fiercest.

Graham met Dmitri at the door and led him to the body. "It's only been a couple of hours, but Teddy tells me there's no scent to be found."

Looking down at the man sprawled blackened and still in the middle of the dirty floor, Dmitri shook his head. "There would not be. This was not an ordinary murder. He was slain. By another vampire."

"That was my first thought, but what makes you so certain?"

"Other than the fact that his heart has been removed and destroyed? And he has been burned, which is how my people dispose of those slain who are not old enough to turn to ash on their own. The only other damage here is from the fire. There are no bite wounds, and no obvious signs of a weapon. A shifter would have used teeth and claws in a kill; a human—a gun, a knife, or a blunt object. I see no evidence of any of those."

"True. I guess the blood is what kept me from saying 'vamp' straight out."

Dmitri shrugged. "Had he been older, his killer might have drunk from him, but at his age, his blood has no value. Human blood is nourishing to us, and the blood of a powerful vampire can carry some of that power into anyone who feeds off him. A fledgling, though, is virtually useless— no human nutrients, no power."

Graham nodded. "So at least we know whoever killed him isn't another newbie."

"Of that, I am certain. In fact, I suspect his killer might also be the one who made him." He crouched down beside the shape that had once been Greg Martin and took a closer look at the wound in his chest. "The wound is clean. And do you see his hands and face?"

"You mean what's left of them? I had to ID the guy from his height and weight and the ID we found in the other room. I'm not sure his own mother would have recognized him in this state."

"Even so, you can ignore the shape of his features and look at the muscle and bone left by the fire. There are no marks. I believe he must not have fought back. To me, that indicates he felt comfortable with his killer. He did not see this coming."

"Well, after hearing you talk about him, I got the impression he wasn't that bright." Graham shook his head and looked back at his friend. "So what do we do now? I thought you were hoping this guy would lead us to the rogue who turned him."

"I was. Indeed, I still am."

"How do you figure? If the rogue is also the one who killed him, it's not like they left a scent we can track."

Dmitri pushed back to his feet. "There is more to life than your nose tells you, *bratok.*"

"Like what?"

"Like what your cousin tells you." Logan Hunter stepped into the room from the hallway behind them and handed Graham a scrap of paper. Dmitri didn't bother to protest. There was a protocol among the pack. "It looks like Mr. Sunshine here was using the basement as his hidey-hole during the day. I sent Jamie and Garth down to check it out. They found that shoved into a crack in the foundation."

While Graham examined the paper, Dmitri frowned at Logan. "I thought you were supposed to be trailing the boy from the nightclub."

Logan lifted one dark brow. "And Justin thought you were going to answer your phone. We found the kid. Sort of. It turns out he started an internship with the UN today."

Of course, Dmitri scowled. It had been that kind of day. "Did you speak to him?"

"Nope. And we're not going to either. He's currently on a plane headed for Georgia."

Graham looked up. "Atlanta?"

"Eurasia."

Right. There went one lead on the rogues.

Graham was frowning. "I thought they'd worked out that whole thing with Russia."

"They've been working it out since the eighteenth century."

Dmitri snorted. "Try the eleventh."

The Alpha shrugged. "You're the expert. But since this matter now has your complete attention, why don't you see what you make of that?"

Looking down at the paper, Dmitri read the words and symbols scrawled there and felt a moment of confusion. "This is impossible."

"Does that mean you know what it says?"

"Of course, but it cannot be."

"What cannot be?" the Lupines chorused.

"The symbol on this paper indicates that Gregory Martin was sired by Yelisaveta Chernigov. But that is impossible."

"Why?"

"Because Yelisaveta has been in a prison outside Moscow for the last four hundred years."

"Houston, we have a problem," Graham said.

Dmitri reached for his phone. The call to Moscow went through quickly but was answered very slowly. Considering that it was the middle of the morning in western Russia, Dmitri made an effort to leash his impatience.

"*Allo.*" A voice barked in his ear.

"*Pyotr, eto govorit Dmitri.*"

There was a short pause. "*Vysyo v poryadke?*"

"I'm fine," Dmitri continued in Russian, "but I need your help."

"Name it, friend."

Before he was turned, Pyotr Soliskiy had been a member of Empress Elizabeth's personal Cossack guard. Dmitri had helped to hide him from the empress after his turning.

"I need to know if Yelisaveta remains at Kolomenskoye."

"Of course." Pyotr's frown came across even over the long-distance phone lines. "I received the weekly report from her guards just yesterday. What's going on?"

"I will explain another time, my friend," Dmitri said. "Right now, I have trouble on my hands that needs attending to. *Spasibo, moy drug.*"

Graham barely waited until Dmitri flipped the phone closed. "Well, what did he say? What did *you* say?"

"This symbol is a kind of seal," Dmitri explained. "It has been used for centuries by the head of a powerful Kievan family called Chernigov. Since the death of her older brother in 1447, Yelisaveta Ivanovna has been that person. But she was imprisoned in the late seventeenth century for the attempted slaying of the head of a French vampire clan."

Graham humphed. "I thought you guys didn't bother with prisons. Why didn't you just slay her?"

"Our laws state that the only crime for which a vampire may be slain is the wanton murder of humans. Not only was Etienne du Perigord a vampire, but he remained alive another two hundred and fifty years before he was captured and beheaded by a group of zealous hunters."

Logan blinked. "Okay, but if she's been in prison in Russia since, you know, before electricity, how could she be turning humans in Manhattan—what?—six months ago?"

"That is precisely what I wish to discover."

CHAPTER 16

HALFWAY THROUGH THE APPETIZERS, REGGIE forced herself to admit that Marc Abrahms was a really nice guy. By the time their waiter at the swanky little French restaurant delivered their entrées, she'd even worked up a sense of regret that she couldn't make herself excited about the prospect of sleeping with him.

Smiling at him across their table, she half-listened to his story about his car breaking down in rural Alabama (which was genuinely amusing), and tried to figure out why she couldn't muster up even a flicker of attraction for Ava's friend. She knew Ava would want a full report, even though Reggie hadn't heard from the other woman since Sunday. Her calls had gone unanswered, and she had figured Ava just didn't want to hear any complaints.

Not that Reggie had any right to complain about having Marc as her Fantasy Fix. He was definitely good-looking. In fact, he was more her type than . . . than some other people she'd met recently but who hadn't called her in three days. Blond streaks highlighted his light brown hair, but they looked like the kind that came from hours in the sun rather than hours in a stylist's chair. His skin was lightly tanned, confirming the impression that he didn't spend his life locked up at the office. His blue eyes sparkled with animation, and his face looked just lived-in enough to save him from being pretty. He was built like perfection, strong and fit without being muscle-bound.

All in all, the man ranked up there at "yummy," but Reggie had to work to push away the thought that his eyes would be sexier if they were dark enough to look black in the dim restaurant lighting.

Stifling a sigh, she looked down at her plate and wondered if she could at least work up some enthusiasm for the braised pheasant with haricots verts and baby potatoes. So far, she hadn't had any luck.

"You're quiet. I guess my adventures with De-wayne and Bubba have lost their sparkling allure."

Startled, Reggie raised her head to find him watching her with a raised eyebrow and an expression of faint amusement. "I'm sorry. I've been really rude," she apologized. "You've been a lot of fun, but I guess my mind was someplace else."

And it really was unforgivable of her, especially

since she hadn't heard from the source of her torment since he'd read her the riot act for not realizing they were in a "relationship." Misha didn't deserve her attention, and Marc didn't deserve her rudeness. Even if her enthusiasm for this date didn't threaten to boil over, Marc was a nice enough guy that she ought to be polite. Forcing her distracting thoughts from her mind, she traded her fork for her wine glass and smiled at him.

"I'm back, I promise. No more mental vacations."

Marc returned her smile and gracefully changed the subject. "So why don't you fill in some of the blanks Ava left me with? Where are you from originally?"

Oh, good, small talk. Reggie thought she could handle small talk.

"Why? Is my accent not New Yawk enough?" she teased. "I grew up in Connecticut."

"Ah, that explains it."

When he didn't elaborate, Reggie's curiosity overcame her. "Explains what?"

"You. You've got a little bit of princess in you. Must be that country club air you were born in."

Reggie couldn't get offended when his expression so clearly told her he was teasing. Still, she mocked outrage. "Country club! I'll have you know, not all of Connecticut is Greenwich or Cos Cob, thank you very much. Some of us Nutmeggers come from families that worked for a living. I

certainly don't expect to be treated like a princess."
She gave him a righteous look while she set down
her wine glass and schooled her face into an exaggerated picture of haughty arrogance. "I think
Queen of the Universe is more fitting, don't you?"

Marc chuckled. "Sorry, your majesty." He
drained his glass of wine, but waved the waiter
away when he would have refilled it. When he focused back on Reggie, his expression looked
more serious. "You know, when Ava told me
about you, she said you were just out of a bad relationship, and she worried you didn't get out
enough. But now that I've met you, and seen you
in person, I have a hard time believing you're
lacking for invitations. So it's got to be a lack of
interest on your part."

Reggie took a second to adjust to his honesty
and to digest what he was saying. "Well, it's not
as if I have men beating down my door . . ."

"If you don't, it's not because they don't want
to." She shook her head like she planned to
protest, and he held up a hand. "I hope you're not
going to play at being modest now. We both know
you're beautiful."

He stated it so matter-of-factly that Reggie just
blinked. "Thank you. But not every man out there
shares your taste for women who look like me."

"Sexy?"

"Round."

"Wrong word." He shook his head and ran his

gaze over her. "You are definitely not round. Curvy? Uh-huh. Lush? Yes. Mouthwatering? Absolutely. But not round."

"Certainly not round. And even more certainly not available."

Reggie almost jumped out of her seat when the voice that had been haunting her dreams all week sounded from just above her head. Whipping around, she saw Dmitri standing beside her chair with one arm resting on the back and his gaze fixed on Marc. His posture and attitude had become so familiar, she spoke before she thought about it.

"Misha, you have got to stop doing that."

Dmitri flashed Reggie an amused glance. *I am pleased that you remember how to address me,* dushka, *but you should not contradict me in public.*

Reggie rolled her eyes and prepared to argue, feeling more energetic and alive than she had since Sunday night. So what if he was doing impossible things again, like talking to her in her head? She could deal with that, sort of.

She never got the chance to protest his interruption because Marc pushed back his chair and stood.

The two men eyed each other for a long, strained moment, one dark and mysterious and intense, the other fair and frank and just as intense. They took each other's measure, each evaluating the situation and the other man while the maître d' hovered in the background, clearly unsure of what he ought to do and whether or not he could pull it off even if he decided.

Finally, Marc's mouth quirked in amusement, and he held out his hand. "Marc Abrahms. I take it you're a friend of Regina's."

"Yes, a . . . close friend. Dmitri Vidâme." He shook Marc's hand politely, but his other hand moved from the back of Reggie's chair to the shoulder left bare by her strapless evening dress.

Marc acted as if he didn't catch the movement, but Reggie felt sure he noticed. Damn men. They could always read each other's shorthand.

"We were just about to have coffee," Mark remarked. "Would you care to join us?"

That was going a little too far. Reggie shook her head. "That's really not—"

"Thank you." Dmitri squeezed Reggie's shoulder to silence her. He only had to look back at a waiter, and a third chair appeared at the table. He sat.

Marc, too, resumed his seat, and the waiter poured three cups of coffee before beating a hasty retreat to the relative safety of the kitchen.

Reggie ignored the coffee, infinitely more interested in glaring at the two men. They ignored her and the coffee.

"So, where are you from, Dmitri?"

"I was born in Novgorod, Russia, about one hundred eighty kilometers southeast of St. Petersburg, though I have lived in many places during my life. I have called New York home for many years now."

Christ, they were treating this like a cocktail party! Reggie glared at them both, but neither one was paying her any attention.

"And what is it that you do?" Marc asked, tempting Reggie to kick him under the table. He didn't even blink. He just shifted his legs out of her reach, making her wish she'd worn steel-tipped combat boots rather than sexy, strappy sandals.

"I have a variety of business interests," Dmitri said, "but currently my most absorbing interest is of a more personal nature."

Marc observed the look Dmitri gave Reggie, watched the silent exchange between them, and sighed. "Yes, I imagine it is." He signaled to the waiter and quickly paid the bill. "It was very interesting to meet you, Dmitri; and Reggie, I had a wonderful time." He stood. "But I do have to run. You two enjoy your evening." He grabbed his jacket, shrugging into it while Reggie shot to her feet.

"But what about the opera?" she asked, feeling awful about Dmitri's behavior.

Marc smiled, and when he spoke, his voice was wry. "I don't think the opera would work for us, Reggie. But I wouldn't want you to miss it. Why don't you and Dmitri go and enjoy yourselves?"

Reggie was still trying to wade through all the double entendres when Marc extended two tickets to Dmitri, who refused with a shake of his head.

"Thank you, but it is not necessary," Dmitri said. "I maintain a private box of my own. Regina and I will be using it tonight. You should keep your tickets."

"It's not like I'm going to use them." Marc sighed, but he slipped the tickets back into his jacket pocket. "I guess the box will just have to sit empty for the night. Now, if you two will excuse me, I'm going to go home, pour myself a nice big glass of bourbon, and see if I can catch the last few minutes of the game."

He walked away before Reggie could protest again, so she turned to Dmitri, intending to take her embarrassment and frustration out on him.

"I like this Marc fellow," he said, before she could speak. He rolled right over whatever she had planned to say, bundling her into her coat and pushing her gently toward the exit. "But I do not like that you would think to encourage the interest of another man, *milka*."

"I wasn't encouraging anything," she groused, standing obediently at his side while the doorman hailed them a cab. "It was just dinner."

"It was a date. And my woman will not date any man but me." The slamming of the taxi door behind them punctuated his words, and chased whatever she had been planning to say right out of her head.

"Your woman?"

"Of course. In fact, I believe we already had this discussion. Several days ago."

"Oh, we did, did we?"

Any other man would have listened to Reggie's tone of voice and realized that cracking sound he heard was the thin ice under his big, clumsy feet. Dmitri, though, merely nodded pleasantly.

"Well, you'll have to forgive me if I don't recall," she bit out, "since I would have expected any man of mine to have actually *contacted* me at least once in the last three days. In the age of telephones, cell phones, e-mail, text messaging, and, oh, *being PSYCHIC*, that doesn't sound like too much to ask to me!"

"Yes, I apologize for my neglect, *dushka*. This has been a very busy week for me."

Reggie just stared at him, her mouth gaping open until she imagined she looked something like a landed bass, only with better lipstick. It took her at least three blocks to collect herself.

"Busy? That's it? That's your only excuse?"

Dmitri shrugged, his expression blank and his gaze hooded. "I have many responsibilities, Regina, both professional and personal. Sometimes, what I *must* do must take precedence over what I *wish* to do."

Reggie's rage nearly blinded her. "Right. Well,

it's funny you should say that, because right now what I wish to do is strangle you; but since you're not worth going to prison over, what I must do is get the hell out of this car and wish you a nice rest of your life!"

CHAPTER 17

HAVING SPENT THE ENTIRETY OF THE PAST seventy hours or so in a futile search for a mad vampiress he knew perfectly well was safely ensconced in a comfortable prison in the land of his birth more than five thousand miles away, Dmitri could safely say he was not in the mood to argue with his mate. Since last seeing her, he'd been living on little blood and less sleep, and if he hadn't known about her "date" this evening, he would likely be out right now, combing the city, interviewing vampires, and listening to Graham whine about how bored the Lupine had become with his life and the women he dated.

When Jean-Paul Sartre had declared that "Hell is other people," he'd clearly been referring to a werewolf with a bad case of sexual boredom.

Therefore, when Regina began to rage at him for not having contacted her in three days, Dmitri could admit he might have overreacted. Just a smidge.

Calling on powers he'd technically never admitted to having, Dmitri seized the mind of the cabbie, remotely skidded the taxi to a stop at the curb, and grabbed his mate by the shoulders before she could so much as look at the door handle. With deliberate gentleness and inexorable strength, he pressed her back into her seat, then fisted his hands in his lap. If he touched her now, he knew he might explode.

"*Do not* test me, Regina Elaina," he growled, and when her eyes widened, he could see red flames in his own reflected there. "I am half a breath away from dragging you out of this vehicle, pinning you to the nearest available flat surface, and demonstrating *very* graphically why it would be a serious miscalculation on your part to continue provoking me.

"I have known you for less than a week and already you have pushed me further than any other woman I have ever met. All day, every day, you invade my thoughts when I should be working. You tempt me to forget every responsibility. And twice in this time you have deliberately sought to torture me by making engagements with other men! I ask you, Regina, what is a man supposed to do with a woman like you?"

"You're supposed to talk to me!" she screamed, thumping him on the chest with one tiny fist, then doing it again, and again until she was pounding on him with all her delicate might. "You're supposed to make me forget all the reasons why you scare me so much that I can't even think straight except when you're touching me!"

Dmitri looked down, shocked right out of his anger to see his sweet, gentle Regina reduced to violence. He watched for the space of a full breath until—to his horror—her face crumpled and she began to weep.

"*Milaya*," he groaned, brushing aside her fists and wrapping his arms around her to drag her bodily and resisting into his lap. "Hush, *katyonak. Lyubov moya*, please. Do not cry."

For a handful of seconds Regina continued to struggle. Then he felt the resistance leave her and she melted against his chest and clung.

Dmitri cradled her to him as if she were something precious. To him, she was. He placed his cheek atop her head and stroked her bright, silky hair with one hand, all the while murmuring to her in a hushed, jumbled mix of English and Russian. Only half of what he said made any sense; the rest of it consisted of nonsense words and calming sounds that served no purpose other than to stop her crying before she shattered his heart into a thousand tiny pieces.

For long minutes, Regina continued to cry as if her world were tumbling around her. When she finally began to quiet, he reached into his jacket pocket and produced a neatly folded square of white linen. He pressed the handkerchief into her hand and waited while she wiped her face and sniffled.

"I'm sorry," she hiccuped, avoiding Misha's gaze and turning to repeat the apology to the driver in the front of the cab. "I'm sorry. I don't know why I lost it like that—"

Dmitri took her chin between his fingers and turned her face back to him. "Do not worry about the driver, *dushka*. I am sure he has seen worse, and I will give him a handsome tip if he acts as if none of this ever happened."

And it didn't hurt that Dmitri's push at the driver's mind would prevent the man from remembering that any of this had happened.

"Still, I am sorry. I shouldn't have made a scene. It's just—" She blotted her eyes again and shook her head. "I guess I've been more stressed out than I realized. Meeting you really turned my head upside down. And then there was the thing at the bar with Gregory and me passing out and the argument we had and Ava busting into the apartment. And when you didn't call, I thought—"

Dmitri placed a finger against her lips to stop her babbling. "It is all right, *dushka*. Everything is fine. I owe you an apology of my own. I meant it when I told you I have been very busy this week, but that is no excuse for my neglect of you."

Her frown told Dmitri that his mate was not yet

quite ready to forgive him for that slight. "What were you doing that was so important you couldn't even leave a message on my machine?" she demanded. "Or even just popped into my head. I admit that it's taking me a little while to adjust to the idea that my—" She hesitated. "That the man I'm seeing has ESP," she finally managed, "but I *am* working on it, and I think I've come a long way. So I don't think it would have been out of line for you to send me a little 'thinking of you' buzz now and again."

Dmitri debated with himself for a moment over what to tell her. On the one hand, his instincts told him that his mate was to be sheltered and protected at all costs; but on the other, his intellect warned him that his Regina would not appreciate being kept completely in the dark. He felt obligated to tell her something, especially after seeing how upset he had made her with his silence.

Plus, there was still the problem of Yelisaveta or her imposter. As long there was a rogue out there with a bloodthirsty streak, he did not want his mate involved in the situation. Call him a chauvinist, but he simply couldn't stand for that.

In the end, he settled on a very carefully edited version of the truth.

"I am afraid that part of why I was out of touch over the last few days has to do with that man you used to know."

Regina frowned, confused. "What man I used

to—" Realization dawned. "Do you mean Greg? What on earth could he possibly have to do with you? We broke up more than six months ago, and even if we hadn't he's not the sort of guy you'd have to be worried about. I mean, he's no threat to you."

"I am not the one he threatened, *dushka*."

Dmitri watched her face carefully and saw when memory began to tickle at her consciousness.

"I'm not afraid of Greg, Misha," she said slowly, almost as if she were trying to convince herself more than him. "He may be a low-down, slimy, faithless jerk, but he never hurt me physically."

"Didn't he?"

"No. I told you—" Regina broke off and her eyes widened. "That night at the bar. He was talking about us getting back together. We went outside where it was quieter. I told him no, but he just kept at me."

She shook her head and paused. Her gaze turned inward as she replayed the fragmented memories in her head and tried to make sense of them. Dmitri had seen it many times before. The human mind had an uncanny ability to rationalize, to convince itself that what it thought was impossible could not be true and that what it knew to be logical must be the only alternative, no matter how false or misleading. The Others had relied on that particularly mortal trait for millennia.

"He attacked me," she breathed, raising a hand

to her throat and meeting Dmitri's gaze once more. "I thought—he must have tried to strangle me. I remember being afraid and having trouble breathing. Then I must have passed out."

That explanation suited Dmitri. It was close enough to the truth to fit in with what she actually remembered, and it provided a good foundation for what else he was about to tell her, so he nodded.

"I know you did not remember his attack until now," he said, "but I saw it happen. I was on my way to meet you at the bar when I heard noises in the alley. I went to investigate and found him pinning you to the wall. I only thank God that I reached you in time. I pulled him off you, but he ran before I could summon help."

Regina shook her head. "Why didn't you call the police?"

"I could not. All I could think of was that you were hurt and shocked and that I needed to take you home where I knew you would be safe. But once I calmed down, I realized I could not let Martin get away with treating you like that, so I tried to track him down."

"Oh, Misha!" She laid a hand on his cheek. "Please tell me you didn't do anything stupid like beat him up because of me!"

"I did not," he answered truthfully. "Though I cannot say that was not my intention. He hurt you, *milaya*, and he frightened you. This is not something I can allow."

"Misha, what did you do?"

He mustered a regretful-sounding sigh. "I did nothing, *dushka*. By the time I was able to locate him it was too late."

She frowned. "What do you mean?"

"Dushka." He took her hands and clasped them between his own. "I know your heart is tender, so I am afraid you will be saddened when I tell you that Gregory Martin is dead."

CHAPTER 18

"DEAD?" SHOCK HIT REGGIE HARD, LEAVING HER dizzy and breathless for a long moment. "How? Misha, what happened?"

He frowned at her. "I was not involved in his death, Regina."

"I know that," she assured him, realizing how her questions had sounded. Honestly, the thought that Dmitri might have killed someone never occurred to her. She had every confidence that if he had gotten to Greg in time, he would have pounded some sense into her ex, but she never considered that he might seriously harm the man. "I didn't mean to imply you did. I just—this is such a shock! How did you find out?"

He hesitated. "I was told by someone who knew I'd been trying to find him."

"Do you know what happened?"

"I believe he had become involved with some unsavory characters over the past few months," he said. His answer came easily, but Reggie couldn't shake the feeling that he was holding something back.

"My God, I can't believe it." And she couldn't. Greg might have ranked high among the scum of the earth and she might occasionally have wished that he would come to an ignoble end, but Reggie had never really imagined him the victim of a killer. "Was it some kind of—of . . . hit? Was he involved in something illegal?"

Dmitri shook his head. "I am afraid I do not have those kinds of answers, *dushka*, but I suspect that may have been the case."

"I can't believe it," she repeated. Then a new thought occurred to her and she felt herself pale. "Oh, my God, I wonder if the police are going to want to talk to me? I mean, we did break up a few months ago, and on TV they always suspect an ex-girlfriend! And if anyone saw us have that argument at Captain J—"

"Hush. I am certain you are not a suspect," Dmitri said. "I had hoped to spare you from any upset, but I understand that whoever killed him must have overpowered him, something you obviously could not have done, *milka*."

He sounded so certain and so firm, that Reggie felt herself relaxing against her better judgment.

"Still, they might assume that I asked someone to do it for me," she speculated, but the fear had drained out of her. Somehow when Dmitri held her, she found it impossible to be afraid of anything, and that was the only thing that frightened her.

"I think you worry too much."

He spoke firmly, and Reggie understood that the subject was closed. Really, what else was there to say about it? The news had shaken her, even shocked her, but when she examined her feelings more closely, she realized that the stirrings of sadness she felt had more to do with her regret that any person had to die unnecessarily than with the fact that she had once had a relationship with Greg. She felt sorry for him, sorry for whatever people might miss his presence in their lives, but she couldn't bring herself to grieve. Their relationship had ended long ago, but even more than that, being with Dmitri had taught her that whatever she and Greg had shared in the beginning . . . even that hadn't been love.

Love sat with her now, calm and strong and watchful. It hadn't taken weeks or months to develop, and it didn't care about logic or common sense. It didn't even care about mind reading or secrets or possessive, macho attitudes. All it cared about was Regina and Dmitri and the way they fit together like two pieces of a puzzle finally joined.

In the flickering lights that flashed through the taxi windows, Reggie looked at the man she loved and saw him watching her with a light in his eyes that made her stomach flip and her heart melt. And all the sadness in the world dissipated.

When she spoke, her voice sounded low and husky, and it made Dmitri focus all his attention on her. "So I guess that's why you didn't contact me again before tonight, huh?"

He nodded and brushed a stray lock of hair out of her face, tucking it behind her ear. "It is, though I apologize if my silence upset you, *dushka*. I never meant for my lapse to make you uncertain of me. The only explanation I can offer is that my feelings for you are so strong, I took too easily for granted that you understood them."

Regina tilted her head back to meet his gaze shyly. "And what are your feelings, Misha?"

"Ah, *dushka*, I suspect you know very well how I feel about you," he murmured, unable to resist brushing her lips with his. Once. Twice. "I did not, however, plan to tell you of those feelings in the back of a taxicab on the side of a busy street."

She laughed softly and leaned into him. "Point taken." Her arms twined about his neck. "So what do you say we skip the opera, go back to my apartment, and have a very private discussion?" She interspersed her suggestions with kisses, pressing her lips to every bit of available skin she could reach.

"I think not." He caught her lips in one brief, meltingly sensual kiss and broke away just as her knees began to turn to pudding. "I understand you have been looking forward to this evening for quite a long time, and I would hate to disappoint you." He trailed a fingertip along her jaw, his smile turning wicked and his gaze capturing hers with an intensity that burned. "I want you to understand, *dushka*, that whatever you desire, I will provide. You will never need to turn to another while I live."

Reggie shivered and felt her throat tighten. The words sounded teasing, but they felt like a vow, one that bound him to her for eternity. Shakily, she nodded.

"Good." He pressed a kiss to her forehead and his arms tightened briefly around her. "Then we should hurry before we miss the overture."

At a word from Dmitri, the cabbie put the taxi back into gear and steered them into traffic without a word. Settling back into her lover's arms, Reggie watched the city pass by the windows and thought to herself that the most important overture had been conducted last Friday night. Now she just wanted to sit back and enjoy the story. She had a feeling it would be the most exciting spectacle of her life.

CHAPTER 19

REGGIE HAD ATTENDED THE OPERA AS A YOUNG child—her mother had been a fan—but she'd never before sat in one of the newly built private boxes near the ceiling at the back of the auditorium. If she had realized that was where Dmitri meant to take her, she would have been even more careful in repairing her hair and makeup in the restroom off the lobby. As it was, she had said a prayer of thanks for waterproof mascara, reapplied her eyeliner, swiped on some lip gloss, and piled her hair loosely atop her head, fastening it with a set of carved ebony hairsticks she had tucked into her bag for emergencies.

This definitely qualified.

Looking around while the usher led them to their seats, Reggie reflected on how different this date would have been if she'd come here with Marc. He had been very sweet and remarkably easy to talk to, but it would have made her feel terrible to let him down about her supposed fantasy. At least in Dmitri's company, she didn't have to explain that she didn't feel comfortable having sex with a relative stranger in a public place.

She let Dmitri take her coat and seat her in one of the two luxurious armchairs that occupied the center of the box. When she looked around her, it almost seemed a shame they were there alone, considering that the dimensions of the box could easily have accommodated four or even six people, oversized chairs notwithstanding.

She watched him hand their coats to the usher, who proceeded to move to each side of the box where it bordered their neighbors and release the heavy drapes from their swags. The material formed a visual barrier between the other boxes and made Reggie's eyes widen. The public nature of the box had just been transformed into something else entirely. Something very private.

Centering her attention on the darkened stage, Reggie shifted in her seat and smoothed the silky material of her dress over her thighs. Then she straightened the clasp on her silver and onyx necklace. Then she checked the clasp on her tiny evening bag, gave a tug to her bodice, and patted her hair. When she ran out of fidgets, she stared straight ahead and cursed herself for not wearing opera gloves. They would have provided one more step in her distraction techniques.

The usher left their box, and Dmitri took his

seat beside her. She started to tell him he was crowding her, but before she could speak, he slid his arm over the back of her chair and wrapped it around her shoulders. He didn't even pretend the move had been casual. He meant it as a statement of possession, and that's exactly what she took it for. The man was about as subtle as a jackhammer, but she pretended to ignore him and kept her eyes on the stage.

She probably should have noticed it before, but she'd had other things on her mind. The man fairly reeked of privilege. His evening clothes had definitely been custom tailored; there was just no other way he could have gotten the fabric to hug his tall, well-muscled frame that lovingly. His shoes had the buttery soft look of Italian leather, and now that she studied them, she realized his shirt studs and cuff links shone with the rich, warm glow of solid gold. She'd bet twenty-four karat. Taking a deep breath, she turned back to the stage and crossed her legs primly at the ankles.

Just when the lights began to dim around them, she leaned the tiniest bit closer and, her eyes still fixed on the stage, murmured, "So then, you're pretty much filthy rich, huh?"

"Disgustingly so." He, too, kept his attention on the proscenium below.

"Hm. Isn't that special."

Settling back into her seat, she crossed her hands primly in her lap and concentrated on presenting an utterly calm exterior—to contrast with the chaotic thoughts and emotions beneath the surface. Even before this late-breaking news, she'd had a few moments where she wondered exactly what she was doing with Dmitri. After all, the man was drop-dead gorgeous, sexy as sin, dynamite in bed, mysterious as the hero of a gothic romance, and one-hundred-percent alpha male. Now she learned he was also richer than Midas.

So what the hell had he been doing hanging out at a run-of-the-mill dive like the Mausoleum that night? Why had he fixed his attention on her among all the beautiful women who had been there, available and most likely panting after him? Then she felt his thumb rub softly over the curve of her bare shoulder, and she shivered. Perhaps the why didn't really matter so much, after all. What mattered was that they had found each other somehow.

With the final light extinguished, the first notes of the overture flooded through the auditorium. All around them, attention shifted from conversations with companions and strangers to the action revealed on stage when the footlights went up. Everyone watched while the city of Peking came to life before them, and the Mandarin began to sing of the Princess Turandot and the impossible test her suitors must pass in order to win her hand.

In their quiet box high above the stage, Dmitri didn't bother to win Regina's hand. He took it, by right of strength, twining his fingers with hers and resting their clasped hands together on her thigh, halfway between knee and hip.

Oh, Lord.

In her mind, she heard him chuckle.

Titles are archaic, dushka. *And unnecessary. You need not address me so formally. I have told you "Misha" will do.*

Though she didn't look away from the stage, Reggie felt a rush of relief. He still didn't seem mad at her. Maybe he was going to let the date with Marc go after all.

As soon as she relaxed, she couldn't help rolling her eyes. Despite his teasing, the autocratic tenor of his words suited him and rang with an underlying truth. He probably did see himself as some sort of feudal lord, demanding tribute from the peasants while he sat in his castle and counted the spoils of war.

I have always preferred the spoiling to the counting. Mathematics can be so tedious.

Would you be quiet? And get out of my head. I'm trying to watch the opera. Barbarian.

She felt his laughter along with her own sense of satisfaction when he finally deigned to actually look toward the stage.

Of course, milaya. *Because watching the performance was your only intent in coming here tonight.*

He just had to have the last word. She frowned, her attention straying from the touching reunion between the aged Timur and his son, Prince Calaf. Something in his tone made her a little uneasy, but he sat quietly enough beside her, and she soon found herself drawn into the world of the haughty Princess Turandot and her determined suitor, Calaf. The determined part sounded familiar; it was the suitor she was having trouble relating to.

The image of Dmitri petitioning for her hand popped into her brain, and she had to stifle her laugh. Despite Marc calling her a princess, she didn't really think she had much in common with Turandot, but she guaranteed that Dmitri was nothing like Calaf. He would never follow the dictates of a spoiled princess, never play along with her game. If he wanted her, he would take her, as he had taken Reggie.

The memory of it made her squirm in her seat, and she glanced at him from the corner of her eye. In the dark, she saw the smile curve his gorgeous mouth. She held her breath, waiting for his reaction, but Misha simply raised their joined hands to his lips and brushed a whisper-soft kiss along her knuckles. He turned his attention back to the stage and watched while love battled with anger for the princess's heart.

In Reggie's heart, relief battled with pique to make her decidedly uncomfortable. For some insane reason, she felt disappointed he paid more attention to the stage than to her. What was she thinking? She ought to be relieved the man had decided to behave himself for a change; she shouldn't be brooding because he'd been with her for a good hour and hadn't ravished her yet. Clearly, he had driven her over the edge. She could no longer claim to be sane. She needed to get her mind back on the opera and off the hunk at her side.

Or did she?

Casting Dmitri a sidelong glance, Reggie considered a few salient points. During the cab ride from the restaurant to the opera, her world had turned upside down. She had fallen in love, or at least realized that she'd been falling in love for the past week, and somehow the romantic tribulations of a spoiled brat in a fictionalized, medieval China couldn't compare with the real-life adventures of her experiences with Dmitri.

Now, an opera about the two of *them* . . . That might just be able to keep her attention.

"I believe it would be illegal to perform in most countries," he murmured, leaning forward to nuzzle the hollow beneath her ear. She could feel his smile against her skin. "Such things are still generally considered ill-suited for public consumption." She blushed hot enough to burn, and he drew back to grin down at her. "Though the audience would surely fall in love with whatever actress portrayed you, *dushka*, especially if she blushed as prettily as you do when she came."

Embarrassed to her pink-polished toes, Reggie decided Misha had spent a bit too much time during their brief relationship playing the role of charming, self-controlled rogue. He definitely needed to learn that some of the time, the submissive partner was the one with all the power.

She took a moment to check on the action on stage and threw a glance at her watch, thankful there was enough light to see. It looked like they had about forty minutes left until the intermission, which should be just enough time for a little judicious lesson-teaching. Her lips curved in anticipation.

For the next several moments she pretended to be absorbed by the story on stage. In reality, she was waiting for Dmitri to relax and shift his own attention off her even briefly. It took a few minutes, but finally he seemed to content himself with holding her hand in his, and he watched while lack of sleep began to wear on the fictional people of Peking.

She started by leaning closer to him, snuggling against his side and laying her cheek on the warm silk of his lapel. She shifted their clasped hands from her thigh to his, then stilled and waited. His arm slipped around her shoulder to cradle her to him, and she thought she felt his lips brush over her hair, but he continued to watch the stage.

After a few more minutes, she cast a furtive

glance around to be sure no one could see into their little boxed-in cocoon and took a deep breath. Time to make her move.

With a feather-light touch, Reggie slipped one of her hands free and sent it gliding up Dmitri's inner thigh. Unfortunately, due to the nature of men's fashions, cloth muffled her touch, but she could still feel his muscles bunch and tighten beneath her hand. When she reached the vee of his legs, she skirted her fingers around the very interesting bulge behind his fly and headed straight up to the hook at the top. Slipping it free of its catch, she grasped the zipper between her fingers and waited. She felt his anticipation as keenly as his heartbeat pulsing against the back of her hand. When the secondary soprano hit an extended high note, Reggie tugged and lowered the zipper. Her hand slid under the straining cloth and found him, warm and hard and heavy beneath. Her murmur expressed her approval, and her fingers gladly curled around his length, feeling him thick and smooth and eager for her touch.

Leisurely, she began to stroke him, scraping her fingernails delicately against the skin at the base of the shaft and squeezing lightly when she moved toward the tip. She tortured him with a few of the teasing strokes, or at least, she meant them to be teasing, but a quick glance at his face revealed no particular strain. He looked way too calm for her taste. Eyes narrowing, she continued to watch him while she tightened her grip, pumping her small fist and using her index finger to rub circles around the sensitive head. His erection twitched, but his face remained impassive. This meant war.

In a flash of movement she slid off her seat and onto her knees to take him between her lips in one smooth movement. That at least made him draw in a deep breath, but when he let it out, he wore the same polite expression he would use during a stockholders' meeting.

Well, since they were here to enjoy the performances, Reggie decided she might as well show him what being a virtuoso was all about.

Freeing her left hand from Dmitri's grip, she spread open his evening trousers. One hand closed around the base of his cock, while the other lifted the heavy pouch below from confinement, cuddling him tenderly in her palm. Watching his face from beneath her eyelashes, she leaned forward and delicately nibbled the skin of his glans.

Dmitri shuddered.

Reggie smiled. The man just might not be made of stone after all, she mused, though you'd never know it from this angle. He felt hard as granite, but infinitely warmer. His pulse throbbed against her lips, and she parted them to take the first few inches into her mouth, closing around him like a moist heaven. One hand continued to cradle and massage his sensitive skin, and the other wrapped around the base of his shaft, stroking what she couldn't fit in her mouth.

Dmitri watched the stage.

Acknowledging the challenge, Reggie applied herself to her task, and a very pleasant one she found it. He filled her mouth, his thickness stretching her jaw just enough to make her acutely aware of what she was doing. He pressed against her tongue, filling her with his salty, earthy, intensely masculine flavor. He smelled the same, fresh and clean and earthy, the essence of a man, like forests after spring showers. Humming her approval, she suckled at him like a tasty treat, and he rewarded her with a hiss of indrawn breath.

Yes, milka. Sosi mne. *Suck me.*

Ah-ha. Now she had him. Reggie complied, her head bobbing while she drew him deep into her mouth and released him, over and over, swirling her tongue around the head with each pass. Her eyes had drifted shut, but she felt his hands reach out to cup the back of her head, holding her to him. The possessive gesture excited her.

Bystraye. Faster.

Oh, no, she thought. This time, *she* was the one calling the shots.

Deliberately, Reggie slowed, drawing back until just the tip of his erection remained in her mouth so she could lash the sensitive underside of the head with her tongue. Just let him try to give her orders now.

Dushka! he panted.

She removed her hands from between his legs and braced her palms on his thighs, depriving him of her massage. She wanted all his attention focused on her mouth, on the way she could make him feel. On the way she held his very life inside of her.

Pazhalsta!

Please!

His thoughts flooded her, a tangled mass of need, lust, affection, understanding. She felt him reach out, felt his urgency in the way his fingers tightened at the back of her head, and she knew she could deny him nothing.

She worked faster, tightening her hand at the base of his shaft, massaging with a firmer motion. He pressed against her tongue, hardening even more, if that were possible. His hands clenched in her hair and even the small pain of it aroused her. She whimpered, the sound muffled around his cock, then hummed in the back of her throat so the vibrations traveled through her tongue and palate to provide another layer to the sensation that already threatened to send him over the edge.

Ah! Bozhe moy, ya umirayu! *My God, I'm dying!*

Even in his thoughts, Reggie sensed his urgency. A moment later, he stilled, every muscle in his body tensing as he hissed out a cry and exploded inside her. She tried to pull back, but his grip held her close, his free hand sliding around to cup her face.

Zagloti, dushka. *Swallow for me, baby. There's a good girl.*

Reggie obeyed. His hand on her skin and the tenderness in his tone soothed her, made the alien experience seem safer and less threatening, brought her somehow closer to her lover.

When she finished, he adjusted his clothing and pulled her back up to her seat to kiss her, his dark eyes glinting in reflected stage lights. "Thank you, *milaya.*"

Suddenly shy—which was ridiculous considering what she'd just been doing—Reggie smiled at him and snuggled against his side. He wrapped his strong arms around her and held her close, resting his chin on top of her head while Turandot wept with joy at Calaf's kiss.

Reggie watched the scene on stage and smiled against Dmitri's lapel. Turandot might think her prince was hot stuff, but she clearly didn't know what she was missing.

CHAPTER 20

REGGIE HAD BEEN SO PREOCCUPIED WITH HER thoughts—and memories of their intimacy—she'd lost track of the story on stage. When the house-lights came up, she started and sat up straight in her seat, blinking while her eyes struggled to adjust to the brighter lights.

"Come, *milaya*." Dmitri rose and tugged her to her feet beside him. "Let us stretch our legs for a few moments."

Reggie trailed obediently after him—how did he always manage to make her do that?—as he led her out of the box. They passed other attendees while they walked, women who eyed Dmitri's lean, muscular form with avid appreciation and men who quickly averted their eyes from Reggie's curvaceous figure as soon as they glimpsed Dmitri's threatening scowl.

"Do you have to do that?" Reggie hissed when

he dropped his hand to the small of her back to urge her into a reception room ahead of them.

"Do what?"

An opera employee greeted Dmitri by name when they passed. Misha acknowledged the young man with a nod and attempted to sculpt his features into an innocent mask.

"Your dog-in-the-manger routine."

"An inappropriate analogy," he dismissed, accepting two glasses of red wine from the bartender and handing one to her. "While I may have warned a man or two to keep his distance, I assure you that I have no intention of doing the same."

Reggie gazed up into his deep, black eyes, and her stomach flipped. She'd managed to convince herself during the first half of the performance that Dmitri's failure to make her pay for accepting a date with another man meant he no longer felt a need to make her pay for her poor decision. But if she were to judge by the heat of his gaze, she'd have to reassess her conclusion. Rapidly.

Hastily, she raised her glass to her lips and sipped the crisp, dry liquid. Dmitri responded with a smile, but let her enjoy her strategic retreat. He seemed content to watch her take in their surroundings.

As she watched the glittering crowd around them mill about the room, it occurred to Reggie that these weren't your average a-pair-of-tickets-once-in-a-while opera-goers. Come to think of it, she felt pretty sure they weren't your average season-ticket opera-goers.

Oh, my God! Was that a Rockefeller?

Dmitri gazed down at her, clearly amused. *I believe it is. In fact, I'm sure of it, because he is great friends with the Vanderbilt and the Kennedy you see him speaking to.*

She almost choked on her wine. Swallowing quickly, she took another, more searching look around her and felt a little light-headed. Unless she missed her guess, not one person in the room with her possessed an annual income with less than seven digits. Before the decimal point.

The sound of a woman's rather braying laughter drew her attention, and Reggie looked over to see a well-known television personality conversing with a communications tycoon and two heirs to a real estate fortune. When she examined the quartet in a new light, she realized the tuxedos were definitely not rentals, the gown was a designer original, and the rocks around the TV personality's neck had about as much in common with paste as she had with the people in this room.

Suddenly self-conscious, she glanced down at her hunter-green gown and simple silver jewelry and felt woefully underdressed. She clearly ought to be down in the penny pit with the other peons and not breathing the same rarefied air as the debs and celebs up here at the private bar.

"Do not be silly. You have no need for shame.

You look magnificent," Dmitri murmured, leaning down so his breath tickled her ear when he spoke.

To the other people in the room, he probably looked like a doting lover, she thought.

"Is that not what I am, *milka*? Your lover?"

Chimes interrupted their dialog and signaled the end of intermission.

Taking her empty glass, he set it alongside his on a small table and returned his hand to the small of her back. *Your luck and your timing never cease to astound me*, he drawled into her mind. *I begin to wonder if you have some strange powers of which I am not aware.*

Reggie walked sedately at his side as they joined the crowd leaving the bar area. Meanwhile, she mentally used a whip and a chair to subdue the emotions he had wrought inside her. "I think you're just too spoiled and too used to getting your own way."

"Ah, but I do always get my way, *dushka*, and I see no reason to let that change."

"You wouldn't," she murmured, keeping her eyes on the crowd. It was the only way she could resist sticking her tongue out at him.

To keep her mind otherwise occupied, she took one last opportunity to goggle at the crowd as they passed through the bar and into the hall. In the brighter environs of the passageway, one particular head reflected the glare of the lights off a smooth, silky curtain of pale golden blond.

Lisette, the Limber Latvian.

Reggie froze in place and stared. "Holy crap!"

Startled, Dmitri looked down at her, his brow creased in concern. "What is it, *dushka*? Are you ill?"

"No, I'm just—" She shook her head and pointed discreetly. "Do you see that blonde over there? Talking to the balding man with the pot-belly? That's Lisette Lesaius. She's the woman Greg cheated on me with. The one I caught in the act with him anyway." She blanched as a terrible thought struck her. "Oh, no. I wonder if she knows? I wonder if anyone told her that Greg is dead?"

JUST WHEN DMITRI HAD BEGUN TO ENJOY HIS night away from business, with his mate at his side (Well, all right. He had already begun to enjoy it before the intermission, when Regina had knelt before him and turned him into her willing slave), fate struck an unexpectedly cruel blow. One moment he was humming along peacefully in the back of Regina's mind and the next he was flooded with images of Gregory Martin intimately entwined with a blond woman atop a disarranged office desk. Both had lost at least half of their clothing, and Martin had a dark crimson smear that stood out boldly against the fair skin behind his loosened collar.

At first the haze of Regina's perceptions clouded

his own judgment of the scene. The smear wavered in his sight, first taking on the waxy, grainy appearance of a lipstick smudge, then glistening thick and liquid like fresh blood. Once the truth clicked, the image stabilized and Dmitri knew at once that Gregory had been bitten by a vampire. Turning his attention to the woman, he followed the pale curve of her arms to where her hand clutched the edge of the desk. On her left wrist, she bore a similar wound, fresh and shining, and Dmitri saw a trace of blood in the sheen on Martin's lips. It was the woman who had turned Martin. Dmitri felt certain that he had never seen her before, and yet something about her face seemed vaguely familiar.

Dimly, Dmitri heard Regina speaking, but he couldn't focus on her words. He was too caught up in the scene that played behind his eyes. It wasn't until she squeezed his arm and began to walk away from him that he realized what she had told him.

I have to find out if she knows, and if not, I have to tell her. I'd hate for her to learn about it from someone who didn't even know him.

She was halfway across the space before Dmitri could stop her.

CHAPTER 21

FIXING A SMILE ON HER FACE, REGGIE MADE herself a solemn vow that she would be pleasant to Lisette no matter what the other woman said to her. This wasn't the time or place for old grudges, and she had no desire to create a scene.

She left Dmitri near the entrance to the bar just as the second gong sounded and the hallway lights flickered to indicate that the second act of the performance was about to start. Since she had already missed a good portion of the first act, Reggie didn't figure it was all that important to rush back.

Neither, apparently, did Lisette. As the hall emptied of people, the blonde continued to stand where Reggie had first noticed her. The man she'd been speaking to had deserted her, but she seemed content to stare at a small, framed piece of art that hung on the wall beside her. She gave no indication that she sensed Regina's approach, but as soon as Reggie got within a couple of feet of her, she spoke without prompting.

"It isn't that I mind talking to you, Reggie," the blonde purred in her sex-kitten voice. Or maybe sexy, man-eating-lion voice described it better. "After all, we have so much in common. But I didn't stay out here to talk to you."

Confused, Reggie eyed her warily. "What do you mean?"

"I think she means, *dushka*," Dmitri rumbled from just behind Reggie's shoulder, "that she was waiting for me."

Lisette turned to face them, and the eyes Reggie remembered as round, blue, and rather vague were narrowed, and they glowed with an unearthly orange light. Reggie took an instinctive step backward.

Lisette laughed. "Timid little thing, isn't she? I'm surprised at you, Misha. I thought you always preferred women with backbone, and from what Gregory told me, this one can't have much of it. If she did, she would have broken things off when he fucked the caterer during their engagement party."

Only the fact that Reggie could see how much Lisette wanted her words to hurt kept Reggie from gasping. She'd known Greg was a lowlife—well, she'd known eventually—but she hadn't realized exactly how long he'd been screwing around on her. It wasn't that she minded because she still cared about Greg, but no woman wanted to see herself betrayed.

Dmitri lifted his hand to rest it on Reggie's shoulder and squeezed gently. "I find it hard to believe you know what I prefer, since we have never before met."

"Perhaps not, but I have heard very much about you." Dark marscaraed lashes swept down and the tip of a pink tongue swept out to moisten ruby-tinted lips. "In fact," the woman purred, "I was instructed to convey to you the most particular regards of an old acquaintance of yours."

Okay, the subtext here ran deep and thick, and even though she didn't understand half of it, Reggie knew for sure that she didn't like any of it. Especially not the way Lisette eyed Dmitri, as if he were something tasty and exotic. Even though that was the way Lisette eyed every man with a pulse as far as Reggie could tell, it still made her want to rip the floozy's hair out by the roots. And choke her with it.

Of course, Dmitri was earning his own personal mark on her fecal-material roster. Not only wasn't he smacking Licentious Lisette in the face as she deserved, but he was also gently steering Reggie behind him, as if he didn't want anything coming between him and the buxom bimbo.

"Who?" Dmitri demanded. "Who sends me this message, Lisette?"

The smile that spread across Lisette's face made

Reggie think of knives and blood and thick, dripping acid. It did not inspire her to smile back.

"Why, my sister, of course," Lisette purred. "Her name is Yelisaveta."

ALL IT TOOK WAS THAT ONE REVELATION AND the jumbled pieces of information in Dmitri's mind filed into place like a column of soldiers. Yelisaveta Cherginov was behind everything, just as the paper they had found in Martin's lair had suggested. While physically, she might remain safely confined in a prison in Russia, her influence could not be so easily contained. He should only be surprised that it had taken her this long to find a way to make trouble on the other side of the world. She had always been on a constant lookout for new playgrounds.

"I did not know that Yelisaveta had a sister," he said, stalling for time. Now that he knew what kind of threat he faced, he needed a way to get Regina to safety in order to deal with it. "She never spoke of you."

"Of course not. Why should she provide her enemies with a means of gaining power over her? I was born to another mother when my sister was barely sixteen. I was raised in France until Liza found me, only five years after she herself was turned. She brought me to Riga when I was ten, and when I turned eighteen, I begged her to turn me. She knew I would be safe and undetected across the border from the mighty Kievan princes." Lisette scoffed. "Liza always had too much cunning for men like you."

Dmitri raised an eyebrow. "If that is true, then why has she spent more than four hundred years in a prison designed and guarded by men like me?"

Behind him, he felt Regina start at his words. He cursed that he did not have time now to explain.

"I defy any of you to escape from a prison guarded every moment of every day for centuries," the woman said, sneering. "You set an impossible task and then mock the one who cannot complete it. Hypocrites, all of you!" She spat at his feet.

"I do not find it hypocritical to punish one who has proven herself a menace to the society she claims to be part of. If your sister had not plotted to kill the master of a clan, she would still be free. She has brought about her own downfall."

"My sister is not fallen! Even in her isolation, she has more power than you know, *ublyodok*! Or do you imagine someone else has been able to turn the screw over your Council's thumbs from nearly five thousand miles away?" She sneered. "Did you think your own people had made such rogues as I made? The weaklings in this city are too concerned with playing by your rules to realize the potential of our people. They think the humans should be respected! Bah! I would sooner respect a sheep. Your people do not have the courage to destroy this Council of yours."

"And why would Yelisaveta wish to destroy it? The council is not responsible for her imprisonment. It had yet to be formed when her sentence was handed down."

Lisette's laughter held a ring of madness, something besides her facial features she clearly had in common with her sister. "*Durak!* You understand nothing. The only interest Liza has in the council is that it is significant to you! You and your disgusting family who robbed her of her rightful place among the masters of Europe. A curse on all of you!"

Dmitri opened his mouth to respond, but Regina's voice stopped him cold. As did the horror that welled up in him when she stepped out from behind his protective cover and gave Lisette a skeptical once-over.

"You know, I knew you were stupid when you let Gregory screw you," Regina said, her tone reeking of disdain. "But I didn't realize you were completely batshit crazy into the bargain. Do you have some little pills in your purse you're supposed to be taking? Because, sweetheart, I'm about to call the white coats on you."

Unpredictability, of course, was a madwoman's greatest weapon, and Lisette sprang before Dmitri could even reach out to draw Regina back. He heard a jumble of sounds, the vampire's cry of fury, his mate's own instinctive grunt as the air was knocked out of her, the thud as the impact of Lisette's attack sent both women crashing into the passage wall. He almost wished the noise would bring security running, but he knew the volume of the music in the auditorium would mask the noise.

Terrified and furious, he watched as Regina's head slammed into the plaster and ricocheted back for a second solid blow to the skull. He saw the fight sap out of her, her eyes going dazed and unfocused as her attacker grabbed a handful of her upswept hair and yanked her head aside to expose the tender skin over her carotid artery.

He launched himself forward with a guttural shout of rage.

Catching Lisette by the shoulder, he jerked her backward before her fangs so much as grazed his mate's flesh. Even for that, he vowed, there would be hell to pay.

Lisette screamed and released Regina, turning on Dmitri in a flurry of claws and fangs. She fought not like a woman but like a demon, intent not on winning or losing but on inflicting as much damage upon her opponent as possible. Her hard sharp nails raked across his cheek, leaving bloody furrows in his skin, but he ignored it. All that mattered now was keeping the bitch away from his Regina, his mate. His partner.

His love.

He turned to keep his own body between them, making himself into a shield for the woman who had accomplished the impossible—she had made him feel in a way he'd never expected to feel. She made him want to be as she perceived him, strong and noble and just. She made him want to keep her settled on a satin cushion, safe and protected, but more than that, she made him want to let her do anything she pleased, so long as the pleasure made her smile.

Except, of course, if she wanted to put herself in any kind of danger. That sort of behavior he could not allow. Which was why when he saw her rise to her feet, swaying and trembling, and shake off the effect of her fall, he saw his entire life—all eight centuries of it—flash before his eyes.

REGGIE HAD THOUGHT SHE WAS LOSING HER mind when she saw Lisette's eyes glowing red, but when the woman came at her with nails like a Siberian tiger's and canine teeth longer than an actual canine's, a whole bunch of things suddenly made completely perfect sense—not only was her ex-fiancé's tramp a bloodsucker; she was also a bona fide vampire.

The going-straight-for-the-neck thing only confirmed the worst.

What didn't make sense to Reggie was when Dmitri grabbed the monster by the shoulders and hauled her away as if she were no more substantial than a Raggedy Ann doll. Or the way her previously mysterious but presumably human lover now seemed to be sporting some serious dental additions of his own.

Holy shit, she marveled. *I've fallen in love with a vampire.*

The psychic mind-reading thing made so much more sense now—in an intensely creepy way— and so did a lot of other things. She only saw Misha at night, he could make her melt with one touch of his hand, he'd even been able to glue her feet in place that first night they'd met. No wonder Ava had been so against Reggie hooking up with Dmitri. She must have known something Reggie didn't. But why hadn't she just said something? That's what friends were for, right? To help pick out clothes, and to inform each other when one person in the friendship might be forming an emotional attachment to an inhuman, bloodthirsty creature of the night.

Duh.

The only problem Reggie could see now was what came next. What was she supposed to do now that she knew he was a vampire? After all, the love thing was a moot point. She'd already fallen, and somehow her traitorous heart seemed fairly unconcerned with the revelation. According to what it was telling her, he could have been a little green space alien and she would still go right on loving him.

Talk about an emotional kick in the pants.

Taking a deep breath, Reggie squared her shoulders and considered her angle of attack. Once she realized the truth of her feelings for Dmitri, it was no longer a question of whether she would try to help him, but only of how she would offer her assistance. She settled on providing a distraction to split Lisette's focus. Not only was it a time-honored tactic, but it was probably the least likely to end with Reggie's tonsils being ripped out through her neck.

With her eyes on the fighting vampires, she began to sidle along the wall, looking for a good place to implement her strategy. She hadn't planned on being grabbed roughly from behind.

"Hey, Reggie," an eerily familiar voice rasped in her ear. "Did you miss me?"

Gregory.

Reggie froze. "But you're dead!"

He chuckled, a rough, evil sound that made her blood run almost as cold as the feel of his hand wrapped around her throat. "Oh, no, sweetcheeks. I'm a little harder to kill than your average bear. The body your boyfriend thought was me belonged to the poor fellow who thought he'd try to set up camp right above my lair. I don't take kindly to squatters, you know."

Reggie glared at him from the corners of her eyes and wriggled to test his grip. It held firm. "So what do you want? Since you didn't pay this much attention to me when we were engaged and living together, I'm pretty certain it isn't me."

"You're meaningless, Reggie," Greg agreed, giggling almost maniacally. He sounded almost insane. "The only value you have to my mistress is that Vidâme seems to feel some affection for you. If it were up to me, I'd have drained you and killed you already."

"And instead?"

"Lisette is going to drain you while Vidâme watches, and then we're going to kill him. Once we do that, we'll be able to bring Yelisaveta here to Manhattan to start over again. She'll be able to build a new clan from the ground up, and once she's done that, no council, man, or government will be able to halt her plans."

Okay, more than almost insane.

"Her plans? Which involve what? A worldwide ban on garlic? You can't mess with peoples' immune systems like that."

She could feel the tension rising in Gregory, spiraling up and up until he fairly vibrated with suppressed madness and excitement. "Shut up, bitch," he hissed. "Or I'll tell her I'm draining you myself while she takes Vidâme. We'll make sure to feed in a way that lets you watch each other die."

Heart beating a mile a minute, Reggie reached up to brush away a hair that had fallen from the mass atop her head. "I'm sorry, Greg, but that just doesn't work for me. How about we try this, instead?"

With what she hoped was no warning, Reggie reached up, snagged one of the sharp, ornately carved ebony sticks securing her hair, and thrust it hard into the chest of the man behind her. She could only pray that she had hit somewhere in the vicinity of his heart.

"You fucking bitch!" Gregory howled, his grip softening enough for Reggie to struggle free and run as fast as she could toward the opera auditorium where there were people. Lots and lots of people, who would be happy to summon the police, or the National Guard. Or maybe an exorcist. Whoever you were supposed to call when you and your boyfriend had just been attacked by vampires.

She had gotten only a few feet when a sharp bellow sounded behind her. She knew it was Misha. Turning around she saw that instead of following her, Gregory had turned and joined Lisette in what looked like her attempts to rip Dmitri's heart out of his chest.

"No!"

Reggie had kicked off her heels and was halfway back down the hall before the echo of her shout even reached the place where she'd been standing. With no thought for anything but Dmitri, she grabbed the second stick from her hair, raised her arm, and ran with the pointy end of the wooden tool aimed directly at Gregory's glowing red eye.

She missed. Her ex-fiancé raised his head and turned at the last minute, and instead of shoving the hair stick into Greg's eye, Reggie was carried by her momentum to the spot where his eye had been a moment before and her stick punctured the back of his neck, driving four solid inches into his brain stem. He crumpled so fast that he pulled her down with him before she could remove her hand from the stick.

Lisette screamed something in Russian—something Reggie felt pretty sure Dmitri would refuse to translate even if she asked—and turned her attention from trying to rip out Dmitri's heart to trying to rip out Reggie's throat. She succeeded at neither. As soon as she turned her attention from Dmitri, the larger, fiercer vampire took instant advantage, grabbing the female's skull between his hands and wrenching it hard to the side. Reggie heard the popping and felt her stomach give a sick roll in response. Her eyes stayed glued on the blonde's limp body as it fell slowly to the floor and shattered on impact like thin, brittle glass. Within seconds, nothing remained of the madwoman's body but a thin layer of ash on the thick hallway carpet.

For several moments, neither Regggie nor Dmitri spoke.

Finally Reggie shivered and wrapped her arms

around herself to hug in her body heat. A detached voice in her head whispered that this was what going into shock felt like, but she ignored it.

"What happens to him?" she asked, jerking her chin in the direction of Gregory's body.

Dmitri took his cell phone from his pocket. "I will call and have someone take care of it. It is only because he was so newly made that he did not turn to ash like Lisette. Most vampires do after fifty or sixty years."

Reggie nodded, as if that made perfect sense. "Right. Well, you go make your call. I'm going to—" She shivered again. "I'm going to go to the ladies' room."

She felt Dmitri's eyes on her as she walked to the far end of the hall and pushed open the rest-room door. As soon as it closed behind her, she felt simultaneous waves of relief and nausea crash over her. Two seconds later, she bolted into the nearest stall and declared the nausea the official winner.

CHAPTER 22

DMITRI FOUND REGGIE FIFTEEN MINUTES LATER, clinging to the sink and shaking as beads of water dripped off the end of her nose. She looked as pale as milk except for her eyes, which were wide and dilated, and the faint green tinge to her complexion. Meeting his gaze in the mirror, she blinked slowly and shook her head.

"You're a vampire," she whispered, using her palms to wipe away the worst of the water she'd splashed on her face once her stomach had stopped trying to turn inside out. "I screwed a vampire."

"Actually, I believe if you wished to be technical, the vampire screwed you." His expression encouraged her to laugh.

She didn't. Instead she grabbed a handful of paper towels and busied herself with not having to look at him. "And we didn't even use condoms. Does that mean I have some kind of vampire disease now?"

"You're perfectly healthy," he assured her, turning his back to the mirror and leaning his hips against the marble counter. "Not to mention tasty."

"How do you—?" Reggie cut herself off, remembering the hickey from the other day, the one her friends had given her such a hard time about. Instinctively, she pressed her fingers to the spot, then pulled them away and inspected them as if she expected to find residual bleeding.

"Dry as a bone," he assured her, looking amused. "Even if it hadn't been days since I last fed from you, the wounds close up almost immediately. I won't apologize for the hickey though. I could have fed without marking you, but I found the idea of you bearing my 'love bite' too tempting to resist."

"Har-har." Reggie stared at him and waited for the panic to replace the numbness of shock. It didn't happen. Instead, the memory of how it had felt when they'd been together, when he'd sucked at her neck, when she'd found the mark he'd left behind . . . All she felt when she remembered that was horny.

Well, horny and wary. He was a bloodsucking fiend, after all, but he hadn't killed her, and he'd had plenty of opportunities. In fact, he'd actually saved her life at least twice when Lisette had wanted to kill her. So really, the question she had to ask herself was, how did she feel about dating a real-life, genuine, honest-to-goodness vampire?

Could she look at him the same way knowing he wasn't quite human?

Before she could answer that question, Reggie decided she needed to ask a few questions.

"Did you turn me into one of you?" she demanded, crossing her arms over her chest and scooting back to put a little bit of distance between them. Less because she was actually afraid of him and more in case she turned into a bat or something. She'd already killed someone today—granted an insane, immoral, violent, murdering fiend, but still—and while she didn't regret saving Dmitri's life as well as her own by doing so, it wasn't exactly a habit she wanted to get into.

"Of course not. More is required to make a vampire than a simple bite. If that were all it took, the world would be overrun—by us 'bloodsucking fiends.'"

He appeared more amused than insulted, but Reggie was distracted by a memory. "That's why you can read my mind! You've got some vampiric power of mind control, or something."

Dmitri chuckled. "Or something. I cannot control your mind, *milka*. I can influence your decisions, but only in the direction your subconscious already wishes to go. If I could truly control you, you never would have attempted to date that Marc person. But I can read your thoughts, and I can speak to you in your mind."

"Can you read everyone's mind? Can I?" Now that would be a useful little skill.

"You can read only me, unless you have other talents you have been hiding from me," he teased. "Were you to become like me, your talents would strengthen with time. I can read your mind with true clarity. Some others I can read fairly easily, some barely at all. I do get impressions from most humans though. I am an infallible judge of character."

"Too bad I'm not."

He reached out and tucked a lock of hair behind her ear. "I am really not an evil monster, *dushka*. I am just a man who has lived an unusually long life."

"Yeah, and who lives off drinking other people's blood. That hardly sounds like Prince Charming." She scowled at him.

"The prince is a fairy tale. I am real, and I do drink blood to survive. I am not ashamed of it. I do not kill those I drink from, and I do them no lasting harm. I have lived too many years not to be at peace with what I am, Regina."

Reggie really wanted to ask how long he had lived, but his talk of "lasting harm" had brought a more pressing issue to her mind. "So you're sure I'm not a vampire now?"

He grinned. "Positive. In order to become a vampire, you would need to drink from me as I have drunk from you. Unless that happens, you remain my very human, very stubborn, very adorable Regina."

"Flattery is not going to sweep this all under the rug, bucko." She humphed to cover up the warm fuzzies his words gave her. "*You* are a vampire. That's big news in my world. I don't generally date the living dead."

"What sort of dead do you usually date?" He ducked her punch and laughed. "I'm really not all that different from any other man. I have the needs any man has."

And then some, she thought, remembering their nights together. "Other men don't drink blood," she insisted.

"No, but among human men there are those who are greater monsters than I am. That Martin fellow was a perfect example. The reason he was so evil as a vampire is because those traits existed in him even when he was a man. He hurt you then, did he not? I would never betray you, *milaya*, and I would die rather than cause you harm. You are precious to me."

That brought the fuzzies back, but she ignored them. One thing at a time. She needed more information. "You could hurt me though. You're really strong, and fast as hell. I've seen you move."

Dmitri shrugged. "I am a man. I could have hurt you when I was human. But yes, being a vampire does give me additional strength and speed. Still, these are things I would never use to harm you."

"What else can you do?"

"Am I a trick pony?"

She scowled. "You know what I mean. Like, are you going to turn into a bat or something?"

He rolled his eyes. "Why would I want to transform myself into a disease-carrying, winged rodent?"

"How should I know? I can't understand why you would want to drink blood."

His eyes fastened on the curve of skin bared by her neckline, where her neck met her shoulder. Suddenly his expression turned from lazy amusement to heated interest. "Ah, but your blood is intoxicating, *milaya*. Shall I describe for you its sweetness? Its warmth? The way it goes to my head like aged whisky?" He met her gaze, and his eyes filled with wicked intent. "Shall I describe the cries you give when I drink from you?"

Reggie remembered coming apart in his arms perfectly well without that look of heated sin he was giving her. She blushed. "Don't change the subject. I'm trying to get some answers. I want to know exactly what I've gotten myself into here."

Dmitri sighed and folded his arms across his chest. He wore a long-suffering expression as he closed his eyes and began to recite facts.

"You have watched too many movies and read

some lurid novels," he said. "Vampires are not the monsters humans like to portray us as. We are different by our very natures, but we are no better and no worse as vampires than we were as men. We are stronger and faster, this is true. Our senses are also keener, and our lifetimes can be prolonged indefinitely. In order to survive, we must drink blood. But we are not harmed by crosses or garlic or holy water or any of that non-sense. We can be killed if you destroy our hearts, for that is the organ that supplies our bodies with the blood we consume. And, of course, if you be-head us or severely injure our brains, we will also die. I know of few things that could live without their heads."

"Few?" Reggie squeaked, floundering for a grip on reality and therefore able to focus on only one statement at a time, and that was the last one. "You mean there are things that can?"

"I always assumed politicians could do so. They so seldom seem to use them."

Her jaw dropped open for a second, until she noticed how intently he watched her reaction to his teasing. She closed her mouth with a snap and glared at him. Somehow the things he told her actually reassured her. She couldn't understand why, but her reality had just shifted and found a new foundation. Her belief system had made room for an unexpected addition, and now things looked to be getting back to normal.

If you could call having a flaming affair with a vampire "normal."

Reggie took a couple of hesitant steps forward and raised her chin defiantly. "Wooden stake and sunlight?" she asked, her tone now more curious than frightened. "I think I missed Gregory's heart that first time, so I couldn't tell."

"If you drove a wood stake through the heart of any living thing, I imagine it would not live much longer," he said. He didn't touch her, but somehow she felt the intimacy of his company. "And sunlight is painful, but not usually life threatening. We cannot absorb the melanin in the blood we drink," he explained. "And we do not produce our own. Therefore, we burn easily. But I have yet to burst into flame."

She humphed. The man had a way with sarcasm. "So, basically you're telling me you're a totally average guy with superhuman strength, the ability to read my mind, and a very selective diet."

He grinned at her. "Precisely."

"And you'll never grow old or die."

"It is unlikely to happen for a very long time."

"Don't you get bored? I mean, after a century or two, I'd think you'd have seen it all."

"I have many varied interests that keep my attention," he informed her, still grinning. "Human culture is a fascinating thing. It evolves constantly and with dizzying speed. And if you wish to know my age, you have only to ask me."

Apparently, her fishing hadn't been as subtle as she'd thought. "Fine. How old are you?"

"I was born in Novgorod, as I told your date this evening"—his eyes met hers, and that damned eyebrow quirked again—"in the year 1199."

Reggie shrieked and leaped backward. "You're eight hundred and five years old!"

Misha clearly decided to ignore the fact that she sounded like a fishwife. He merely raised that eyebrow and reached down to give a light tug at the hair that had tumbled over her shoulder. "Eight hundred and four," he corrected calmly. "The anniversary of my birth is not until October."

"Oh, well, pardon me. That makes everything perfectly all right. Those few months are incredibly important to me. I'd hate it if I broke my rule of not dating older men by that wide a margin."

"Sarcasm does not become you, *milka*. Besides, what does my age matter? Do I look eight hundred and four?"

"Of course not. But that . . . that's not just old—not just dead—it's compost!"

He sighed, beginning to look impatient. "And I am very much alive and very much desirous of touching you again. Come, let us go home. It has been a difficult night."

"I'm not ready to." She scowled, all but digging her heels into the tile floor. "I've still got questions."

"You can ask them at home. Come."

He took her by the hand, pushed up from his slouched position against the counter, and began to drag her toward the door.

"Misha, cut it out!" She tugged against his grip and refused to go any further, for all the good it did her. "I'm serious. I've got to figure out what I'm going to do with you."

"I have several suggestions for you, which I will explain in very great detail. At home."

"I'll just bet you will, but that was not what I meant." She tried to inject a tone of firmness and resolution into her words, but that wasn't so easy when the man swept her into his arms like Rhett Butler and began carrying her down the hall toward the opera lobby. "I just found out my lover is a vampire. I've got some decisions to make."

Dmitri tightened his arms around her until she could feel the heavy beat of his heart against her chest, but it was the tender heat in his eyes that captivated her.

"*Dushka,*" he murmured, leaning down to brush his lips softly over hers. "I am afraid your decisions have already been made. I will not allow you to leave me. You are mine, and I intend to keep you."

CHAPTER 23

"KEEP ME?" SHE BLINKED. IT WAS TWENTY minutes and dozens of blocks later and Dmitri was just opening his front door to let them inside. It had taken her all that time to stop gaping like a rubbernecker at his unprecedented, dictatorial declaration. "You can't just decide to keep me."

Dmitri opened the door to his gorgeous, old brownstone townhouse in a hideously expensive, historic neighborhood on the Upper East Side. "And who shall stop me?"

"I will!"

Dmitri ushered her into the entry hall, which was a dirty tactic on his part. How was she supposed to keep yelling at him when there was so much to look at in this beautiful place? The golden glow of the entry lights gleamed on the warm, hardwood floors and period wainscoted walls. Above the paneling, the walls were papered in the sort of embossed wall covering that had more in common with expensive fabric than generic wallpaper. She tore her eyes away from the artwork on the wall (which really looked like an original Degas charcoal sketch), and let Dmitri take her coat. He draped it along with his over a settee and took her arm.

"Welcome to my home, *dushka*," he said formally. He stared down at her and tucked a stray curl behind her ear. "You honor me with your presence."

She had to fight hard not to melt into a puddle of goo at his feet right then and there, but now wasn't the time. There were a few important matters that she felt the two of them still needed to clear up.

"Thank you, it's lovely. But don't think it's going to distract me. I'm serious about this. I've never let a man tell me what I can and can't do, and I'm not about to start now, Mr. Dictator. I've got a mind and a will of my own, and I am not your possession!"

"But I have possessed you, *milaya*."

"Big frickin' whoop," she growled. "That doesn't give you any rights to me. I might like to let you have your way in bed, Dmitri, but outside of it is a whole 'nother story. I'm sexually submissive. I'm not a doormat."

Dmitri sighed. "I never thought of you as a doormat. And I have never treated you as one. I love your fire and your stubborn streak. I would not want to rob you of those."

His words convinced her to at least stop shouting, not that she seemed to be making any sort of impression on him anyway. "Dmitri, if you love those things about me, then how can you ask me to let you make these sorts of decisions for me?"

"Regina, how can you expect me to let you go?"

His softly spoken words and expression of weary longing almost made her melt. She nearly gave up the ghost right there, nearly wrapped her thighs around him and said, "Sir, yes, sir." But her mind saved her, beating her heart back into its rib cage and holding it at bay until they cleared the rest of this mess up once and for all.

"Dmitri, you barely know me. We've spent a total of about twelve hours together over the course of one week. Why am I supposed to think you want me? For this?" Stepping close, she arched her hips against him and ignored the flash of pleasure it caused. "Somehow I don't think you have much trouble getting laid."

His eyes flashed.

"Do you think this is merely 'getting laid' to me?" he demanded, his frustration clear. "Do you think I feel this way with other women? That you would feel this way with other men? You are my mate. The woman I have never found in all my centuries of living. The one I thought I would never find. And I will not let you go."

That was almost good enough, Reggie acknowledged to herself over the flood of pleasure and
wonder the statement caused; but *almost* didn't
count. She wanted the whole shebang. So she
prodded the wounded lion.

"Why not, Dmitri?" Self-preservation be
damned. This was her future they were tap-
dancing around. If she had to make him furious to
get what she wanted, so be it. "Why not let me go?
Why not write this off as a couple of nights of good
sex and move on to your next conquest? Why not
let me move on? Why not let me give Marc a call
and arrange to have a real date this time? The kind
that doesn't end at the restaurant but in a bed or on
the floor or in the back seat of his car. Why not?"

"Because I love you!" he roared. "And no man
will ever touch you but me!"

A smile curved her mouth until she probably
looked like an idiot. She didn't care. Especially
not when he swept her back into his arms and carried her up the stairs, stalking all the way like an
angry bear.

"Well, okay, then," she murmured as he shoul-
dered his way into a bedroom and somehow
flicked on the light switch.

"You are going to be my wife, and I refuse to
hear—" He jerked to a stop mid-tirade and
dropped her without warning onto a pillowy mattress. "What did you say?"

"I said okay, you big goob." She grinned. "I

love you too. I don't want anyone else to touch me. And incidentally, if that was a proposal—and if it was, it was a god-awful excuse for one—then the answer is yes."

"Yes?"

"Yes," she repeated and tugged impatiently at his hands, tumbling him down to the mattress beside her. "I'll marry you, provided you ask me again properly. And since I plan to celebrate our five-hundredth anniversary at the very least, that means you'll have to make me a vampire too. Let's get started. I'm not really looking forward to the blood-drinking part, so do you think we could get that over with first?"

The man looked positively shell-shocked. "You want to marry me and become a vampire."

"Isn't that what I just said?" She finally tugged her hands free—or, he let her tug her hands free—and wrapped them around his neck. "Now let's hurry up before I lose my nerve. Not about the marrying part, about the vampire part. I'm really not good with blood. I faint at the sight of it. I won't have to look at blood when I drink it, will I? Because that might make things kind of tough for me . . ."

While she babbled, Dmitri's expression went from stunned to satisfied. When she finally trailed into silence, his expression shifted into its natural state—wicked.

"You may keep your eyes closed if you wish,"

he purred, pushing her thighs farther apart and settling his hips deeper into the cradle of hers. He hooked a hand into the neckline of her evening dress and tugged it down to expose her breasts to his avid gaze. "But if you do, you might miss something."

Reggie groaned and buried her fingers in his thick, dark hair when he lowered his head and latched on to her puckered nipple.

"Oh, no," she moaned. "I wouldn't want to miss a thing."

CHAPTER 24

NO MAN SHOULD BE ABLE TO MAKE HER THIS horny this fast, Reggie thought while she melted under Dmitri's warm mouth and skilled fingers. And no man should be wearing his evening clothes while he got her this hot.

Forcing her hands to give up their compelling nest in his hair, she slid them over his shoulders and between their bodies to the button at his waistband.

Dmitri chuckled and lifted his head from her breast. "Is someone feeling impatient?"

"Someone is going to remove your pants with her teeth if you don't get them off in the next fifteen seconds," she grumbled, already tugging at the zipper.

"Promises, promises," he teased. Levering himself back onto his knees, he brushed her hands away and finished the job himself, stripping away his dark suit and dropping it over the side of the bed.

Reggie had to take several deep breaths just to keep from screaming "Take me!" like the heroine of a melodramatic romance novel. Ye gods and little fishes. Would she ever get used to the way this man looked? From the top of his tousled, black hair to the soles of his leather-clad feet, the man oozed masculine perfection. And he was all hers. She offered up a quick and fervent prayer of thanks while he prowled toward her on his hands and knees.

"Help," she whispered, a small smile curving her lips while lust darkened her eyes. "I think I'm about to be ravished by a wicked vampire. Help. Somebody please help me."

"There is no one to hear your screams, girl." He grinned at her, wicked and sexy, while he forced her legs wide apart and crawled between them. "I have you at my mercy."

"And will you be merciful?" Her question made it clear mercy was the last thing she wanted. She reached out to trace a line down the center of his chest before she wrapped her hand around his erect cock.

"Not even if you beg, *milka*."

Reggie heaved a happy sigh. "Oh, good."

"Did you miss me, *milaya*?" Dmitri asked, his voice a stir of gravel and sin. "While we were apart, did your body ache for me?"

His hand slid down to palm her breast for an instant before it continued over her stomach to cup her through the fabric of her dress. "Did you dream of me?"

His touch drove the breath from her lungs. She arched her body, pressing herself against his hand.

God, if he only knew what she had dreamed.

"Tell me."

She tried, she really did, but the only sound she could make was a whimpering sort of gasp when he touched her. Her eyes drifted shut, and her lids became a screen on which the film of her fantasies ran in all their Technicolor glory.

She heard Dmitri laugh, a low, rumbling sound. "Ah, *milaya*, you are a wonder to me. You have such passion behind your conventional little exterior." His hand moved to the zipper at the back of her dress. "It pleases me."

The material gave way beneath his hands, and he tugged the dress away from her and tossed it aside, leaving her sprawled out before him in lewd abandon. She'd gone naked beneath the dress, since the bodice had a built-in bra, and she couldn't seem to forget his order that she forgo panties even when she wasn't with him, so now all she wore was her pale skin, her white flesh a stark contrast to the darkness of the man looming over her. She opened her eyes and found him staring, his glance like a pair of hands running over her, raising gooseflesh on her skin.

"Lovely," he murmured. He released her hands and sat back, resting against the carved headboard with indolent grace. "But I think I am intrigued by this dream you have had of me, *dushka*. I would like to make it come true for you. And for me."

His eyes glinted with an intensity his lazy drawl had managed to conceal. Reggie twisted into a sitting position and faced him. He raised his eyebrow and remained still. A thrill of excitement ran through her. He expected to lie back and be pleasured, like some pasha with his slave girl, and Reggie's normally independent nature remained cheerfully silent, offering not a single protest. It shocked her to realize these fantasies of hers—these submissive feelings she'd always felt were so antithetical to her real personality and beliefs—were maybe not so foreign to her nature after all. They certainly felt completely natural in that moment.

Taking a deep breath, she scooted forward across the mattress until she knelt before him, perched hesitantly between his thighs. She reached up to his collar and tugged loose the knot in his tie. Silk whispered against silk when she drew the fabric free and tossed it on the floor beside the bed. Dmitri merely smiled.

Her fingers fumbled a little on his shirt studs, but eventually she got the tiny gold clasps unfastened. When she started to slide off the bed so she could set the studs down on the bedside table,

Dmitri fastened his hands around her waist and stopped her.

You are not permitted to get up just now.

Reggie read the challenge in his eyes. Once he knew she understood, he dropped his hands. Nibbling her lower lip, Reggie hesitated for a second. She braced one hand against the mattress and leaned across him. If she stretched as far as she could without tumbling over, she could just reach to drop the studs on the edge of the table. Stretching in that direction, though, meant she had to drape herself across Dmitri's torso, bringing her breasts within an inch or two of his face.

He noticed. His lips latched onto her nipple and tugged in a sweet suckling motion. Reggie moaned, a shiver of pleasure shaking her. Blindly, she groped for the nightstand and dropped the studs onto the corner. She vaguely heard them make contact with the wooden surface and fall, scattering across the floor with tiny pinging noises. She couldn't have cared less. She wrapped her arms around Dmitri's head, pressing him closer to her. As soon as she did so, he pulled back.

"How clumsy of you, Regina," he murmured, pushing her back to a kneeling position in front of him. "I expect you to take better care of my things. I trust you will not be so cavalier with my cuff links." He extended his arm to her, wrist turned to expose the decorative clasp.

Reggie hurried to unfasten it, repeating the

operation with the other cuff. She leaned forward toward the nightstand, but this time she twisted her body so she presented Dmitri with her shoulder blade, rather than her breasts. If he went for her nipples again, she'd be totally useless.

She heard him chuckle, and his hand slid swiftly between her legs, penetrating her with two long fingers. She froze in place, dropping her head on a groan. "Are you trying to kill me?"

"Only in the French sense of the word, *dushka. Seulement le petit mort.*"

"Oh. Only a little death," she translated in her high school French, panting as she set the cuff links carefully on the table. "I feel so much better now."

Dmitri laughed, his lips brushing against her nipple as he brought his thumb into play, using it to draw tight little circles around her already aching clit. *No, no, milaya. Le petit mort is . . . well, allow me to demonstrate.*

His free hand slid to her side, cupping one breast and shifting her to face him fully. He raked his thumbnail over the erect nipple even while his teeth nibbled delicately at the bud in his mouth. Reggie shuddered and tried to pull away, but succeeded only in pressing herself harder on the hand between her legs. His fingers sank deeper, and he curled the tips to caress her slick inner walls.

She felt trapped and overwhelmed and dizzy

with the sensations pounding at her. She grabbed desperately at his shoulders, needing an anchor to hold her steady. The pressure inside her built with ridiculous speed, winding tighter and faster with each stroke of his fingers, each glide of his tongue. She became an extension of his touch, existing only for the fingers in her cunt and the mouth on her breast.

"Misha," she whimpered, feeling him guide her inexorably to the edge of an enormous cliff. What would happen when he drove her over, she couldn't imagine. "Please. I—I need . . ."

I know, milaya. *I know.* His thumb pressed harder on her clit, and his fingers closed sharply around her nipple. *Come for me,* dushka. *Now.*

She obeyed, her body drawing tight while the tension inside her peaked and broke, flooding her with pleasure and flooding his hand with the evidence. She slid boneless against him, leaning her cheek against the front of his shirt while her hands still clutched at his shoulders.

She struggled to catch her breath, shuddering delicately with the aftershocks that still rippled through her. Dmitri comforted her, petting her back with soothing motions and brushing soft kisses against her hair. He gave her a few minutes to compose herself, but his hands soon moved to her hips and sat her back on her heels again.

"I do not believe you had yet finished your task, Regina," he said, glancing down at his shirt, which hung open but still covered his arms and broad shoulders. "I would not want to think you neglect your chores."

Because undressing him is such a chore, she thought, biting her cheek to keep from rolling her eyes. She waited for one of his smart comments, but Dmitri remained silent. He was waiting.

Sliding her hands beneath the two open shirt halves, Reggie took her time, savoring the warm weight of his muscular chest beneath her hands. She savored the feel of him, smooth and hard near his shoulders, rougher and somehow less civilized in the center of his chest where a blanket of masculine fur arrowed down toward his waistband. She leaned forward to strip the cloth from his shoulders and gave in to the temptation to rub her cheek against the sensual, contrasting textures. She felt the rippling of his muscles beneath her touch, but he kept his hands at his sides and let her continue.

She pushed the shirt down his arms and tugged it from under him, tossing it away near his tie. She sat back to survey what she'd uncovered.

Great googly-moogly.

Lord, but the man was gorgeous. He had the musculature of a Greek statue that had decided to take up bodybuilding. She could see the definition of his muscles when they flexed and shifted, and appreciated that they stopped short of exaggeration. His shoulders looked impossibly broad while he lounged there in graceful splendor. His chest was wide and strong, his waist lean and stomach firm. And suddenly she couldn't wait to see the rest of him again.

The fingers she lifted to his waistband trembled before she managed to force them into steadiness. Just to be sure they were prepared to obey her, she caressed them down his sides, her thumbs brushing over his nipples before gliding south to his tuxedo pants. She undid the top catch and gripped the zipper tab between her thumb and forefinger and slowly began inching the fastening open. Her eyes were glued to her task, her head bowed, the tension of a child on Christmas morning filling her. She felt his eyes on her while she pulled the zipper down the last few millimeters and spread open his fly.

He wore nothing beneath but his skin, a fact she'd appreciated at the opera and reveled in now. She tugged at the fabric, and he cooperated by lifting his hips so she could pull it down. She eased back toward the foot of the bed, stopped just past his feet and quickly stripped them as well. Grabbing hold of his slacks, she tugged them down and off him, casting them aside behind her. She lowered her head, set her tongue against the hollow of his ankle and slowly dragged it upward along the inside of his leg.

She loved the taste of him, warm and salty and solid. He tasted like man and earth and desire, and she paused occasionally on her journey to enjoy the flavor. He let her have her way and lay still beneath her lazy exploration, but she heard his breath catch when she reached his knee and stroked her tongue along the crease behind it. When she reached his thighs, he gave in and buried his hands in her hair, fingers massaging her scalp while her tongue darted out to stroke the smooth skin she found there. Here his taste was stronger, darker, even more enticing. She let her tongue glide up and up until it flicked over the sensitive skin between his legs in a warm hello.

Her eyes drifted shut in pleasure, and she rubbed her cheek against his erection like a cat, enjoying the knowledge she'd caused him to harden, that she had brought him pleasure and made him want. She parted her lips to take him inside, but he had other plans. Grasping her arms, he dragged her up, bare skin sliding over bare skin, until her face came level with his.

His black eyes gleamed in the candlelight—candles that hadn't been lit a moment ago—and his lips curved in a wicked smile.

"Not this time, *dushka*," he whispered, brushing his lips against hers, returning a heartbeat later for a deeper kiss. He nibbled her lips apart, stroked her tongue with his, conquered her mouth and claimed her for his own. When he drew back, her breathing had turned into excited panting. "I have seen your desire for me, seen how you dreamed of me. That is what I want from you now. Will you indulge me?"

Leaning down she brushed her lips against his, against his throat, his nipples, and the tip of his erection. She sat up and turned her back to him, kneeling between his spread legs and bracing her hands against his hard thighs. She perched on her heels, her back straight and graceful before him, and turned to send him an enticing look over her shoulder.

Dmitri rumbled out a sound of appreciation. He moved closer and slid his hands over the smooth skin of her back, briefly cupping her ass before he wrapped his arms around her and pressed against her.

"You are so lovely, *milka*," he murmured, and his breath tickled her ear even while his hands slid up to cuddle her full breasts in his palms. "Soft and lush and sweet." His tongue flicked her earlobe, followed by gentle nibbles, and one of his hands slid down the center of her body, over the soft curve of her stomach and down between her thighs. "Warm and wet and giving."

His fingers slipped easily over her damp flesh, tracing each curve and fold, probing at her entrance as if testing her readiness. God, how could he doubt she was ready for him?

"It pleases me that you take pleasure in my pleasure," he whispered, sinking two fingers deep inside her. "You were made for me. Can you not tell?"

He trailed kisses from the hollow behind her ear, along her throat to the curve of her shoulder. Reggie's head fell back, resting on his shoulder while he sent waves and waves of pleasure coursing through her.

"Can you not tell you were born for me, Regina? Born to please me and to be pleasured by me?"

Reggie groaned, her mind blank of everything but Misha and pleasure and need. Her fingers tightened on his thighs, dug into his flesh, her whole body tensed with wanting. "Misha. Please."

"Can you tell, Regina?"

His black-magic voice only added to the chaos inside her, only layered another level of sensation on her already-overloaded nervous system. Her body arched, pressing into his hands. "God! Misha, I want . . ."

His hand at her breast abandoned its massage and slid up her shoulder to the nape of her neck. His fingers caressed her briefly before they firmed on her skin and pressed, urging her forward. She followed his silent command, easing forward to brace her weight on her hands and lift her hips, until she knelt on all fours before him and trembled.

He bracketed her hips with both hands and leaned over her, covering her with his heat and his presence. His lips brushed the nape of her neck, making her shudder. She could feel his lips curve into a smile.

"What do you want, *dushka*?" He teased her, knowing the answer, but forcing her to say it.

Reggie's head bowed, her long hair falling forward to curtain her from everything else. She didn't know if she could talk, didn't know if she still controlled her body, since it seemed so intent on doing Misha's bidding. She tested her tongue, tried to speak. Nothing emerged but a whimper, and she pressed back against him instead, her ass cushioning his insistent penis.

His hands pressed her forward, separating their flesh. She groaned at the loss of the contact.

"What is it you want?"

Reggie moaned and tried to sit up, to turn toward him, but his hand just cupped the back of her neck again and pressed her back down.

This time he held her there while he repeated the question. "What do you want, Regina?"

Frustration and the pain of wanting him gave her the power to speak, barely. Her words tore from her on a moan. "You! God, Misha, I want you!"

He hummed his approval, and his hand lifted from her neck. It trailed down the length of her spine, slid between them. His erection nudged at her tight opening, demanding entrance. She wanted him to thrust, needed him to take her, needed to feel him inside her. But he wasn't done torturing her.

"I can feel what you want, Regina," he crooned, his hands reaching to cup her breasts where they hung beneath her. He pressed against her back, her breasts, her thighs. She felt surrounded by him, overwhelmed and helpless. And, Lord, but it felt good. His breath caressed her cheek, and he nuzzled her hair out of his way so he could touch his skin to hers.

"But what are you willing to give me in return?"

Moaning and shaking and needing him more than her next breath, Reggie turned her head enough to touch her mouth to his. Parting her lips against his, she breathed her answer into his mouth, as if she could gift her soul to him.

"Anything," she whispered urgently, willing him to know how much she meant it. "I would give you anything."

"Yes."

He took her mouth, claimed it, marked it as his. His tongue swept over hers like a conquering warrior, even though her surrender came swift and willing. When he finally drew back, she could see his intensity and his lust in the harsh cast of his features. His savage look caused her no fear, but made her tremble with the thrill of anticipation.

"You will give me everything, *dushka*," he growled, hands grabbing her hips to hold her still. "And I will take all you have. For you are mine."

As he spoke, he thrust, claiming her physically even as he claimed her verbally. Reggie gasped at the intrusion, her body shocked at the feel of him after a week-long absence. Her muscles clenched to ward him off, but it was much too late. He was already buried to the hilt, his thickness stretching her, pleasure and discomfort blending into an indistinguishable maelstrom of sensation.

He released her hips long enough to grab her wrists and guide her hands to the rail at the foot of the bed. She had to stretch to reach it, moving forward on her knees until she leaned past them, shifting her center of gravity to her torso and throwing herself off balance. Misha followed her motion, embedded in her clutching pussy, and wrapped her hands around the cool wood, squeezing a warning that she leave them there. The position was awkward. Her weight had shifted forward and now was supported mainly by her grip on the railing and Dmitri's grip on her hips. If she moved, she would collapse. All she could do was kneel there, still and submissive, and let him take her.

He did.

He leaned forward to place a tender kiss on her spine just at the small of her back. He reared back, withdrawing until only his tip remained inside her; then he braced her hips before him, and plunged.

Reggie screamed. She barely heard herself, too caught up in the feel of him pounding inside of her. Her head jerked back even as the force of his thrust pushed her forward. She braced her arms, locking herself in place, not wanting to lose even a fraction of the force. She tried to spread her legs further to give herself a better sense of balance, but his calves were braced on the outside of hers to keep her exactly as he had positioned her. All she could do was whimper and accept him.

He drew back slowly, making her pant. She could feel each inch of him while he pulled out of her, feel her passage collapsing back on itself, relieved of the merciless invader. It felt like a massage on her most sensitive tissues. She thought wildly that nothing could feel better, but he surged forward again, filled her again, and she knew how wrong she had been.

Misha settled into a rhythm, fast and hard and desperately deep. Each thrust brought him inside her to the hilt. She'd never felt him this deep, this hard. She loved it, wanted more, and even while she thought it, he gave it to her.

"Misha!"

She screamed his name. Her body shook with his thrusts. The tension was unbearable. She needed him to stop. She needed him to never stop. She needed to get away. She needed to get closer. Her hands clenched so hard on the bedrail that her knuckles ached. Her elbows had locked, stretched out before her, and she used her braced position to thrust herself back onto him, desperate to take everything he had.

He obliged her with a grunt, and somehow he grew impossibly larger inside her, stretching her abused pussy even further. She shuddered, and her head fell. Her hands remained braced on the railing, but her upper body sank down until she rested her cheek and her shoulder on the mattress, her hips still angled up to take Misha's fierce, pounding sex.

She gulped in oxygen, desperate and out of breath. If he didn't stop, he would kill her. If he ever stopped, she'd die.

Misha leaned forward, curling his body around hers, his hips still hammering hard and rhythmically into her. She felt the slight roughness of his cheek against the sensitive skin of her neck, heard the irregular sound of his breathing, felt the heat of him like a firebrand against her. She heard his voice, deep and harsh and frighteningly intense.

"What would you give me, *dushka*?" he growled low and bestial.

Reggie tried to moan, but she didn't even have the breath for that. She couldn't speak, couldn't think, could barely hold herself up for his possession.

Anything, she thought desperately. *I would give you anything!*

Anything?

Everything.

She heard a rumbling growl of pleasure, felt him shift, fill her more deeply, surround her more completely. She felt a sharp pain at her throat, and she shattered.

The pleasure inside her exploded and she came, spasming around him, milking him of his seed, sharing her ecstasy, as she had shared her body. The orgasm lasted forever, her inner muscles clenching in time to the rhythmic draw on her pulse. She felt him tense, heard another muffled growl when he spurted inside her, still feeding on her pleasure as he fed on her blood.

CHAPTER 25

I THINK I PASSED OUT. I THINK HE FUCKED ME until I passed out.

I fucked you until we both passed out.

He nuzzled her breast and planted a soft kiss on her tender nipple, the one he'd fed from. He lay sprawled half on top of her, his weight pinning her in place. He seemed absolutely disinclined to move. Frankly, Reggie couldn't blame him. Staying right where they were sounded pretty damned good to her too.

A smug, and probably goofy, grin curved her mouth. "Yeah. And it was fantastic."

Dmitri chuckled. "I'm glad you enjoyed it, *dushka*, because I don't think I will be capable again for at least half a century."

Reggie tickled his ear with her finger and hooked one leg over his hip. Her grin turned wicked. "Wanna try for half an hour?"

This time, he laughed straight out, and the

rumbling noise shook the bed. "You are an optimist. It is impossible."

Her hand slid down his back and between his thighs to tickle his scrotum.

He amended his opinion. "Highly unlikely."

She squeezed gently.

"Almost inevitable."

Reggie laughed and leaned down to nibble at the flat disc of his nipple. "That's what I thought you'd say."

"Enough, wench," Misha growled, levering off her and sitting up to once again lean against the headboard. When he pulled her into his lap, Reggie winced.

"Not this way again," she protested. "My hips are still too sore from last time."

"As flattering as your confidence in me is," he laughed, "your reprieve will last a while longer. We have other matters to tend to than our bodies' cravings for each other."

Reggie blinked. "We do?"

"We do. You have agreed to marry me, Regina. Do not tell me you've forgotten already."

She grinned at his expression of mock disapproval. "Well, I admit I was distracted, but no, I remember." She kissed his firm lips. "I may even be looking forward to it."

"And you asked me to turn you into a vampire." His dark eyes searched her expression.

Reggie made it easy for him and grimaced. "Not so looking forward to that part."

Dmitri hugged her close and stroked her back with soothing motions. "You do not have to do this, *dushka*. It is not necessary. We can manage quite well if you wish to remain human."

Realizing what a silly git she'd be to turn down a man who was that hot in bed and gave a damn or two about her feelings, Reggie shook her head and raised a determinedly cheerful face to him.

"And let you go off chasing after sweet young things as soon as I start wrinkling?" she teased. "Not a chance. Like I said, I want a five-hundredth anniversary. What is that? Raw platinum? What comes after silver, gold, and diamond?"

He grinned as if her answer pleased him. "I am entirely unsure. However, it would be my pleasure to discover this with you."

He kissed her soundly and left her perched in bemusement on his lap while he reached into the nightstand drawer and pulled out a sheathed dagger.

"Because you do not yet have fangs," he explained. He pulled off the protective leather, and her eyes widened.

That looks awfully sharp . . .

He cupped her chin in his hand and forced her gaze to shift from the knife to his face. "You do not have to do this," he repeated with firm authority.

"It is forever, *milka*, and I would rather lose you than have you come to hate me."

Somehow, the freedom of that choice made her decision to bind herself to him all that much more definite. She kissed him tenderly, lingering over it, showing him without words how much she loved him and how much she wanted to be with him always.

When she pulled back, her expression held warmth and love and humor. "Forever may not be long enough for me," she warned him, half teasing. "I might follow you into the afterlife. Maybe *you* should think twice about this."

"You would not have to follow me. I would not go without you, *dushka*."

Reggie smiled, her nerves giving way to a sense of peace and excitement. "Then let's get this done, bucko, before you decide to back out. What do I need to do?"

He searched her face one last time before nodding, apparently content with what he'd read there. "As I said, you will have to drink from me. I will make a small cut in my flesh. You will have to drink the blood from it."

"Do I need to drink a lot?" She was willing to do this, wanted to do this, even, but the idea still seemed a little creepy.

"Not a vast quantity this first time, but enough to set the transformation in motion. You will know when it has begun."

"Will it hurt?"

"It is a . . . peculiar sensation, but you should not find it too painful."

Reggie absorbed that, paused a moment, and nodded decisively. "Okay. I'm ready."

He smiled at her, and before she could blink, he raised the dagger and sliced a narrow cut in his chest above his heart. She couldn't see it at first, but he leaned over to put the dagger back in the drawer and when he faced her again, blood had begun to seep from the wound, dark and thick against his skin.

Reggie bit her lip and looked uncertain.

"Your choice, *dushka*. Either way, I will love you always."

She took a deep breath, inhaling the masculine scent of him along with the scent of sex, and knew he meant it. "Good," she whispered, "because you're never getting away from me now."

She lowered her head, feeling time stretch around her into slow motion. The first drop of blood worked its way free of the welling fluid and trickled down his chest. Reggie got to it just as it reached his nipple. She captured it with her tongue, caressing him while she did so. He tasted familiar and foreign, dark and rich and coppery, like himself, sweeter than his come, saltier than his mouth. She found the flavor intriguing.

She traced the crimson path back up his chest to the wound and dragged her tongue along the length of the cut, cleaning it of the accumulated blood. More welled up in its place, and, when the first drops slid easily down her throat, she realized she wanted more. The flavor of him changed even while she sucked the first mouthful from his wound. It became sweeter and smoother, like some rare liquor. The coppery taste of blood faded, and she found she could savor him like wine. She purred deep in her throat and snuggled closer while she began to drink from him in truth.

He went to her head and made her drunk with the taste of him. She couldn't get close enough to him. Even when he wrapped his arms around her and rolled onto his side, bringing her with him, she wanted more. She wanted to merge with him, to crawl inside him and rest beneath his skin beside his heart. She hooked her leg over his hip and pressed her hips against him, sucking hungrily from his chest. She felt so thirsty, and he was the only thing that could quench her need.

She existed in a black haze, all the world muffled but for her senses, which were acute. She gloried in the texture of his skin and hair, tasted his blood, smelled his scent and wanted him. She heard him moan somewhere above her, and his hand clenched on her thigh and raised it higher. The thick length of him probed at her tender opening and slid deep.

It overwhelmed her. She sank her teeth into his skin, unaware they had lengthened and sharpened while she fed. She pulled him closer with newfound strength, meeting his every thrust when he began to surge into her. She'd never felt anything like this. Before, when Misha had taken her, he'd been the center of her universe. Now, he was the center of *the* universe, and she wanted to weep and howl with the joy of it. Instead she drank deeply and moaned against his skin when he bowed his head and sank his fangs deep into her neck. He drank back the blood she was taking, and passion and power arced between them, a never-ending chain of pleasure and heat and lust and love.

The tension broke over them simultaneously, her body trembling and clenching while he pulsed his release inside of her. She tore her mouth away from his chest and screamed, a banshee sound of ecstasy and transformation. He echoed her with an animal roar of pleasure and triumph. They melted together in a tangled heap of blood and sex and sweat.

When Reggie finally managed to stir a long time later, she realized there really wasn't any blood. Like he'd said, the wounds seemed to have closed even while they'd pulled away from each other. But there was plenty of sweat and plenty of sex.

Reggie wrinkled her nose. "I need a shower."

For some reason, Dmitri found that vastly amusing. He laughed out loud and hugged her close. "I love you, *dushka*. You delight me."

"I'd delight you more if I didn't stink," she said. She sniffed and arched an eyebrow at him. "In fact, I think you'd delight me more if you—"

Dmitri glared at her, though his eyes glinted with humor. "Do not insult me by telling me I stink, Regina Elaina. I may have changed you, but I am still the one in charge here."

"Yeah, yeah. You're the great big alpha male, O Exalted One," she said, pushing at his shoulders until he rolled away from her. "But I am going to take a shower. Turning into a vampire takes a lot out of a girl. Which door leads to the—"

Her chatter ground to an abrupt halt, and Reggie fell back to the bed with a muffled thump. "Oh, wow. I almost forgot. I'm a vampire."

Dmitri surveyed her dazed look with humor. "Almost. It will take a few more hours for the transformation to complete itself, but you are on your way."

"What do you mean, 'almost'?" she demanded, glaring at him. "I drank blood. I had fangs!"

"Those are merely the first stage," he said dismissively, sitting up on the edge of the bed and scratching his chest absently. "In a few hours you will also have excellent night vision, amazing strength, acute hearing, and incredible speed. You're not done yet."

That took the wind out of her sails. "Oh."

She thought for a second, and when she looked

back at him, she looked like she was plotting something. "Will I get as strong as you?"

He laughed out loud. "Not a chance." She pouted, and he kissed the tip of her nose. "Not only am I more than seven centuries older than you, *dushka*, but I am also a man. Even among our kind, nature has weighted the advantage with men when it comes to strength."

Reggie humphed and stood, heading for the door she thought might lead to the bathroom. "Then I guess if it's just like being human, nature compensated by giving women the advantage when it comes to intelligence."

She punctuated her comment by looking back at him over her shoulder and sticking out her tongue. Clearly, she had maturity on her side too.

Dmitri gave a mock growl and started after her, but the thunderous clap of the door slamming back against the wall stopped both of them in their tracks.

"Get away from her, you dirty bloodsucker, before I turn you into vampire shish kebab!"

CHAPTER 26

IT TOOK REGGIE A FEW SECONDS TO PULL HER mouth closed, but the sight of your four best friends bursting through your lover's bedroom door, brandishing crosses and sharpened broom handles, can really shake a girl up.

Danice stepped warily forward to stand beside Ava, a makeshift cross, fashioned from two rulers and some duct tape, held out in front of her. Corinne and Missy stepped into the room and took positions flanking them.

"Come on, Reg," Danice urged, her voice soft and soothing, as if she were talking to a child or a victim of some violent crime. "We're here for you. It'll all be okay now. Just come here to me, and we'll get you out of here. Poor baby."

Reggie just stared at her. "Are you out of your minds? What the hell are you doing here?"

"I believe this is the cavalry, *dushka*. Your friends

have come to rescue you from my evil, bloodsucking clutches."

Dmitri's voice showed exactly how amusing he found the situation. Reggie glanced in his direction and saw him leaning unconcerned up against the bedpost, his arms crossed over his muscular chest and his legs crossed at the ankles. His very bare legs, since he was still completely naked.

And so was she.

"Jeez, guys! Could you maybe knock next time? We're not exactly dressed for company here." Grumbling all the way, Reggie stalked back toward the bed, yanked off a sheet and wrapped it around her in a makeshift toga. When Dmitri made no move to cover himself, she grabbed a pillow and threw it at him.

He caught it and grinned.

"I think he must be using some sort of mind control on her. What do we do now?"

Corrine whispered her theory, but Reggie heard it with no trouble. Her hearing had already improved.

"Dmitri is not controlling my mind, you idiot! And none of you have to do a bloody thing except apologize for barging in on us uninvited and then get the hell out of here so we can get dressed."

Ava ignored her friend's scowl and stepped forward, holding an intricate gilded crucifix toward

Dmitri. "We're not leaving without you, Reggie. We know all about your new lover. He wasn't just at that goth party for kicks. He's a real vampire. You're not safe with him."

"You're out of your mind!"

"No, Reggie, it's true!" Missy, clutching her own cross, moved closer to Regina, her face an earnest picture of concern. "I thought she was crazy, too, at first. But then what she told us started to make sense. Did you know the only recorded photos of Vidâme's ancestors are of adult eldest sons? No mothers, no fathers, no children, no old people. Just men in their thirties who manage to look almost exactly alike."

Reggie started to open her mouth to talk some sense into her friends, but Danice stopped her.

"It's the truth! It's freaky, Reg. Every single picture could be this guy's twin, and in all the photos, the dude is only ever seen at night!" Danice shuddered.

"And what about that hickey on your neck, Reg?" Corinne joined in. "Danice was right all along. It was a bite mark. This monster drank your blood. I'm telling you, he's a vampire!"

"And I'm telling you, I know!"

Reggie's shout cut straight through her friends' protests and even made Dmitri quirk an eyebrow. Reggie thought about smacking the smirk right off his face, but she refused to resort to violence. No matter how good it sounded. She contented herself with glaring at him and snarling before she turned back toward her friends.

Ava took one look at Reggie's expression and stiffened. Corinne screamed and Missy looked ready to faint. Danice jumped back until she hit the wall, and Ava turned her cross toward her friend.

"God, Regina, I'm so sorry," Ava whispered, a mask of agony twisting her features. "We came as soon as I heard from Marc that you'd been kidnapped from the restaurant. But we're too late. He turned you into one of them."

"How do you know that?" Reggie demanded. Ava's reaction kind of hurt her feelings.

"Your fangs," Dmitri explained, dropping the pillow and crossing to Regina's side to wrap his arm around her shoulders. He paid no attention to the cross-wielding reactions of her friends. "You became angry, *dushka*, and your fangs emerged. It is an emotional reaction you will learn to control."

"Yeah, and I hope you'll keep that in mind right about now. That whole control-over-your-emotions thing." Graham appeared in the doorway, looking sheepish. He shrugged to Dmitri. "I did the best I could."

Reggie threw her hands up in the air and turned on Dmitri. "Great! Now we're having a party in your bedroom! Did you invite the neighbors, or just your closest vampire buddies?"

Dmitri spared her an impatient glance before glaring at the new intruder. "Graham is not a vampire. He is Lupine, a werewolf, and I did not invite him at all. In fact, I assumed he would be keeping an eye on your friends and preventing this very event from occurring."

"Give me a break, Misha," Graham said, stepping into the room with a belligerent expression. The four human women scattered out of his path. "I'd like to see you try and ride herd on four humans with estrogen poisoning. They're royal pains. They almost made Rafe want to kick my ass for talking him into helping me with them."

"Actually, I would like very much to kick your ass for that." Another male voice drifted in from the hall a second before an unfamiliar, dark-haired man stepped into the crowded bedroom.

Reggie uttered a choked scream. "Is this another werewolf you didn't invite? Should I expect the entire uninvited population of Manhattan to join us next? Are we supposed to serve refreshments?"

"Werecat," Rafe corrected with a lazy smile. "I'm not a wolf, but 'shifter' is a great nonspecific term that's guaranteed not to offend any of us. And I'm Rafael De Santos. It is my pleasure to meet you."

Regina reflexively shook the hand he extended to her before she remembered how furious this entire farce had made her. She snatched her hand back and used it to poke Dmitri hard in the shoulder. "This is all your fault!"

"What is all my fault?" Dmitri looked offended.

"Everything," she proclaimed. "The fact that I'm losing my mind. The fact that my friends have already lost their minds. The fact that I have half the world in my bedroom, and I just got turned into a vampire. I'm sure global warming is your fault too. I'm just not sure how yet."

"Don't forget the fact that he scared your friends so badly, they're hiding behind the bed," Rafe offered with a grin.

Reggie turned around and saw her friends peering warily over the mattress from the other side of Dmitri's massive bed. She rolled her eyes.

"Actually, that's the one thing I can blame on you two," she said, extending her glare to encompass Graham as well. "They were fine until you showed up. You're the ones they're scared of."

"We're not the ones they were waving crosses at," Graham said. "I think that means they're afraid of you."

"Ha! My friends know me better than that."

Determined to prove her point—since her life couldn't get much more surreal than it had in the past ten minutes—Reggie stalked over to the other side of the bed, and grabbed the crosses and broom handles out of her friends' hands so quickly, they couldn't even think to protest. She grabbed the woman closest to her—Danice—and gave her a great big hug and a smacking kiss on her cheek.

"See? My friends know I would never hurt

them. They're intelligent, modern women who don't fall prey to superstitions."

From the corner of her eye, Reggie caught a glimpse of Corinne's hand sneaking out toward a cross. She reached out casually and planted her foot on it.

"They know crosses and garlic and holy water are nonsense, and vampires are not evil demons from the depths of hell." She ignored the shocked expressions on the faces of her friends and continued. "They also know if I didn't have complete faith in Dmitri, I would never be with him, and that I'm a grown woman fully capable of making my own decisions about who I want to date and who I want to marry."

"Marry?" Ava almost choked on the word.

"And they know that even if I did become a vampire, I'm still the same person I always was, and I still love them as much as I did before. And they know they're not getting out of being the bridesmaids at my wedding, so they might as well get used to the idea!"

By the time Reggie finished her tirade, she was panting, her friends were reeling, and Rafe and Graham were looking chastened.

Dmitri laughed.

"Well, I think you have explained everything to everyone's satisfaction, *dushka*," he said, pulling her into his arms. "I believe they are only waiting for us to set the date."

"Don't think you're getting off scot-free, mister," she grumbled, glaring up at him. "You just stood there buck naked and flashed all that manly muscle at my friends. It's indecent! Would you go put some clothes on?"

He threw back his head and laughed harder. "Why should I?" he teased her. "Our guests are on their way out, and I will just have to strip them off again, because I intend to make love to you as soon as we are alone."

Reggie scowled. "You know what they say about good intentions."

"That refers only to the good ones. I intend to be very wicked, *dushka*."

"Um, I think that's our cue to leave," Corinne said, breaking the tension and dragging herself up to stand on shaky legs. "It's been a really long night."

Reggie dragged her eyes from Dmitri. "You don't have to go. I'm sorry I yelled like that. I was just a little tense. But you could hang out for a while. I could get you guys something to eat."

Ava turned green and shook her head frantically.

"Oh, don't be such an idiot," Reggie said, rolling her eyes. "I meant I'd call for pizza or something. I just had a drink. I'm not going to snack on my bridesmaids."

Missy stepped forward bravely and gave Reggie a hug. "We know that, Reg. It's just going to take a little getting used to. Give us a few days, and I'm sure we'll be fine."

With the last of her anger faded away, Reggie realized she was nervous. What if her friends couldn't accept what she had become? What would she do?

But when she looked into Missy's eyes, she saw the other woman meant every word. Yes, Missy was a bit-shell shocked, but her love for her friend was stronger than her fear. Looking around at the other women, Reggie saw the same truth reflected in each of them. It really would be okay.

EPILOGUE

IT TOOK A WHILE TO CLEAR OUT THE CIRCUS IN Dmitri's bedroom, but they finally managed it around four that morning. There were a few cacophonous minutes of questions, explanations, and discussions when Reggie demanded to know how her friends had managed to research vampires, evade trailing werewolves, and take up breaking and entering. She also wanted to know how they'd accomplished all that, but couldn't remember to knock before barging into someone's bedroom.

Dmitri expressed admiration—or maybe that had been fear—when Ava explained how she'd will-powered her way past his mind games, shimmied out her eighteen-inch-square basement window right under Graham's nose, and gathered up an impromptu army for the cavalry charge.

He also took the opportunity to reemphasize that whole "knocking" thing.

Reggie sat on the side of the bed and heard bits of the conversation that took place when Dmitri escorted his two friends to the front door. It seemed like her hearing was improving by the minute, and a shiver of excitement passed through her. All of a sudden the possibilities open to her in her new life sounded exciting. Letting Dmitri turn her no longer felt like even a minor sacrifice. It felt like a blessing.

Tentatively, she reached out with fumbling, infant senses and tried to share some of her new feelings with Dmitri. She knew the instant he sensed her, knew his pleasure and his affection.

If you wish to take a shower, you should do so now. His voice rumbled in her head, a thousand times clearer and sharper than she'd ever heard it. It left her breathless. *It will be dawn soon, and at the beginning, the sunrise will exhaust you. I will be up in a minute.*

Grinning, she decided to take his advice and headed for the bathroom, or at least for the door she thought probably led to the bathroom. Dmitri still hadn't given her the tour.

She guessed correctly, and felt quite pleased with herself when she turned on the shower. She had barely stepped under the spray before he crowded in with her. Not that he needed to crowd. The shower—and the bathroom—was just as spacious and elegant as the rest of his house. Still, she ignored him while she reached for the bottle of shampoo on the shelf and lathered her hair, but she couldn't ignore him when he slipped his hands into the foamy cap and massaged her scalp with strong, gentle fingers. She gave in and leaned back against his chest on a blissful moan.

"You should call in to work," he murmured while he continued to rub lazy circles in her hair. "After your change, you will need to sleep for most of the day."

"I already took the day off."

His fingers paused, then resumed. "I am going to pretend you did so because you expected me to rescue you from your date. Otherwise, I would have to punish you."

He tugged gently on her hair and leaned down to nip her shoulder.

Reggie grinned, and purred her reply, pressing her hips back against him. "Oh, no. Please don't hurt me."

Dmitri chuckled. "That is good though," he continued. "It gives us all of tomorrow evening and the entire weekend to move your things out of your apartment."

Reggie stiffened. "I'm moving out of my apartment?"

He turned her around and tilted her head back to wash the soap out of her hair. "You have agreed to marry me. That means we will live together."

She jerked her head up and glared at him. "But you're just assuming I'll be the one to move. I just got through yelling like a fishwife at a bunch of people who were making assumptions about me, Dmitri. Don't get me started again. I told you before, just because I'm submissive in bed doesn't mean that—"

Dmitri chuckled and picked up a bar of soap. "I am not trying to run your life, *katyonak*. You may sheath your claws. But your apartment is too small for both of us. My house is much larger and more private. It is also owned and not rented, so it is much safer for both of us. I was being logical, not dictatorial."

Reggie eyed him warily, but couldn't really argue with his reasoning. "I guess you're right. But you'd better be careful with that, Misha. I'm not going to become some plaything. I'm going to be your wife. That means an equal partner."

He slid his soapy hands up over her breasts and squeezed. "I am always careful with you, *dushka*," he purred even as he slid one hand down to cup her between her thighs. "And I do not think of you as a thing, even though I very much enjoy playing with you."

He slipped his fingers inside her, and she laughed around her moan. "Misha, you can't always end our discussions with sex."

"Then do not bore me with discussion when I am hungry for you." He twisted his hand and rubbed his thumb over her clit. "We will make each other happy, *milaya*. What else is there to discuss?"

It took every ounce of her strength and determination to articulate anything beyond a plea for more sex, but Reggie managed it. Barely.

"What about my job?" she demanded, grabbing his wrist in both hands to hold it still. "How am I supposed to go to work if I'm going to be sleeping all day long?"

Misha sighed and withdrew his fingers, reaching for the soap again and lathering her legs. "You could manage it if you wanted, with a lot of effort," he grumbled. "But there is no need for you to work if you do not wish it. As you guessed this evening, I am disgustingly wealthy. I can well afford to keep you for eternity."

Her eyes narrowed warningly. "Misha, you're not thinking of telling me I can't work, are you? Because—"

"Regina! I said it before. The only thing I will forbid you to do is to leave me. Other than that, you may do as you please. I want to make you happy. As happy as you make me. Whatever you want, I will give to you. Wherever you wish to go, I will take you. If you wish to work, you may. If you wish not to work, you may. You may do anything you want." He paused. "Except sleep with another man. Or touch another man. Just to be safe, you should probably not look at any other man."

Reggie laughed and threw her arms around him, hugging him close while the very last of her fears washed down the drain. She peppered his

face with kisses, feeling a sense of exaltation fill
her to overflowing. She wanted to dance and sing
and laugh and cry and yell for joy. But most of all,
she just wanted Misha.

"You never need to worry about that, my darling, jealous, vampiric Misha." She hugged him
tight and pulled herself up his chest, wrapping
her legs around his hips and kissing him passion-
ately. "You are the only man I want. The only man
I will ever want. Why should I ever need anything
else when I have you?"

He smiled at her, the small, wicked grin she
had grown to love. "You do have me, *dushka*. You
will always have me."

"And you have me, Misha. Forever."

"Forever," he echoed and lowered his mouth
to hers. They kissed until the water threatened to
turn cold and they had both turned very hot indeed. Misha switched off the water without dis-
lodging Reggie from her position around his waist
and carried her back to the bedroom.

He tumbled her down onto the tousled sheets
and kissed her again, his hunger making his intent more than clear. At his urging, Reggie loosened her grip around his waist so he could slide
down her body and take a taut nipple between his
lips. She smiled up at the ceiling and hummed
her pleasure.

"You know," she murmured, running her fingers through his thick hair, "if I'm going to be around for a few more centuries than I expected, I'm sure there are some things you'll need to teach me. After all, I've never been a vampire before."

Dmitri grunted and moved to her other breast. Reggie grinned and pulled his face up to hers for a long, deep kiss. When they were both breathless and needy and desperate to come together, she pushed him onto his back and slithered down the mattress to lick his nipples and tease his navel with her tongue.

"Just as an example, I'm sure there are nuances to drinking blood I've never considered before," she purred, gazing at him from beneath her lashes and smiling wickedly. "For instance, I'm sure it's easiest to drink from someplace that has a strong . . . pulse."

She closed her hand around his penis and squeezed. "If I'm going to feed on blood from now on, I should probably know the best ways to sate my appetites."

Her tongue caressed the length of him, and he shuddered. She smiled and slid farther down the bed until she was eye level with his rampant erection.

"Misha?"

"Yes, *milaya*?"

"I think I'm hungry right now," she whispered, tasting him like a midnight snack.

"I will always provide for you." Dmitri buried his hands in her hair and guided her mouth to him. "If you hunger, *dushka*, you should drink."

Reggie parted her smiling lips and took him into her mouth.

Then she drank.

Turn the page for a sneak peek at
CHRISTINE WARREN'S
next pulse-pounding Others novel

You're So Vein

Coming soon from
St. Martin's Paperbacks

THE HEELS OF HER BLACK GINA BOOTS CLICKED on the pavement with the sharp rap of gunfire, which suited Ava Markham's mood just fine. Frankly, she felt as if she'd just fought the Battle of Bunker Hill single-handedly. And without ever letting the enemy know they'd been engaged.

Why she continued to attend these events, Ava could hardly fathom. Certainly it had nothing to do with enjoyment. She'd stopped looking forward to the girls' nights years ago, and she knew perfectly well that she made all the rest of the attendees as uncomfortable as they made her, but Ava wasn't the kind of woman who gave in. So every other Friday evening, as regular as the army, she gathered up a bottle or three of good wine, stopped at the cheese shop down the block from her office, then carried herself, her provisions, and her very forced smile to a party that offered her approximately as much pleasure as an IRS audit.

Of course, she'd be a fool if she didn't acknowledge that periodontal surgery likely held more appeal for the other guests then her awkward presence. Everyone always welcomed her with open arms, but she could see that behind their smiles, her friends clenched their teeth whenever she made an appearance. That could very well have been one of the reasons why she continued to appear. Ava appreciated nothing so much as the sheer perversity of her own character. Knowing herself to be unwanted was the surest way on earth to make sure she planted herself in the middle of the action.

You should have let me call you a cab.

The errant thought, coming out of thin air as it did, made the hairs on the back of Ava's neck stand at stiff attention below the elegant twist of her chignon. Immediately and reflexively, she tensed and forced her mind to go blank. She had rules about things like this, and she made very sure that everyone around her knew about them.

As expected, her cell phone rang less than a moment later.

"I'm serious. It's too late for you to be walking home alone."

Ava pressed the slim, silver phone to her ear and kept walking. "No, actually it's merely too late for unexpected visitors to barge in without so much as knocking. I told you I don't like it when you get in my head like that." Reggie would make far more use of her telepathic gift if Ava let her.

"I'm sorry, but that's what you get for making me worry."

"While I appreciate your concern, Regina, I neither needed nor wanted a taxi. I'm a big girl, more than able to take care of myself."

On the other end of the line, the woman Ava loved—and hated—like a sister sighed. "I don't dispute that, but it's two in the morning, Av, and even on the Upper East Side that is not an hour when women should be walking alone."

"Why not? You've done it. Repeatedly."

"That's not the same thing, and you know it."

Silence.

Regina sighed again. "Look, just tell me where you are, and I'll come meet you. If you won't take a cab, at least let me walk you home."

The image of standing around like an idiot, waiting to be escorted home by a woman at least six inches shorter and two inches softer than herself, struck Ava as ridiculous. No matter how fast or strong the other woman might be.

The Other woman. Vampire to be exact.

"No, I'll be fine," Ava dismissed, shoving her errant thought back into the abyss where it belonged. "Go back to your guests and tell everyone I said goodnight."

"They'll be disappointed that you had to leave relatively early."

"Don't lie, Regina. It can cause wrinkles."

She disconnected before Regina could answer.

It would only have been another lie, and Ava didn't need anyone to pretend with her. She could handle the truth; in fact, she preferred it, and she thought she'd done a pretty damned good job of dealing with it over the last few years. Like she'd told Regina, Ava Markham was a big girl.

Having grown up in Manhattan, Ava knew the city like the rooms of her apartment—well enough to navigate blind, deaf, and wearing three-inch heels. The time of day, or night, wasn't going to give her any trouble. She always kept her eyes and ears open, her pace brisk, and her attitude confident. Attackers would take a look at her and move on to easier prey. But just in case any particularly stupid muggers decided to try for her, she had self-defense training, lungs like an opera soprano, and a can of pepper spray. She'd be fine.

Her heels beat a steady tempo on the pavement as she shoved her hands into the pockets of her cardinal-red trench coat and attempted to walk off her discomfort. Her oversized, black Spade bag bumped her elbow with just enough force to maintain her current level of irritation. Now if only she could decide at whom that irritation was directed.

Some of it had to rest on her own shoulders, of course. It was her monumental stubbornness that kept her running face-first into the same brick wall over and over while expecting a different result. That was the definition of insanity, wasn't it? Or had the guidelines been revised since the news

broke that people who thought they were werewolves hadn't necessarily gone off their meds?

Ava gritted her teeth and glared at the empty
sidewalk ahead of her. Displacement, she admitted, but healthier than confronting what she really
wanted to glare at. She hadn't worked this hard
for this long to retain her friendships—strained
though they might be—just to throw that away
by punching out one of their husbands. And
that was without considering the fact that commit-
ting suicide by vampire, werewolf, or demon—Oh,
my!—had never been a personal goal of hers. In
the interests of her health and social life, Ava had
perfected the ability to pretend that everything
was fine and that the good old days remained
brand spanking new.

Too bad the developing ulcer in her stomach
put paid to that particular lie. Times hadn't just
changed; they'd undergone a metamorphosis that
made Jeff Goldblum's turn in *The Fly* look like
something out of a beauty pageant. It almost made
Ava consider cutting off her electricity and exploring the requirements for conversion to an Old Order Amish church. If it weren't for the fashion
limitations . . .

Her cell phone rang again. After a quick glance
at the caller ID, Ava shoved it back into her pocket
unanswered. This time, Missy was calling, of
course. People always thought that not even Ava
could be so hard-hearted as to ignore the pleas of

sweet, sensible, loving Missy. Her friends believed that if Missy asked Ava to take a cab, so Missy wouldn't have to worry about her friend's safety, Ava couldn't say no.

It was better to walk. She'd be perfectly safe. She certainly *felt* safer than she had in the very swank media room of Regina's townhouse, surrounded by the women she still called her best friends. There had been a time when Ava would have sworn that nothing could come between her and Regina. And Missy and Danice and Corinne. They'd been inseparable, best friends forever, together to the end, one for all and all for one. But that had been before Dmitri had entered the picture. Then Graham. Then Mac and Luc. Before their circle had expanded to include werewolves and witches and even a twenty-four carat, straight out of another dimension, certified Faerie princess. Before Regina had turned.

Before Ava had realized she was alone, completely alone, in a room full of monsters.

Swallowing back the fist that tried to lodge in her throat, Ava stepped up her pace and lifted her chin. She still felt a wave of guilt and shame every time she reflexively used the M word. She didn't want to think about her friends like that. She loved those women like sisters, but she couldn't deny the truth. They had changed, changed in ways that went beyond marriage and starting new families and growing older and wiser. They had become people that

Ava barely recognized sometimes. Some of them had even changed species, and as far as Ava was concerned, you could never trust someone who wasn't quite human.

It always came back to that, Ava admitted. That fact was really the root of her problem, the thing she couldn't get used to, the obstacle she just couldn't get past. How did you relate to your best girlfriends when you realized that some of those girls were no longer human?

Ava sure as hell didn't know. Which was why she'd left when the party was in full swing to walk home alone like the reject from the kickball team. It was an unfamiliar sensation. People just didn't reject Ava Markham. All her life, she had been the girl everyone wanted to be or be with, the golden child. Born to wealthy parents, raised in luxury, a modeling agent had "discovered" her at the age of thirteen, and by the time she hit eighteen, she had earned more money than most people would see in their lifetime. After her retirement and the years she had spent in Europe being chic and bored, she had opened an agency of her own and signed some of the biggest names in the business. And that had been before her twenty-fifth birthday. Now, at thirty-four, she occupied a coveted spot at the top of the Manhattan food chain of wealth, beauty, and success.

Was it any wonder then that she felt angry every time she thought about the way things had turned out? The Fantasy Fixes they'd dreamed up all those years ago had been intended to set them up with the men of their dreams—the *human* men—so that they could live the kind of fantasies that most women spent their whole lives only dreaming about. They were supposed to have hot sex, lose a few clothes and maybe a few inhibitions, not their damned minds.

Shit.

"Breathe, girl," Ava muttered to herself. She had to force her jaw to unclench before she could get the sound out, and then it took another effort of will to draw the crisp night air deep into her lungs without letting it back out in a frustrated scream. If this weren't a quiet residential neighborhood, she might not have managed it.

Ava crossed the street and hopped up onto the opposite curb. Anger had lengthened her stride until she was practically jogging, her slim knee-length skirt stretching against her thighs with each step. With her eyes fixed on the shadowed sidewalk in front of her, she saw she still had quite a distance to go before she reached her elegant little row house in Yorkville. Maybe by the time she got there, she'd have walked off some of this resentment

When her peripheral vision caught a blur of dark movement off to her side, Ava didn't think anything of it. Manhattan was home, to her and about eight million other people, so people rarely made her look twice.

Unless they leapt at her from the shadows and grabbed her by the throat, dragging her struggling form into the alley with the casual ease of inhuman strength.

I knew it! her mind crowed even as her instincts drew breath to scream. *Can't trust an Other!*

Which would be cold comfort when the police discovered her body in the alley. Cold and dead.

But right.